Guy Adams lives in Spain, surrounded by rescue animals. Some of them are his family. He isn't a spy, but he is a boy, so naturally he's always dreamed of being one.

Having spent over ten years working as a professional actor and comedian, eventually he decided he'd quite like to eat regularly, so switched careers and became a full-time writer. Nobody said he was clever. Against all odds he managed to stay busy and since then he has written over twenty books.

Also by Guy Adams:

The Clown Service

The Rain-Soaked Bride

Torchwood: The House That Jack Built

Torchwood: The Men Who Sold The World

Kronos

Hands of the Ripper

Sherlock: The Casebook

Countess Dracula

GUY ADAMS

A FEW WORDS FOR THE DEAD

1 3 5 7 9 10 8 6 4 2

Del Rey, an imprint of Ebury Publishing
20 Vauxhall Bridge Road,
London SW1V 2SA

Del Rey is part of the Penguin Random House group of companies whose addresses can be found at global.penguinrandomhouse.com

First published in the UK in 2015 by Del Rey

www.eburypublishing.co.uk

A CIP catalogue record for this book is available from the British Library

ISBN 9780091953195

Printed and bound in Great Britain by Clays Ltd, St Ives PLC

To Ida Siekmann, Winifried Freudenberg and the needless others in-between

ONE

The gunfire from the jungle distracted Romeo from what the young woman was saying.

'It is our honeymoon,' she told him, 'and it never ends.'

If the woman had noticed the noise, she gave no sign of it, just continued talking while Romeo looked over her shoulder towards the treeline and the dense, wet foliage beyond.

'It was two weeks in Portugal,' she continued. 'The honeymoon. But then the man cursed me. I think he believed this would make us keep away. Make us run. This shows how he does not know us. Toby and I do not run. Not for long.'

There was more shooting. In his thirteen years Romeo had heard too much gunfire. The bandits liked nothing more than announcing their arrival with it, riding into the village in their jeeps, rifles firing into the air. Romeo knew they thought this made them look impressive, it made them seem like an army. They were wrong, the villagers responded with grim indifference to the show of machismo. Nobody was stupid enough to challenge the bandits, they were a way of life, a parasite, mosquitoes with guns. But just because the village gave them the supplies they wanted, and gave them quickly, it didn't mean they lived in terror. They were simply pragmatic. A cut of their meagre belongings traded against the loss of life that would result in saying no. Besides, the bandits were useful too; they policed each other. This part of the jungle belonged to the El Ninos, and at least that kept other gangs – worse gangs – at bay.

'The curse has rules,' the woman was saying. 'If I get close to Fratfield . . . That's his name, or the name we know – he is, I think, a man with many names . . . If I get close to him then the demon appears. It is a thing of wind. Before, he used a woman who brought rain but we beat her. We will beat this too. If I stay back then the demon does not become too dangerous. It is just a thing you can tell in the air, a change in the weather.' She pointed towards the trees as they bent in the breeze. 'If I get too close, the demon takes form. It becomes a thing that is real. Then it is time to move.'

In the jungle there was the harsh sound of branches snapping as someone moved quickly through the foliage. Romeo thought they were coming their way. He wondered if it were, perhaps, time to move to safety. He had no wish to get involved in another man's fight, he had enough problems of his own. They'd lost three chickens in the night and the crops were fighting all attempts to make them thrive. His empty belly, and the health of his mama, that was more than enough for him to contend with.

'This angers me,' the woman continued, 'because it means I cannot fight the man myself. But if we catch him we can break the curse.'

She smiled at Romeo and he found her more terrifying than

he had ever found the bandits. That smile was not a nice smile; he hoped he never had cause to make his own face look such a way. 'Then we break Fratfield. End of honeymoon!'

Romeo nodded, because it seemed to him that was what was expected.

The woman and her man had arrived in the village half an hour ago, bouncing along the dirt track in their hired jeep. For a few minutes the people of the village had observed them, some of the kids had approached them, eager to do a little business, but once it had become clear that there was nothing to be gained from the *extranjeros*, the children had drifted away and returned to the jobs they had interrupted.

'More strangers,' Romeo's mama had said. 'They'll be wanting the man on the mountain.'

The man on the mountain, another invader into their world, had arrived three weeks ago. He hadn't set foot in the village but nothing made its home in the nearby jungle without their noticing. The empty shack on the bank of the river, a place that had been abandoned after the El Ninos drove its previous occupant away (or, as some of the more gossip-inclined villagers would have it, murdered). One day it had been empty, the next it had been occupied.

'I wonder what he's hiding from?' Romeo's mama had said, staring up into the canopy as if her eyes could part the leaves and see right to the shack's front door. 'No white man makes his home up there unless he's hiding from something.'

The jungle fell silent and so did the woman. Romeo looked at the trees as their leaves began to whip more forcefully against the hazy sky. The wind was picking up. He hoped it wasn't a sign of a storm – it wasn't the season for it and nobody in the village would be prepared for such a thing. Storms were worse than the gangs. Storms could not be bought off with grain.

'The wind,' said the woman. 'I think he is coming. You should tell everyone to get indoors.'

In her pocket her phone began to ring. She tugged it free. 'Toby? I have seen.' She sighed. 'I will move.'

She began to run back towards their jeep, the wind building around the village.

Romeo watched her go. She was attractive, he decided, even if she smiled like the devil herself. A shame he didn't speak a word of English.

Toby hated the jungle. The jungle was filled with things that wanted to poison you or slap you in the face. The jungle was like the worst nightclubs of his youth.

Why hadn't Fratfield tried to hide somewhere with wide tarmac roads and decent restaurants?

Because he didn't want to be found, of course. Which just went to show how little he knew about the far-reaching abilities of Section 37.

As soon as it had become clear to Toby and Tamar that the only way to escape the threat of Fratfield's curse was to go on the offensive, Shining had sent Toby a book of field contacts. In it had been the phone number of Angela, a young woman from Tuxtla who did the most awful things with chickens and smoking bowls of incense. She had laughed as Toby had gone green watching her at work.

'You do not like to see blood, no?'

'As long as it's not mine I can stomach it.'

'Voodoo calls for blood,' she explained, 'and sometimes, when you want to find things, you need a bit more than an internet connection and a search engine, though they play their part.'

Indeed they had, an ancient PC computer buzzing along with Angela's chanting and the panicked cries of sacrificial fowl. The ancient and modern fused together via a tatty wooden box that glowed with a sickly blue light. As Angela's rite came to a close, Toby saw the screen on the PC fire up, a map appearing, zooming in on a location.

'I call it Voogle!' Angela laughed, wiping her bloodied hands on her AC/DC T-shirt. She peered at the screen. 'I hope you packed bug spray. I'll grab the location for your satnav.'

And now he and Tamar were in the jungle, and Fratfield was—

Toby ducked as automatic gunfire cut the branches of the tree next to him into fragments. As he moved to better cover, keeping low, he heard howler monkeys expressing their disapproval in the branches above. He knew how they felt.

'Toby!' his quarry shouted. 'What does it take to get you to leave me alone?'

Toby didn't bother to answer. Nothing would convince him to leave the man alone. As long as Fratfield was still loose, Tamar would always be under threat, this new curse hanging over her. They would fight on, however long it took, until she was safe again. He checked his gun and began to move as quietly as he could through the undergrowth. This was something of an impossibility given the dense plant life. Jungle warfare, like so many of his day-to-day tasks in Section 37, had not been covered by basic field training. The closest he had got was a week face down in a puddle on an army assault course in Dorset.

'You're risking her life!' said Fratfield. 'You know that if you get close to me she's as good as dead. Why don't you have the good sense to just leave me well alone? I have no interest in killing her, not really. You stay away and she's safe, you know how curses work.'

Good sense. Toby had long given up on that as a notion. The man's question had only one real purpose: to pin down Toby's location with his reply. Good sense? Right now, good sense was to keep his mouth shut and his eyes open.

He looked towards the sound of the voice, catching a flicker of movement. He raised his gun and fired. He would have preferred a solid target but knew the danger he was in and time was of the essence. He didn't stand a chance in a fair fight; the man's abilities went far beyond being able to wave a rifle around. Toby's only real hope had been to catch him unawares. Now that was off the cards he'd fall back on good luck and bloody-mindedness.

There was a low grunt in reply to his bullet. Toby hoped that meant his shot had found its target.

There was no returning fire and Toby counted out the seconds, not wanting to be caught out, fooled by a lure.

Silence. Toby began to move towards where he had glimpsed Fratfield.

As he walked towards the higher ground, the jungle seemed to crackle around him. For a moment he thought he was surrounded on all sides. Perhaps it was the El Ninos, in which case his only option would be to turn on his heels and hope he could keep ahead of them.

It wasn't the El Ninos.

The jungle itself was moving, branches flexing, vines curling.

The soft ground beneath his feet was undulating as roots strained against the soil. Yes, this man could do much more than just fire a gun.

He heard the crack of a quad bike motor starting up and felt the entire operation fall down around his ears.

He began to run back towards the village, the jungle reaching out towards him as he pulled his phone from his pocket. He was damned lucky to get a signal – a few miles south and he'd have been completely out of contact.

'Tamar,' he shouted, not waiting for his wife's voice, 'he's on the run and heading towards you, the wind's picking up, you need to move!'

He heard the quad bike streaking past him some distance away, the wind around him wrestling with the living plant life. He really missed the days dealing with enemies you could just put a bullet into.

A creeper latched on to his arm, yanking him off balance. He pulled against it, crying out as he felt something tear in his shoulder. His only hope was to keep moving – once the jungle got a solid grip on him he'd never break free.

An idea suddenly struck him and he shifted direction, cutting back towards the shack. All around him the air was filled with the snapping of greenery and, above that, the ever-increasing howl of the wind.

Tamar got into the jeep and turned the ignition. She had to put some distance between herself and Fratfield, both for her own sake and that of the village.

The wind was bending the trees towards her as she drove along the dirt road. She kept her speed as high as she dared, the jeep bouncing off the rough ground and lifting her out of her seat as she fought to keep a grip on the steering wheel.

Slowly, the wind began to die down. The buffeting against the jeep lessened as the road dipped before her, revealing a valley of jungle. A decent road was still a good thirty kilometres away but the track widened ahead in a junction with two other trails.

Just as she began to consider turning around to check on Toby, the wind rose again sending her veering towards the trees to her left. Ahead, at the junction, she saw a quad bike burst from one of the other tracks. The driver halted, and she slammed on the brakes, recognising him. Fratfield.

She wrestled the gear stick of the jeep into reverse, fighting her natural urge to close the distance between them. This was the first time since Portugal she had seen the man who had cursed her and nothing would please her more than to drive the few hundred yards between them and slam her jeep into him. She knew she'd never make it that far, though. Already the wind was so strong it was getting hard to move. Unless she retreated, this would be the last time she ever looked her enemy in the eyes.

Fratfield watched her for a moment, wondering, no doubt, whether it was worth pursuing her and seeing an end to this chase. Then he shifted his arm awkwardly, Toby's bullet having cut through his right shoulder, and decided that self-preservation was best served by getting out of there.

Tamar had the jeep halfway through a three-point turn when the wind began to lift the vehicle from the road. It was just a wobble to begin with, the jeep rocking from side to side. Then she felt the entire jeep lift. She jumped out. As she rolled on the ground, the wind beating at her with the solidity of booted feet, she saw the jeep rise up, spinning through the air, and crash into the trees.

Through squinting eyes, she saw Fratfield continue to retreat as she was lifted up and hurled towards the treeline. She collided with the trunk of a sturdy Piich tree, its rough trunk cutting into her back as the wind forced her against it. She fought to turn, reaching for one of the branches so she could hold on.

She could barely keep her eyes open but she saw a portly figure appear in the middle of the dirt track. Its flesh was as pale as cooked chicken, its belly bloated and distended, hanging below its thick knees. Its mouth was a round 'o' as it forced the wind from the void inside itself.

This was it, she thought, the unearthly creature held over her as a suspended death sentence. The rain-soaked bride had been a tragic figure but one that had, at least, appeared completely human. This did not. This was a creature from legend. This was the demon of the storm.

The tree she was holding on to began to bend, its lesser fellows already snapping and twisting around her as they gave in to the pressure of the wind. When would it cease? Surely Fratfield had retreated far enough away by now?

Toby burst from the jungle, a snatching mass of creepers surrounding him as he fell through the air and into the river. He glimpsed Fratfield's shack for a moment before he sank beneath the surface, fighting against the rushing current. His feet hit the riverbed and he forced himself upwards, his arms reaching out. As his hands hit the air, something whipped around his wrist and he felt himself being yanked back as one of the creepers attempted to fish him back onto dry land. He was stretched between the two opposing forces, the river's current and the hostile jungle. The river won, the creeper snapping and sending Toby coursing through the water, his lungs aching for air.

He hit a rock, and the last of his breath spat from him as the stone cut into his knees. He twisted with the impact, banging his forehead and sending a sharp burst of pain right through him. With the last of his strength, he grabbed hold of the rock, using the current to help him pull himself above the surface, gasping for air as he climbed out of the grip of the river. His head spun and he touched his wound, feeling blood.

He looked up into the sky and wondered whether his wife had escaped. Then he passed out.

'That went well.'

Toby opened his eyes and immediately closed them again, the pain in his head worsening with the light.

'Brilliant,' he replied. 'We showed him.'

Tamar took his hand and held it in her own, shuffling to a more comfortable position on the rock beside him. 'We will find him again,' she said, 'and next time he will not run.'

Toby dabbed at the cut on his forehead. 'Feel like I've split my head in half,' he said.

'It is a small cut,' she told him, as if ashamed he should even feel the need to mention it. 'While you were having a swim I was thrown at a tree.'

'A swim? He set the whole jungle on me!'

'A jungle is not a thing.'

'This one was.' Toby pulled himself slowly into a sitting

position, groaning as the movement made the pain in his head pulse even harder.

He sighed and for a few moments they just sat there, side by side, holding hands, watching the river.

'You'll have to drive back to the town,' Toby said after a while. 'I don't think I should be allowed behind the wheel of a car until my head clears.'

'That will not be a problem.'

'Thanks.'

'You misunderstand. It will not be a problem you being behind the wheel of a car. The jeep blew away. I think maybe it is in Guatemala now.'

'Oh.'

'We will have a nice romantic walk,' she told him, 'because when you marry a woman you treat her like a princess.'

'Sorry.'

Tamar smiled. 'I'm not. Yet. But by the time we have swum to the side of the river I will be calling you bad names, so enjoy my love while it is still there.'

TWO

The Assassin walks steadily through the crowds of disembarking passengers. Groups of tourists, jaded and miserable in the hangover stage of their holiday, return to the cold of their real lives to fold up the brightly coloured shirts and thin dresses of another climate for one more year. Foreign students hoist backpacks and gaze out of the panoramic windows onto a grey landscape of Gatwick concrete. Refuelling trucks and people in high-visibility waistcoats busy themselves around the aeroplanes, long since numb to the sense of magic this place holds for the holidaymaker.

The Assassin strolls through them, balancing his natural impatience with a professional awareness that a good killer never runs. He should never need to.

At passport control, he leaves the crowds behind and heads towards the e-passport machines. A slightly impatient customs official moves between the barriers, repeatedly explaining the process to people still confused by this old technology. The Assassin needs no assistance. He slides his passport onto the reader where its electronic chip – provided, at considerable cost, by a Lithuanian contact who worked miracles with illicit tech – is scanned. The Assassin looks straight ahead into the small camera, letting its software analyse his face, compare it to the stored imagery and make its decision. A soft hiss and the door opens.

He moves quickly through the shopping concourse, buying himself a takeaway coffee, a newspaper and a new SIM card for his phone. He dislikes giving clients contact information and makes a point of using a different card for each contract, sometimes even changing it mid-job. Information is his enemy, the modern-day lichen of existence, accreting with every phone call, email or card purchase. Whenever he feels that build-up begin, he sheds it like dead skin.

He catches the Brighton train heading into London, reads his newspaper and drinks his coffee, just like a normal human being. Which, of course, he is not. Normal human beings don't kill each other for money.

Arriving at St Pancras, he folds up the paper and dabs the cappuccino froth from his upper lip. It leaves a brown, chocolate kiss on the complimentary napkin, like a lover's goodbye. He stares at it for a moment, feeling paranoid, then pockets both the cup and napkin. He'll dispose of them later.

Leaving the station, he finally feels he has stepped out of the hinterland of travel, that false world of airports and train stations, and been delivered into the real world. This had been his city once, a home when he had enjoyed the luxury of a real life, removed from the constant travel from one country to another, swapping names and languages, invisible, transient, unreal. Here he had had friends – well, as close as he had ever got to such a thing – lovers, hobbies, a job. Here he had been real. It feels disconcerting to be back.

He sends a text message to the client, breaking the phone's pure, new state. Now it exists, and him with it, the clock is ticking.

The reply is less than a couple of minutes coming. A location. Not a meet, thankfully. The Assassin doesn't approve of face-to-face encounters. He prefers to handle all contracts remotely. Anonymity and murder should always go hand in hand. The location is for a locker linked to an online store. Alongside the address is the pin code he'll need to access the locker.

He buys himself a day's travel card for the Underground and heads to Waterloo. Exiting the station past the seemingly endless row of taxicabs he descends into Lower Marsh street. Finally, he is out of the heaving crowds and walking along streets sparsely populated with real, normal people. These are people who have never choked someone to death or slit a throat. The dislocation he felt earlier is multiplied a hundredfold. He is an impostor. A man at odds with his surroundings. He looks at the office creatures, the market shoppers, the simple, definable human beings with their basic needs, their simple narratives, and he feels utterly alone. Here, in the city he once called home, there seems to be nothing left of the man he had been, the fiction he had carried to keep himself safe, the fiction that had acted as if the world was a simple place to be. That fiction, fragile as it was, has rotted away. He is a shell. He is a hollow man.

Walking into the grocery store listed in the text message, he stares at shiny packaging and advertising faces, perfect and happy, and begins to wonder if perhaps it is the world that is false and him that is real.

The locker is set up against the back wall. A small control

panel invites him to enter his passcode. He does so, copying it from the text message, and there is a click as the door of a locker opens. Inside there is a large Manila envelope. He takes it out but doesn't open it. This is neither the time nor the place.

'Got something nice?' asks the shop assistant as the Assassin makes to leave.

The Assassin stops. He glances up at the security camera on the wall above the door, turns and sees a second above the counter. Is the footage they record stored locally or held on a server by the security company? Paranoia. That old friend. He feels exposed. He keeps his face low, unseen.

'I don't know what it is yet,' he says.

'Surprise, huh?' the assistant smiles. 'Nice.'

The Assassin takes another quick glance at the camera. It's cheap. The store is independent, not blessed with the financial support of a multinational company. The camera footage will be stored locally. Hell, it might even be on tape. He's willing to bet one of the cameras might even be a dummy.

Easy. It will be easy. Then the paranoia will go away. He can kill this man. Choke the life out of him. Beat out his skull on the hard wood of the shop counter.

There is no need, the calm, professional part of him insists. Do that and you only add to the information. You make people look. And what of the footage from the cameras in the street? London is lousy with cameras. If this man dies, people will look at the information on those cameras. He will exist as a person of interest.

'Get you anything else?' asks the assistant, and the Assassin realises he's been stood, staring at the man. Drawing attention.

'No,' he says, 'I was just wondering if I had enough phone credit but I'm fine. Thanks.'

He walks out of the shop.

'No worries,' says the assistant, completely unaware how close he came to dying during his low-paid shift.

The Assassin returns to Waterloo, the envelope zipped up inside his jacket. He catches a train to Bank and then walks the short distance to the hotel he has picked for his stay. He always stays at chain hotels. They are nondescript, cheap and the constant flood of guests means the staff have grown blind to faces.

The receptionist barely looks at him as he books his room using one of several disposable credit cards he keeps for just such occasions. It will pass a cursory check through the machine but can't be used to trace him. These places insist on a card imprint for security but when he comes to leave, he'll pay cash and the card won't be charged. No trail.

His room is identical to so many others he has stayed in during his life. Deep red carpet and white sheets. The companies keep the permanent fixtures dark to hide the grime, distracting you with the lightness of the removable sheets and towels. The furniture comes in flat-packs. The desk, one of hundreds of thousands scattered through this chain, is littered with glossy literature inviting him to part with his money. He dumps it all in a drawer, sits down and sends a text message to his client confirming that he is in receipt of the envelope.

The reply is, once again, quick. 'Handle naturally. Your friend should be surprised and completely unaware of your efforts. Timing and location for the meet will follow. Precision is vital.'

This means that he is to use traditional means to eliminate

the target. This is not his speciality; people usually hire him to create a piece of theatre, a shocking and well-publicised death. It doesn't concern him – he's happy just to pull a trigger if that's what the client wants. The talk of surprise is common enough and usually suggests a twinge of guilt on the part of the client. They want him to kill quickly and suddenly. The target should be dead before they even know what's happening. No threats, no fear, just a flipped switch. Easy enough. The Assassin is a renowned marksmen and a high-velocity round through the forehead will do the job adequately.

He opens the envelope and, for the first time in his career, feels a moment of indecision. Not because he doesn't wish to kill the target – that is far from the case, the face is all too familiar and the Assassin relishes the idea. No, the regret he feels is that the man will die quickly. It is something he would have far preferred to take time over. Momentarily he wonders whether to ignore the directive but then, as in the shop earlier, common sense prevails. He has no wish to gather more enemies, and whoever wants this man dead is likely to be a dangerous client indeed. He will carry out his job to the letter.

The Assassin leans back in his chair and looks into the face of the man in the photograph. The shot has been taken from some distance, a telephoto lens aimed through traffic, but the target's face is all too clear as it gazes into the window of a gentlemen's outfitters.

'August Shining,' says the Assassin, 'looks like your past is about to catch up with you.'

THREE

August Shining stared at the photographs on his wall and remembered better days. It wasn't nostalgia, his feet were too firmly placed in the now for that, just an awareness of happiness lost.

'You being all maudlin again?' April, his sister, was piled on one of the sofas like a collection of unwanted bric-a-brac someone hadn't yet dumped outside a charity shop. Sometimes the pile of mismatched clothes and cheap, garish jewellery would shuffle or exude menthol cigarette smoke, sometimes it would speak. Either way, the air was a little worse off.

'I am not,' Shining replied, aiming a poisonous look at her. 'I was simply thinking.'

'Amounts to the same thing these days. You're barely there. Half a man.'

'I haven't a great deal to be jolly about, April, as I'm sure even someone as self-obsessed as you must have noticed.'

'Self-obsessed? Well, if you're going to be rude . . .'

'Please don't feign offence, darling, we both know you better.'

He settled down behind his desk and tried to find something constructive to do on the computer. It was like walking into a room having forgotten what one wanted to do when there. A minute's aimless spinning of the cursor mouse led to him emptying the recycling bin and staring once more at the walls.

'They'll be fine.' April said. 'They're both horrendously capable, you know. Probably even more so than we were at their age, though I hate to admit it.'

'I don't doubt their capabilities, just wish I could be more proactive in helping them. Is that so strange?'

'Of course not, but sometimes one simply has to accept one's powerlessness and find something else to rail at. Haven't you got any godawful manuscripts you should be publishing?'

She was referring to Section 37's cover as Dark Spectre, a small publishing house of horror novels that didn't sell. In actuality, Shining left all of the work to a young man in Milton Keynes who brushed up submissions and slapped questionable covers on them. Occasionally the young man became irritated by his boss's lax attitude towards the business but never so much so that the power and minimal freelance wage didn't compensate.

The telephone rang, saving August the need to argue. The caller did nothing to improve his mood.

'Shining?' said a voice that seemed to resent being there, despite the fact that it was making the call.

Shining recognised the voice and his mood slumped even further. Sir Robin, a particularly vocal opponent of Section 37. The man filled the hours he avoided his Whitehall desk by breaking the springs of an armchair at the Cornwell's Club. Shining suspected that would be where the pompous old sod was dialling from, that dusty old graveyard of colonials and kings. The call would be a chaser to another large brandy.

'I'm sorry?' Shining replied. 'I think you may have the wrong number. This is Dark Spectre publishing, can I help you?'

'Oh piss off, Shining, you know damn well who I am.'

He did, but knowing the pleasure Sir Robin would take should he ever catch Shining breaking security protocol, he was damned if he was going to turn a blind eye.

'Actually the line is rather bad, could you hang up and try again?' Shining put the phone down and enjoyed his very first smile of the day. Its brevity made it no less enjoyable.

The phone rang again.

'Dark Spectre?' asked Shining, keeping his voice perfectly civil.

'It's a secure line, you hateful old bastard!' shouted Sir Robin. 'There's a car coming for you in half an hour.' Sir Robin hung up first this time.

'Problem?' April asked.

'Yes,' admitted Shining, 'I think there must be. Sir Robin is sending a car for me.'

Shining made a point of being early, not because he wanted to seem eager but rather because he wanted to keep the buggers out of his office. There was no particular reason, nothing specific he wished to hide, he just didn't like the idea of unknown officers poking around in his private space.

As always, the main road was busy, shoppers weaving between one another as they made their angry way from one shop to another.

Oman, the owner of the mobile-phone shop beneath the

Section 37 office (and occasional technical adviser, cash paid, questions asked but answers never given), was stood in his doorway, attempting to stuff a limp kebab into his mouth.

'Didn't have time for lunch,' Oman explained through a swamp of meat and yoghurt.

Shining might reasonably have pointed out that the man had found time for it now but he wasn't going to take his irritations out on a friend.

'Off somewhere nice?' Oman asked.

'I doubt it,' Shining admitted. 'A mystery tour. They're never good news.'

'My old mum went on one of those once, ended up trapped in a bus just outside Eastbourne. Twenty pensioners fogging up the glass and staring at the rain while waiting for the AA.'

'Sounds charming.'

Shining was distracted by a figure across the road. A man staring at him from behind the window of a sandwich takeaway shop. The reflection on the glass distorted his features but Shining was quite sure that the man was watching him. Perhaps aware that he had been spotted, the other man looked away, turning his back on the window and retreating inside the shop. Shining, still feeling combative, had half a mind to walk over there and take a look but then the car arrived and he had more immediate irritations to contend with.

It was a suitably innocuous hatchback in metallic grey. Four men were inside, all wearing nondescript business suits from high-street stores, people designed to be forgotten. One of the men sat in the back climbed out and stepped to one side so that Shining could climb in. He did do, annoyed to see the man close the door on him and walk off towards the Section 37 office, ignoring a stare from Oman completely. So much for not having his office invaded.

'Should I have warned your chap that the office isn't empty?' Shining asked, wondering who was designated to reply.

'I'm sure your sister will be happy to help,' replied the man sat next to him on the back seat. Shining was only too aware that the man was scoring points. They knew who was in the office. Fine, bully for them. It hardly mattered. He looked at the man, ex-military most likely, eyes constantly scanning the world outside the car as if expecting an attack.

'I don't suppose anyone is cleared to tell me where it is we're going?' Shining asked.

'No,' the man replied, watching a young mother push her child across a pedestrian crossing. Shining couldn't tell if his gaze was appreciative or whether he suspected the woman represented a threat. Perhaps the man had been in the security business so long he could no longer tell either.

They drove north towards the A10 and an escape from London, Shining no longer bothering to maintain the pretence of civility as a pregnant silence filled the car with the breathless atmosphere of a gym locker room. Instead, he took a few moments to analyse his companions and decide what had brought the car to his door.

The men reeked of special forces. UKSF had a bearing, a solidity that never waned, even when not involved in anything more intimidating than the act of filling out suits. Whatever meeting he was on his way to was therefore both secret and outside the normal channels of any specific department. These men were on loan. They probably knew nothing more than that they were to collect him and deliver him to his destination, wherever it may be. Outside London, that much was obvious, and equally worrying. This wasn't to be a simple debrief by one of the other section heads; if that were the case he'd have been called to the meeting, not ferried in ignorance. This was the sort of treatment reserved for the enemy.

Petty animosity aside, he couldn't imagine what he'd done to earn himself that status. If anything, Section 37's last operation should have seen their reputation in the ascendance. Naturally, a good many of the details would be hidden away in obscure files, known by few, believed by fewer. Those facts aside, their involvement in the recent trade talks between the UK and South Korea had saved lives and unearthed an MI6 traitor of long standing. Shining could fully imagine Six were somewhat irritated by the fact – nobody liked it when outsiders discovered these things. If there was a bad apple, better you found them yourself, hopefully in a manner that might suggest you had always had your eye on them – but that wasn't due cause for victimising Shining. Right now, the last thing Six would want to talk about was Mark Fratfield.

They had left someone behind to poke around his office. Why had they done that? What were they after? What files would the man be trying to lay his hands on at this very minute? Had April already killed him? Shining couldn't help a brief smile at the thought.

FOUR

The moment the security officer entered the Section 37 office, April had him tagged as a problem. The only thing she was uncertain about was how best to solve it.

'Can I help you?' she asked. She smiled at him in precisely the sort of way that a mad old woman might.

April Shining had gone a long way in her various careers. She had done so thanks to a number of different skills, not least of which was knowing when to seem unimportant, annoying or mad.

'April Shining?' the officer asked, fixing her with a stare that suggested he was considering how easily she'd fit in a bin bag.

'That's me,' April replied. 'He lets me stay here when my boiler's on the blink. My boiler's always on the blink. I don't suppose you're any good with old boilers?' She winked in case the double entendre was lost to him. You never could tell with security officers.

'I won't be in your way, I promise,' she said, taking him by the arm. 'What are you looking for? Perhaps I can help? He has all manner of old rubbish here: old books, old papers, old sisters.' She laughed again.

'I'm just retrieving some paperwork,' he said, 'nothing important.'

Which meant it obviously was, decided April. Some people were just no good at lying.

She looked the man up and down. Solidly built, ghost of a tan. Recently divorced – or, at least, recently stopped wearing a wedding band – some men took time before the message finally got through and they ditched the jewellery. He had flinched slightly when she'd taken his arm though it moved easily enough as he gave it a squeeze and a shake. It hadn't been a gesture of awkwardness so she decided to be brave and test an assumption. She patted him on his bicep and he flinched again.

'You've muscles on you,' she said flirtatiously. 'Bet you get in a lot of fights.'

'Not for a while,' he admitted. He sounded sad about the fact.

'Got any good tattoos?' she asked.

'A few.' His mood brightened. 'Just had a new one on my arm, actually.'

April looked surprised, though she wasn't. If he was sore on his arm the most likely reason was either a wound or a tattoo. He hadn't been in any fights lately, apparently, so . . . 'Oh go on, give us a look!'

'I'm really busy at the moment.'

'Oh come on! It'll only take a minute!'

He looked around, as if expecting his commanding officer to have come into the room unnoticed, then grinned and pulled off his jacket. She helped him, lifting his wallet out of the jacket pocket as she did so, dropping it on the floor and nudging it beneath the sofa with a gentle backwards kick.

He tugged at his tie so he could unbutton the upper half of his shirt and expose the tattooed arm. Lifting the thin gauze, he revealed a particularly awful picture of a character from a popular fantasy TV show.

'I'm a fan,' he explained.

'It's gorgeous,' April lied, wondering how the actress in question might feel about being reproduced in a manner that made her breasts larger than her head. 'Sexy.'

The officer nodded and made no move to cover it back up, as if April might need a little more time to fully appreciate it. She didn't but she tried to pretend to bask in its wonder for a few more seconds.

'Wonderful work,' she announced finally, helping him cover it back up. 'I'd love to have something as brilliant as that.'

'It was expensive,' he replied, as if that were all the proof needed to grant it artistic merit.

'I bet.'

'I really ought to get on.'

'Oh, do, don't let me hold you up.'

She stooped down in front of the sofa to pick up her handbag, snatching the man's wallet while she did so and dropping it inside. She disguised the action by pulling out a packet of menthol cigarettes.

'I'll just sit here and mind my own business,' she said, taking out a cigarette and lighting it. 'I hope you don't mind but August does insist I never leave the office unattended.'

The officer looked as if he might argue for a moment but

then remembered how much she liked his tattoo and just smiled. 'I won't be long. Maybe you can even help?'

'Darling, I'm at your service completely.'

He moved over to the pair of large filing cabinets on the far wall of the office, tried to open a drawer and discovered it was locked.

'I don't suppose you. . .' He turned to April.

'A key?' April replied, dropping her cigarette packet on top of the set she kept in her bag. 'I'm afraid not, he never trusts me with anything other than the office door.'

The officer sighed and moved over to the desk. He tried one of the drawers there and found it was also locked.

'My darling boy,' said April, 'it just isn't your day is it?'

FIVE

The car had now left London behind and was cutting its way through the Hertfordshire countryside.

The further it travelled, the worse Shining's mood became. The fact that they were driving him so far out felt ominous.

Finally, after a run of narrow roads, they pulled into the long driveway of an old farmhouse and drew to a halt. The house was surrounded on three sides by trees, which would have provided excellent cover in the summer, but the season had stripped their branches bare. Shining looked to the sky, noting the lack of phone and electricity wires. This was clearly a safe house for extremely sensitive subjects, isolated and secure.

'Charming spot,' he said as he was marched up to the front door. 'I wonder how many bodies are buried in the back garden?'

Naturally he was offered no reply, just ushered in through the front door. The hallway beyond was utterly bare: this was not a house used for habitation, there would be no pictures on the walls, no ornaments on the shelves. This building was a place of practicality, somewhere to store secrets that still breathed.

'Mr Shining,' said the only officer to have spoken to him, 'my name is Jennings.'

'I believe you,' Shining replied, in a manner that made it clear he didn't.

'I'm afraid I'm going to need you to empty your pockets,' said Jennings. One of the other officers handed him a small cardboard box. 'Your belongings will be quite safe but, for reasons of security, I need to ensure you have nothing on you.'

Like hell it was security, August thought as he dropped his wallet, keys and phone into the box. It was about stripping him of his possessions.

'Your watch too, please, sir,' said Jennings.

Shining sighed, removed his watch and dropped it into the box. 'Are you sure you don't want my glasses?' he asked, half-removing them. 'I'm sure the manual recommends taking them as a further aid to disorientation.'

'That won't be necessary, sir,' Jennings replied, walking off with the box.

August was led through into what would once have been a dining room but was now used for what a politician would call 'interviews' but everyone else would term 'interrogations'. A medium-sized table, four wooden chairs and a sideboard with recording equipment. A small digital camera was mounted on a tripod, pointing towards the table. The windows had been boarded up so that its inhabitants couldn't see outside. This was also why they had taken his watch of course, the hope being that, after a couple of days, the subject would no longer have a firm grip on what time of day it was.

Sat at the table was a tall woman in her early forties. She was doing her very best to appear severe: pinstripe trouser suit, black-framed glasses perched on the end of her nose, her dark hair pulled back into a ponytail. She was reading from a large dossier and made a point of not looking up when Shining entered. Not being a naughty schoolboy or nervous job interviewee, Shining cheerfully ignore the theatrics, sat down at the table and smiled.

'We both know that if there's still sections of my file you haven't read then you're an idiot,' he said cheerfully, 'and I like to think the best of people so let's assume you're not. In which case, we can skip all this nonsense and get on with having a useful chat.'

She looked up, and Shining revised her age. She was much younger but trying to hide the fact. Which made her seem a little insecure, a fact he filed away should it later be useful.

'And what do you think we're here to talk about?' she asked.

'No, no, no . . .' Shining shook his head. 'I'm sorry but I'm not playing silly games about this. You've been tasked with interrogating me about something; fine, do your job, I have absolutely no problem with that. But I have grown ancient in this business and been sat in your position countless times. As I said before, working from the position that you know what you're doing – and I have no doubt that you do – let's skip all the nonsense they teach us during training and get on with it. I haven't the first idea what you want to talk to me about so might I suggest you tell me, Ms . . .?'

She stared at him for a moment before answering. 'Ryska.'

'Excellent. I know they say we shouldn't give our names either but we both know that's hogwash, you get far more out of an interrogation if you just sit down and talk. All this gamesmanship is counterproductive as anyone who's actually been in the field knows only too well.'

'Lucas Robie,' she said, and Shining felt as if the chair beneath him had given way.

'I thought that might shut you up for a minute,' she continued. 'I appreciate you have been in the service a considerable time, Mr Shining, but that doesn't mean I'm going to sit here and be lectured, is that understood?'

'Yes,' Shining said. 'Lucas Robie is dead.'

'Yes,' Ryska agreed, 'and that's precisely what we want to talk to you about.'

'Thirty years after the fact?'

Ryska didn't reply, just closed Shining's file and continued to stare at him. After a moment, Shining tired of the pointless silence. If he was the only one willing to fill the vacuum then so be it.

'What do you want to know?'

'Your mission to Berlin.'

'It's all on record.'

'Nonetheless, I'd like to hear about it.'

Shining sighed and leaned back in his chair. 'Fine. I just hope you've filled the larder because we're likely to be here some time.'

SIX

Was there ever a golden period for espionage? I've hovered over this hateful business for decades, the Ghost of Intelligence Past, Present and Future, and I've never really known one. I remember old Len Sampson bemoaning the state of the department and taking it out on an onion he was dicing (when Len wasn't lying to someone in a distant corner of Europe, he was in his kitchen, making something delicious). 'What we need, August,' he said, 'is a bloody good war. Then perhaps we'd see an end to the petty games and an Intelligence service that works together rather than constantly poking itself in the eye.' Maybe he was right. Or maybe a job that requires duplicity, emotional coldness and an obsession with 'the bigger picture' is always going to encourage a lion's share of bastards.

That accepted, the early Eighties seemed even more hateful than usual. All the old soldiers were being pensioned off and the young bucks were spending as much – if not more – of their time spying on and manipulating each other as they were handling external threats. It was a selfish time the world over.

I suppose it would be naïve to expect the service to be any different.

I'd been increasingly sidelined over the last few years. The brief boost of my professional fortunes following Operation: Stoker began to fade when Callaghan came into power, becoming even more insubstantial under Thatcher. I could hardly claim to be alone in that.

My office was moved to its current location in Wood Green and, for the first six months of 1982, I'd lived in the safe house on Morrison Close, having been forced to siphon some of my own money into operations and therefore failing to keep up the rent on my own flat.

The call from Oswald Battle came as something of a surprise. It was the first interdepartmental communication I'd had for knocking on three months and, to begin with, I assumed he had the wrong number. My friends at Six just didn't call in those days. You may not remember Oswald but he was one of the fading old guard. Ex-military with a name that sounded like a Sussex village. Straight as an arrow but so set in his ways it was a wonder he hadn't been shuffled into a private office somewhere to slowly expire. It was generally assumed this could not be long in coming. In the late Sixties he'd lived a charmed existence, renowned for his intelligence. Now he was running a single network out of Berlin, the meat of which was becoming particularly thin. He had always had his eye on the Berlin desk but that had gone to someone far more well connected. Instead he was left with his token offshoot. In the old days it had been a valuable resource, run as an adjunct to our main Berlin operations, independent and totally under Battle's control. As the network began to dry up, he was stranded with it, neither a solid part of the Berlin office nor the respected private player he'd once been. It was a matter of open knowledge that his network was soon to be closed down, putting both him and his agents out of productive work.

'How are you fixed at the moment?' he asked, once I'd confirmed he really hadn't been meaning to speak to someone more important. 'I could really do with borrowing you for a few days.'

In the old days this sort of assumptive behaviour used to irritate me. Several section heads had treated me as a resource to pick up and drop whenever the need arose, regardless of what other work I might have had on my desk. When Oswald asked, I was so surprised I forgot to be angry with him.

'I might be able to spare you a little time,' I admitted. 'What's it all about?'

'Lucas Robie,' he said, and with that any pretence of playing hard to get was lost.

SEVEN

Luxembourg is a wonderful place. It always struck me as the lovechild of a Gothic fairy tale and Wigan. Lucas and I had first met there in 1974. He'd been drifting around the friendly parts of Europe, leading a charmed, indolent existence. I'd been looking into a reported labour camp for telepaths, the usual dead end of course, nothing but hearsay and imaginative writing in small press magazines. Once upon a time I had the patience to investigate all these things.

I'd spent a pleasant but fruitless day hiking, before returning to my pension hotel, a tiny place that didn't ask too many questions and was happy to accept me as a visiting lecturer on ferns (always pick a boring cover story; nobody wants to draw you on it for fear of expiring from boredom as a result). I was sat in the hotel's small restaurant staring miserably at some mushroom soup when Robie entered. He was one of those people that altered a room simply by entering it. Quite literally, as I would later discover.

The hotel owner metamorphosed completely from being a sullen misery, staring at a damp patch in the corner of the room and wishing everyone would just eat their damn food and leave, to an exuberant bundle of neurotic excitement.

'Good evening, Mr Robie,' he said, his voice gushing as forcefully as the hotel showers didn't. 'I'm so glad you could join us for food. I'll have chef create something special just for you. Cutlet? Dumplings?'

I looked around at the other diners, wondering how they were taking such blatant favouritism. To a one, they were gazing towards Robie with looks of undisguised admiration or even, in the case of a couple of the more shameless diners, lust.

'I'm not all that hungry actually,' said Robie. 'Perhaps just a small steak and salad?'

The owner panicked for all of five seconds before giving a low bow and dashing out of the room. Less than a minute later I saw him running up the street, tugging on his coat, clearly making a dedicated shopping trip in order to satisfy the desires of his most preferred resident.

I turned my attention back to Robie, who was flicking through a copy of *Jaws*. He seemed utterly ignorant of the effect he was having on his fellow diners, blind to their attentions.

It was difficult to pin down the attraction. He wasn't ugly but was certainly not attractive either. Mid-thirties, his hair a thin, light brown mess that was receding early. His nose was larger than the rest of his face could comfortably accommodate and his lips had a thin sneer to them as if he found everything around him ridiculous. Perhaps he did – living with a talent like his, it would have been no great surprise if he'd developed a critical view of the world. His best feature was most certainly his eyes, made all the more striking by the fact that they were each a different colour, one light blue, the other brown.

He caught me observing him and smiled. For a moment I wasn't quite sure how to respond. Look away and pretend I hadn't been staring or return his smile? In the end, I plumped for the latter.

'A fellow Englishman abroad?' I said.

Robie folded down the corner of the page he had been reading and placed the book closed on the table. 'I've been seeing the world,' he admitted. 'Well, Europe at least. I haven't crossed many oceans yet.'

'There's plenty to see without getting your feet wet,' I told him. 'Where've you been so far?'

'I've been working my way east,' he said. 'Portugal, Spain, France, Italy, skirting past Austria and Czechoslovakia.'

The notion of anyone working towards the East set a spy's heart fluttering, but Robie seemed so open, so guileless in his manner, that I took him on face value, a tourist with a surfeit of time and money.

'Sounds delightful.'

'It's been fun,' he admitted. He pointed at the spare chair at his table. 'Come and join me, saves us shouting across the room.'

I did so, curiously aware of the looks of jealousy on the faces of a number of the other guests. By joining Robie at his table, I had upset the rest of the room. I looked at him and saw that he had noticed. He hid it well, returning his attention directly to me. He was always very good at that, seeming to focus on you so strongly, so completely, that you felt special. A charmer, that's what I thought. Later I would capitalise it and use the word to define his gift.

He stared at my soup, thin and filled with fungus.

'You enjoying that?' he asked.

'I've eaten worse.'

'Not exactly a glowing recommendation. "Try the soup, there are more unpleasant foods."'

I took a sip of it. 'Maybe I'm wrong too, now I come to think of it. Still, we don't all have your skill for avoiding the menu.'

Robie smiled. 'He asked me what I wanted and I told him, honestly.'

'Simple as that.'

'Yes.' Robie continued to smile and we both knew he was lying through his teeth.

'Perhaps I might join you for breakfast,' I said, 'as long as you do the ordering.'

'Bacon and eggs all round.'

'You read my mind,' I replied, wondering if he had. Always the problem with being open to the unusual, any old thing seems possible.

We talked about his travels, me trotting out a few vague details about my cover story but always, thankfully, managing to return the subject to him. After a while, he seemed to give up trying to avoid it and settled into describing his various adventures.

The hotel owner returned, hot and stressed from having run to the butchers and back. He was far from happy to see that I had joined his favoured guest but was polite enough to synchronise our meals. The sum result being that I was able to thoroughly despair in their differences. Watery stew is bad enough on its own, but especially depressing when seen next to a well-cooked steak. It's like putting a morris dancer onstage with the Bolshoi.

He had the good grace to look slightly sheepish as he ate, watching me stirring my stew in the hunt for content. I felt like a Wild West prospector, sieving for solid vegetables. He tried to pretend the meat was past its best but I didn't believe a word of it.

Vodka was provided, and the evening grew warmer and more vague. Robie and I decided to decant ourselves from the goldfish bowl of the hotel restaurant, tired of the attention we were getting from the other guests, and head out into the city.

As we settled into a bar, already half cut from the generous helpings of vodka we'd drunk after our meal, I decided to use the last few threads of sobriety to try and pin Robie down. What sort of person can afford to be wandering around Europe, seemingly without a care in the world? Students on gap years and wealthy ancient aunts managed it. His clothes were good but not exceptional; that didn't necessarily mean he wasn't independently wealthy, but I knew few millionaires who happily walked around with a plastic Seiko on their wrist. As much as they might pretend towards indifference, millionaires' bank accounts usually revealed themselves in either their wristwatches or their shoes.

His conversation was open and, while it naturally benefits a spy to give that impression, it also takes one to know one. He was, I was sure, almost exactly what he seemed: a genuine, charming man who somehow afforded to travel the world. In the end, emboldened by drink, I asked him how he managed it.

'It barely costs me a penny,' he admitted. He looked at me for a moment and smiled. 'I use my charm.'

'Most people saying that would be deflecting from the true

answer,' I replied, 'but in your case you actually mean it, don't you?'

He nodded. 'I know you've noticed. It doesn't seem to work on you – which is rare, but you're not the first. If you're not influenced by it, then I imagine it seems really obvious when other people are.'

'People just bend over backwards to please you.'

'Sometimes literally,' he laughed and we found ourselves presented with two more drinks that we hadn't actually asked for. The barman smiled at Robie, clearly lovestruck and only able to express as much by offering free spirits.

'On the house,' he said and slowly backed away, aware that he had no further reason to stand there but equally reluctant to exist in a space without Lucas Robie in it.

Robie raised his glass to him and took a sip. 'You're most kind,' he said. The barman lit up like a nuclear blast. For a moment I thought he might cry with joy.

'So how do you do it?' I asked.

Robie shrugged. 'It just happens. It's not something I consciously affect. Ever since puberty I seem to attract . . .' He struggled to think of the word.

'Adoration?'

He winced. 'That sounds awful, though, doesn't it? When I was a teenager I loved it, of course. Then I went through a period where I found it oppressive. Perhaps that seems stupid but, as wonderful as it may sound, having strangers fawn over you actually becomes cloying after a while. It doesn't boost your ego because you've done nothing to earn it, it's just attention you haven't asked for. I wanted people to leave me alone.' He took another sip of his drink. When he continued his voice was awkward, uncomfortable. 'Of course, they wouldn't. It's hard to avoid the entire human race – you have to go to work, go shopping, sit on buses . . . Wherever I went, people would stare, offer me things, try to get close to me. It was suffocating. Look at this place now . . .'

I did, glancing around the bar. It was a tiny place, all decorative glass bottles and badly scrawled chalkboard menus. There were another ten or twelve drinkers dotted around the place. All of them were doing their best to stare at Robie without being obvious.

'And the kicker,' he continued, 'the thing that really sticks the knife in if you think about it too much, is that once I leave none of them will even remember I was here. It's as if I affect the subconscious, a momentary attraction that lasts as long as I'm in view. Once I'm gone, everyone scratches their heads and wonders precisely what it was they'd just been thinking about. It's all surface. Imagine how that feels when you want something genuine from someone. When you want real love. Because I can never get it. Fabulous, you think, I can get anyone I like into bed! I just can't get them to really want to stay there. That's really rather horrible. A life of superficial attraction. No life at all, is it, really?'

'I can see how that would be difficult,' I admitted, though I could have argued a life in espionage offered much the same result.

'Once that really struck home, I actually tried . . .' Now he really squirmed in his seat. 'I have no idea why I'm telling you this. The last thing you want is to listen to my self-pity . . . You probably think I'm an idiot for complaining.'

'Not at all,' I assured him. 'Please go on.'

He shrugged, trying to make light of it. 'I tried to commit suicide. Pathetic, I know, but it just . . . the realisation of it all got on top of me.'

'What happened?'

He smiled. 'My landlady. Never have so many medical staff worked so devotedly to try to save the life of one of their patients.'

He finished his drink. Within seconds he was presented with another.

'I didn't try again,' he continued, 'it seemed insulting, somehow, looking at all these beaming faces, so glad to see me alive. I know they didn't mean it. That their enthusiasm was a direct result of my ability, but still . . . For that one moment they were overjoyed just to see me breathe. It felt offensive to ignore that, somehow.'

'And since then?' I asked.

'Since then I have done my best to make the best of it, to appreciate what it does give me rather than what it doesn't.' He looked at me, a quizzical look in his eyes. 'Why do you believe any of this? Am I affecting you after all?'

'Not that I'm aware of,' I told him, 'but you'd be surprised at the things I've seen, the people I've known. You're not alone in possessing unusual abilities.'

'You have something?'

'Not that I'm aware of, though I must admit, the frequency with which I bump into those that have sometimes makes me wonder. I do seem to attract gifted individuals.' I laughed. 'Maybe that's my special power!'

Having not been included in the last act of generosity from the barman, I ordered myself one last drink and, from that point on, Robie and I became firm friends. I didn't enrol him that night, it came later, once I was assured he could be trusted. It was a formality, though. I like to think I'm a good judge of character – certainly my faith in a person, when I really feel it, has yet to prove misplaced. I made a good friend that night and, though our careers ensured we drifted apart, I will always consider myself lucky to have known him. For him, I think it was a relief to finally possess a friend who was there purely because he wanted to be.

EIGHT

Ryska held up her hand, instructing Shining to stop.

'You're lying,' she said.

'A character trait I'll admit to,' Shining replied, 'though I have no idea why you think it's the case at the moment.'

'We know that you and Robie had a sexual relationship. Why are you trying to hide it?'

Shining smiled and looked towards Jennings, who had taken up an uncomfortable position by the door. 'If you're bored,' Shining said to him, 'I wouldn't be offended if you decided to fetch some coffee. It's obviously going to be one of those days that drag on.'

Jennings looked to Ryska, and she nodded. 'Fine.' He quietly left the room.

'Embarrassed talking about it in front of him?' she asked Shining.

This time Shining actually laughed. 'Oh dear, if one of us has an issue over sexuality, I think it's quite clear that it isn't me! I just fancied a coffee, that's all.'

'So why were you trying to hide the nature of your relationship with Robie?'

'I wasn't. I just didn't see how it was relevant.'

'Surely that's for me to decide? Considering our suspicions, I would say the fact that you were lovers could prove to be extremely relevant.'

'Suspicions? You're actually poring all over this again because you have suspicions? It's decades ago and he's dead.'

'But you're not.'

Shining finally began to see the design behind this conversation. 'Ah . . . so it's me you're suspicious of. Because I chose to defend him?'

Ryska rolled her eyes as if Shining was stating the pitifully obvious.

Shining didn't rise to the bait. 'That shows how little you know me, which is understandable. What is more difficult to forgive is that it also shows how little you understand the nature of our job. Do you really think I would only stand by one of my colleagues if I was sleeping with them?'

'I'd say it could be a deciding factor.'

'Then I'm glad not to have to rely on you in the field. Trust is a hard commodity in our profession, and it certainly isn't earned through a damned orgasm.'

'I'm not just talking about the sex,' she insisted, slightly flustered, Shining was pleased to notice: a little victory but he'd take whatever he could get. 'You and Robie were obviously close. You loved him.'

'Did I? And how on earth do you know that?'

'It's obvious from the way you talk about him.'

'It's only obvious if you know me, which, as we've clarified, you don't. Again, expressing consideration and admiration for a fellow officer isn't proof of romantic feeling. The fact that you consider it so makes me worry terribly over the state of your social life. Or love life for that matter.'

'My love life isn't the subject of conversation here.'

'Neither is mine, which is precisely my point. Maybe I did love Lucas. Maybe I didn't. Let's get to the point, though. Your concern is as to whether I may have been under Lucas's influence. You're wondering if I was being controlled by him.'

'That's part of it.'

'If I was, don't you think I would be eager to have you think so? It would make life a lot easier for me, wouldn't it? I could protect myself from any suggestion of wrongdoing, couldn't I? Present myself as a helpless pawn in Lucas's plan, whatever it may have been.'

'So why don't you?'

'Two reasons: firstly, I am quite convinced I wasn't under his influence. Secondly, I still stand by my belief that Lucas was innocent. I don't distance myself from people that I consider innocent. Unfashionable in our job, I know. So many of us refuse to ever stand by our colleagues, it's a wonder we have any friends at all, isn't it?'

The door opened and Jennings returned with coffee.

'Good man,' said Shining, taking a cup. 'I think we've finished discussing my bedroom habits. In fact, I'm pleased to say we never really started.' He looked at Ryska. 'Shall I continue?'

She waved her hand in agreement.

NINE

I met Battle at what the codebook called Blake Hall (the current wheeze was for naming locations after disused Underground stations). The location – a room above a grotty cafe off the Vauxhall Bridge Road – didn't match the splendour of its name. They so rarely did.

'I nearly ended up in bloody Bayswater,' Battle moaned. 'I wish they'd stop changing the book every damn month.'

'Bayswater? The bookies? You were thinking of Brill.'

'I don't know, I'm sure. Secrecy's one thing but I've more important things to do than memorise location codes. What was that nonsense last month?'

'Flavours of ice cream.'

'Bloody hell. "Make it five at rum and bloody raisin." The service is going to the dogs, I tell you.'

'Dogs will be next month.' I looked around at the fat-licked black and white tiles and Formica. In the corner a pallet of sugar was turning to sweet concrete in the damp. 'They can label this place Shitzu.'

'Tea's not bad,' he said, taking a large mouthful. 'Milky and sweet.'

Two goals tea should never aim for in my opinion, but I let it pass. I was impatient to move beyond the small talk.

'So,' I prompted. 'Robie.'

'You knew him well, I believe?'

'Yes, I recommended him for the service.'

Battle nodded and took another sip of his creamy, sweet water. 'Shouldn't reflect badly on you.'

'What shouldn't?'

Battle wasn't being intentionally enigmatic, not like some in this damned business who held on to their secrets for as long as possible, as if aware they were worthless without them.

'He's gone quiet.'

'He could have his reasons.'

Battle shrugged. 'None good. He's been the local lad for my Berlin network for the last five years. No complaints. Regular reports. Good co-ordination.'

Battle had fallen into the ex-military trap of short sentences. If I didn't break him out of it, I feared he'd never savour the joys of a comma again.

'He was always reliable.'

Battle nodded. 'Until last week. He missed his scheduled call and nobody's heard from him since. Seems to me we have two choices: he's either dead or no longer ours.'

'Robie wouldn't turn. He has no interest in the Russian way of life. He was never political.'

'Who knows? His screening didn't ring any alarm bells but I can't say I ever really felt I knew him.'

This was back-pedalling. Battle was already trying to distance himself from any fallout should Robie have turned traitor. I hated that sort of thing. When did we give up on loyalty in this business? Nobody but me was aware of Robie's specialised skills – I hadn't seen the benefit in revealing them. When Robie had expressed interest in signing up, they would have stood against him, whatever their practical advantages. Someone was bound to have questioned the impartiality of the screening process. When dealing with a man that could get people to do whatever he wanted, how could anyone say for sure that he hadn't cheated his interviews? If Robie had gone quiet then it was for a damn good reason.

I decided it was time to get to the point.

'Why are you telling me this? Are you after my opinion of him?' I knew it was more than that – Battle had asked if I could spare him a few days.

'Actually, I was hoping you might pop over and see if you could ferret him out.'

'Pop over? To East Berlin?' Battle was making it sound like a weekend's holiday.

'You spent a little time over there in '73.'

'A week in West Berlin. I barely glanced at the Wall, let alone crossed it.'

'You'll be fine, I'm sure.'

'That doesn't reassure me one jot.'

'You know Robie better than anyone.'

This was probably true but Battle didn't actually know that.

'I've barely seen him in six years. Let's not dance around the truth of it; you want me to go because I'm seen as disposable.'

'I'm sure that's not the case.' Which was a rubbish denial and he knew it. I couldn't get too angry at him, a decision like this didn't come from Battle. He'd filed his report and one of our paymasters had put my name forward. They didn't want this old soldier blundering around, he'd probably start a war, but the network wasn't vital enough to risk anyone important. Send Shining, someone had decided. If he turns anything up then we're happy, if he doesn't come back then we've made a sizeable saving on our annual expenditure. I could just imagine the celebratory round of drinks that had been raised at the brilliance of the suggestion.

'When do I go?' There seemed little point in tilting at windmills.

'This afternoon. I've booked you on the military flight.'

'Then I suppose I'd better pack a bag,' I said, putting aside my full mug of awful tea and getting to my feet.

Battle opened his battered briefcase. It was like watching an ancient brown cow yawn. He pulled out a thin dossier. 'Here's everything I could bundle together for you. The secure stuff, anyway. I've prepped a local boy to give you a hand once you get there.'

'What local boy? Why isn't he looking for Robie?'

'Bit above his pay grade. He's a decent lad, though, Engel, got his head screwed on.'

'Which puts him one up on me.'

TEN

I made the flight, but only by the skin of my teeth. I sat amongst a cheery bunch of squaddies. Having run to catch my plane, my body was cooking inside my suit and shirt. I loosened my collar, trying to let out some heat, a hot updraft cooking my chin. The suit clung to me like an unhelpful shower curtain. What I really wanted to do was strip off and get cool, but I doubted that would go down well.

The soldiers were discussing Berlin in the boisterous terms of students on a rag-week outing. You might almost think their time back home had been a hardship.

Disembarking at RAF Gatow, I was met by Engel, Battle's 'decent lad'. Dressed in narrow-legged faded jeans and a voluminous sweater, he looked like a dandelion seed with acne. He seemed so youthful I wondered if he possessed a valid driver's licence. If he didn't, he saw it as no obstruction, throwing my bag onto the back seat of a fragile Volkswagen and inviting me to occupy the passenger seat.

When flying to Germany, you gain an hour yet seem to lose

five years. Berlin has always had a well-deserved reputation as a vibrant and culturally explosive place, but the overall impression is of an austere, cold city dressed in yesterday's clothes. Brutal concrete punches to the eye leavened by modern extravagance.

It had snowed, much of it turning to dirty grey slush, which didn't help the aesthetics.

'You speak German?' Engel asked.

'Yes, but you'll have to forgive the accent.'

'It's fine, my English isn't very good and I worried. Mr Battle only speaks English and conversations are hard.'

I found it difficult to believe that in all his years of running the network, Battle had never bothered to pick up the lingo. Perhaps he considered it a bulwark against German supremacy. No doubt he tutted at passing Mercedes. You never could share the mindset of old soldiers unless you were one.

'German is fine,' I assured Engel.

'Brilliant. I just have to make a quick stop on the way, hope that's OK?'

I shrugged. 'I'm in your hands.'

I alternated between taking in the busy streets and my driver. If I really was in the young man's hands, I wanted to know a bit more about him. I had never developed much professional paranoia. Working in the distant backwater of Section 37, I could afford to be more casual than most. Here, I was paddling in more dangerous waters and I wanted the reassurance that Engel was someone I could rely on.

'How long have you been working for Battle?' I asked, trying to remain casual even though the car was shaking us up and down as if we were on a fairground ride. Battle must have been extra stingy on his budgets to let Engel drive around in that clapped-out old thing.

Engel smiled. 'Only six months. He needed a driver and I needed money. My father knew him during the war.'

'They were on good terms, I hope?'

Engel laughed. He was always laughing, I liked that. People who laughed easily were usually good souls.

'They hid in all the same tunnels together. Father was part of the resistance.'

We cut down a side street and Engel parked the car skew-whiff on the kerb. It was a relief to be still for a minute. He reached past me to grab a brown parcel off the back seat.

'I won't be long,' he said, jumping out of the car and jogging down the street towards a bar at the far end. I wondered what sort of agent was so confident in himself that he indulged in smuggling during the initial meeting with a superior. A terribly young one, I supposed. I wondered what the package had contained. Drugs? Money? Cigarettes? He returned a couple of minutes later and climbed back into the driver's seat. I decided to face the question head on.

'What was in the package?'

'American chocolate.'

'Chocolate?'

'The owner of the bar has a brother on the Eastern side who occasionally feeds us information. Nothing important really, but Lucas always felt it was worth keeping him. One day he might have come up with something useful.'

'Chocolate?'

'The brother really likes chocolate. Hershey bars if possible. Personally I think they taste like plastic but each to his own.'

They were running a network based on confectionery.

'Do we have any other payments to make? Perhaps a kilo of jelly babies to a ticket collector at the Ostbahnhof?'

Engel laughed again. 'No, that's it for today. I was going straight to your hotel. That OK?'

'Fine by me.'

The hotel was a guest house by British standards, a concrete rectangle struggling to protect its naked modesty behind the leafless branches of a handful of trees.

I was introduced to the landlady, a fading ruin of ancient splendour, dyed black hair, make-up thick enough for Kabuki. She wore black satin and cigarette smoke. The ghosts of decadent nights in cabaret bars clung to her drooping shoulders and she navigated the corridors as if slowly dancing to a lovesick piano. When we reached my room, she croaked something indecipherable and sprawled against the door jamb, offering an inch or so of wilting, fish-netted thigh. She was utterly adorable.

'Thank you, Frau Schwarz,' I said, taking in the box-like cubicle of ancient fabrics and damp. It was the sort of room a Trappist monk might stay in if he wanted to punish himself. 'It's delightful.'

'It's awful,' she said, her thin voice crackling like a Geiger counter, 'but we make do.'

I always enjoyed people who wallowed in misery, so I smiled and began to unpack my bag.

I hadn't brought a great deal, perhaps subconsciously hoping that the less underwear I carried the briefer my visit would turn out to be. This is the peculiar attitude of Englishmen everywhere, refusing to carry an umbrella in the absurd belief it might encourage rain.

For a couple of moments Frau Schwarz observed from the doorway and then, deciding my belongings were of no interest, she wandered away to refresh her cigarette holder.

'She's reliable,' said Engel, as if I might have doubted it.

'I'm sure she is.'

I finished putting my things away and pocketed the room key. 'Office next?'

'Sure thing.'

I still hadn't mentioned the disappearance of Lucas Robie. Perhaps I was hoping Engel would bring it up. Perhaps, like the lack of underwear in my bag, I just hoped that the more I ignored the situation the less real it could be. Enough, however, was enough.

'Tell me about Robie,' I said, trying to keep the subject as open as possible. I wanted Engel's genuine thoughts both on the man and what might have happened to him.

'Lucas was a good friend,' Engel replied. 'I will tell you now, I don't believe what Battle is saying about him. It's easy to accuse someone from behind a desk in another country but I worked with Lucas every day, I knew him. He would not defect.'

Which was nice to hear but didn't really get me anywhere. Of course he liked Lucas, who didn't?

'So what's happened to him, then?'

Engel shrugged, trying to look casual and failing. He was worried, that much was clear, and when he spoke his words carried none of the conviction he was aiming for.

'He's probably chasing something down,' he said, 'following some lead or opportunity. Lucas had a great nose for that sort of thing.'

Which may well have been true. I knew little of Lucas's career.

'Might he be in trouble?' I asked, forcing my way into that little crack of insecurity he'd shown.

'Lucas can look after himself.' He seemed even less believable this time.

'But if he were in trouble,' I pressed, determined to get something useful out of him, 'who would have their finger on the trigger? One of the men in the car following us?'

I'd first noticed the car shortly after leaving Frau Schwarz's charming guest house. It was a black Audi that positively reeked of government expenses. I could guess which government.

'They're not important,' Engel replied. 'You shouldn't have come in on the military plane; someone was bound to follow us.'

He didn't look in the rear-view mirror, and I believed his show of having known the car was there all along. If I'd been a better spy, perhaps I would have remained undecided as to whether this showed skill on his part or a possibility of collusion. I've always been someone who takes people too much on face value – perhaps that's why nobody ever tried to push me towards a promotion.

'They're only bound to follow us if your security's as flimsy as the suspension on this damned car of yours.'

'Sometimes it's no hardship to have your enemy follow you,' he said. 'Lucas always said that. You let them see what you want them to see, and get your real business done while they're looking the other way.'

'And you want them to see me?'

'Does it matter? As long as they don't know why you're here.'

'That rather depends on what's happened to Robie, doesn't it? If they've enrolled him then it's not rocket science to guess.'

'I told you, there's no way Lucas has gone over to the Russians.'

'I'm glad you're so convinced. We may be gambling my life on the fact.'

I kept an eye on the car, paying particular attention to the driver and his passenger, two men I wanted to be able to recognise – for all the good it might do me – if I suddenly met them in a dark Berlin alleyway. If I survived such an encounter, it would make writing the report so much easier.

The driver was in his mid-forties, with the sort of pale, deathlike skin that could only come from a life led under strip lighting. He wore narrow glasses over a nose far too big for them, the overall effect being of a man whose face was swallowing its own spectacles. The passenger was a little older. He wore a large corduroy cap pulled low over a pugilist's face, the sort of vegetable features that looked as if they'd been pounded into place by a god who used his knuckles. The filing clerk and the bruiser, they wore their specialist skills clearly.

'What do we know about these two?' I asked Engel. 'As we're obviously such good friends with them.'

Engel glanced at the mirror, confirming the officers

in question. 'The driver's new but the man with the cauliflower for a head is Ernst Spiegel. Believe it or not, he's one of their sharper men. Dislikes a life behind a desk, otherwise he would probably have a better career. Mother's Russian, father's long dead, he seems an earnest party member, enjoys his work. . .'

'Even when it's just clinging on to our bumper?'

Engel shrugged. 'You know what it's like. They follow us, we follow them, sometimes we make a show of it, more often we don't. It's like cats squaring up to one another, all big fur and bared teeth. If you want me to lose them then I will.'

'If you do that then it'll only make me seem more important. I'm in the open, perhaps it's best to leave it that way.'

I didn't like it, but I disliked putting a target on myself by panicking even more.

We pulled up outside a grey office block and I did my level best not to stare as the pursuing Audi drove slowly past us.

'Another delivery?' I asked, looking up at the building.

'I said I was taking you to the office, didn't I?'

'The Berlin office is in the Olympic Stadium, even I know that. As, I'm sure, does Herr Spiegel.'

'Battle's network is run separately from the station office. I thought you knew that?'

'I didn't realise it had its own office.' I chose not to labour the point but considering how little Battle's superior's thought of his network I was baffled – and, yes, perhaps a little jealous. It may have been independently run but it was still part of Berlin operations. I had to spend a week arguing the toss over a filing cabinet.

Engel led me up the concrete steps to a revolving door. He

walked past the reception desk, smiling at the guard stationed there, a bored-looking man working his way through a crossword. He used a pen: you can always spot a show-off. We walked straight past a pair of lifts and on towards the stairwell. Engel headed down. It was obvious from the smug smile on his face that he was enjoying this piece of theatricality, so I chose not to question him, just followed as he led us into the basement.

He weaved his way through stacks of office supplies and ancient, mothballed equipment until we were in the far corner, barely within reach of the low light afforded by the heavy glass skylights that funnelled thin sunshine down from the pavement above.

He dropped to his haunches in front of an empty wooden pallet, grabbed it, lifted it up and propped it in place with a length of scrap wood clearly left there for the purpose. Beneath there was a manhole cover.

'Oh joy,' I said, fearing for the future happiness of my rather nice suit.

'Don't panic, it's not a sewer. Grab those flashlights.' Engel pointed to a pair of torches on a nearby shelf and lifted the manhole cover.

I descended first. Engel hovered at the opening, knocking the makeshift prop out of the way so that the pallet fell down on top of the manhole cover as he manoeuvred it back into place.

I descended the rest of the metal ladder, turning on my torch once my feet hit the ground.

'The U-Bahn?' I asked. In the distance an underground train rattled along a nearby tunnel, making my question redundant.

'Service tunnel,' Engel agreed, leading the way. 'It's away from prying eyes, has private access to the rest of the city . . . all of the city in fact, though we try not to make a habit of it.'

Various parts of Berlin's underground networks crossed the border. After the Wall had been built, an uneasy compromise had been in place. Some lines had been closed altogether but some West Berlin routes that strayed into Eastern territory remained open, the Eastern stations closed to travellers and manned by barricades and security guards.

'If we make a habit of using the tunnels as a crossing route,' Engel continued, 'we increase our chances of getting caught and the last we thing we want to do is draw attention to a useful route.'

This was also strangely English, I thought. We have a good thing so we'd better not use it in case they take it away from us.

We walked for maybe ten minutes, distantly surrounded by the coming and going of Berlin's commuters. Eventually, Engel stopped next to a locked grating in the wall, pulled a large set of keys from his pocket and opened it. Beyond, what appeared to be a rack of dusty fuses and cabling revealed itself to be nothing of the sort as Engel twisted one of the fuses, a latch no less, that allowed the whole to swing back revealing a dark corridor beyond.

'Someone's been watching a lot of Bond movies,' I said.

'You're just jealous because your office is boring.'

'Actually,' I lied, 'my office is lovely. And you don't have to walk through half an hour of tunnels to get to it.'

Engel smiled and gestured for me to lead the way.

The short corridor turned a corner and I found myself faced with a pair of double doors. I swung them open and was suddenly bathed in the sound of KC and the Sunshine Band. The office was tiny, three desks surrounded by the sort of distressed metal grating low-budget sci-fi shows favour when attempting to build the future. One of the desks was occupied by a transistor radio and a young woman who looked at me over a pair of spectacles with quite astonishingly red frames. 'Herr Shining?'

'You make me sound like a beauty product.'

She turned down the radio slightly and stared at me in confusion, the polite look on her face souring with every passing second.

'An awful joke,' I explained, 'that only really works in English, sorry. Yes, I'm August Shining.'

'I'm sure it was very funny,' she said, proving it really wasn't. She handed me a key. 'For the outside door,' she explained. It dangled from a heavy wooden fob of the sort commonly used by hotels. Embossed in gilt was the number forty-two.

'My age,' I noted.

She didn't reply. Possibly she was still recovering from my brilliant joke.

'If you manage to lose it,' said Engel, 'nobody should look at it twice. There's also a tracker in the fob.'

'So you always know where to find me?'

'That's one of the benefits,' he admitted.

'I presume Robie wasn't carrying one?' It seemed slightly insulting to ask.

'He was, but it was tracked to a Neukölln bar, abandoned next to a half-drunk glass of American beer and a lit cigarette.'

'Which rather suggests he was interrupted.'

'Or saw something that made him run,' Engel suggested.

I nodded. 'I'll want to visit the bar,' I told him.

'Easy enough,' he said.

'Without the presence of our Eastern friends,' I clarified.

'Also easy enough,' he assured me.

I hoped that would be true.

ELEVEN

Berlin had a number of American-themed bars, enterprising Germans swallowing their pride in the name of cashing in on the Yank soldiers stationed in their city. I suppose Budweiser does at least sound vaguely German. Here in 'The Rodeo', one certainly got the impression they liked the beer – signs for it were slapped over the walls. I suppose they had to break up the tatty saddles and steer horns with something. On the jukebox, The Eagles were taking it to the limit one more time; I mentally raised a glass to their consistent endurance.

'I hate this place,' muttered Engel. 'It makes me want to defect.'

'Have a nice glass of Jack Daniels and feel better,' I suggested.

We took our place at the bar next to a group of enthusiastic members of the US Air Force. They were approaching the stage of the evening when each drink had to be accompanied by a boisterous game, preferably with some form of bet involved. It was half past seven, God bless American enthusiasm.

The barman wore a stars and stripes shirt as if it were burning him, fixing us with a stare that suggested it was all our fault.

'What can I get you gentlemen?' he asked in English.

I ordered us a couple of draught beers – in German, as if pathetically trying to curry favour. It didn't make the barman love us but at least he poured them without spitting in them.

We took our beers to a small table in the corner and muscled up the enthusiasm to make a few enquiries.

'So,' I said to Engel, 'fill me in on the last movements of Lucas Robie.'

'He was preparing to cross back over,' said Engel, by which he meant that Robie was planning to return to East Berlin, where, by all accounts, he spent much of his time. 'Usual business, plus,' he added almost as an afterthought, 'he seemed to think that there was something interesting going on involving a Russian soldier.'

I chose not to think naughty thoughts. 'What sort of interesting?'

'Man by the name of Anosov, rising star, young lieutenant, predicted captaincy within the year.'

'Good for him.'

'He went crazy, climbed naked onto the Wall and began machine-gunning passers-by.'

'Bad for him.'

'By all accounts, it took half an army to take him down. His body was little more than tatters under gunfire but he fought on. Nobody could believe it. He seemed superhuman. I dare say it was exaggerated, you know what people are like.'

'I do.'

'There was no history of mental illness, no sign of anything that might have contributed to a breakdown. He went from loyal son of Mother Russia to shocking embarrassment within the space of a day.'

'And Robie thought he knew why?'

Engel shrugged. 'He wasn't very forthcoming but he seemed to think there was something more to it than just a madman and a gun. Lucas liked to chase the unusual stuff sometimes. In all honesty I think he found the day-to-day stuff boring, so when something more interesting came along he jumped on it. I doubt it would have come to anything, it was just a way of him relieving the boredom.'

I could imagine that was true. Lucas's 'day-to-day stuff' would have been the co-ordination of information from the network, arranging meetings and payments and then funnelling back the goods to Battle. For someone like Lucas, especially given the charmed life he led, that would have been child's play, despite the need to spend a good deal of time on the 'wrong' side of the Wall with all the dangers that could bring. He must have felt wasted dealing with the poor results of Battle's network, eager to move on to more exciting opportunities. If he'd believed the actions of Anosov might lead to something exciting, he'd have been all over it.

'Tell me precisely what he said about it.'

'As I say, he wasn't very forthcoming. I don't think he wanted to discuss it until he had something concrete to pass on.'

'All the more reason to know the little he did say.'

'I think I asked him what was so interesting about a crazy guy. People go crazy sometimes, you know? He made a comment along the lines of, "Who says he was crazy?"'

I nodded, encouraging Engel to continue.

'So I said, "The guy strips off and kills a bunch of people, he obviously isn't in his right mind." I definitely phrased the last bit like that because he laughed and said, "If he wasn't in his right mind, what was?"' Engel shrugged. 'I had no idea what he meant and told him so. He just shrugged and changed the subject.'

'What was?' I wondered aloud.

By the bar, a group of American soldiers were arguing good-humouredly about a game of cards they'd recently played. One of the soldiers was bemoaning the fact that he was owed money by someone else in the camp. The others were egging him on with his string of threats as to what he planned doing to the man if he didn't pay up.

Engel stared at the men and grumpily tried to hide behind his drink. 'People that threaten and never do,' he said, 'hot air and empty promises.'

'That's espionage all over,' I told him. 'I wonder if they're regulars? Another drink?'

Engel, whose beer was barely touched, made to decline but I was already on my way to the bar, placing myself right next to the Americans.

'Two more,' I told the barman, this time speaking English.

I turned slightly towards the Americans hoping one of them would take the opportunity to talk to me. A large, red-cheeked man with teeth so large he could bring down a bison on an open plain, offered me a terrifying smile.

'Now, either you've turned your back on that lousy English beer you guys drink or you're new in town. Which is it, feller?'

'Bit of both,' I said, shaking the man's hand. 'Dennis Theakston.'

'I'm Jerry Franks.' He pointed to each of his colleagues in turn. 'This is Lester Reynolds, Tom Hurwitz and Billy Shepherd.' Each shook my hand in turn, big, assertive shakes to let me know they were both happy to meet me and capable of beating me in a wrestling match should the occasion arise. I love Americans. Unlike some of my countrymen, I don't see openness and enthusiasm as qualities to frown upon.

'I'm over here on business,' I said. 'My company imports wine and I have to sign the paperwork and shout at the packaging people. It keeps my boss happy.'

'Who's sat on his ass back at home, I bet?' asked Reynolds, scratching at a moustache you could have comfortably stored a family of thrushes in.

'You've got it,' I agreed, and they all laughed at my fictional boss's expense.

'You drink in here often?' I asked.

'Most nights,' Franks admitted. 'It's close to the base and they play decent tunes. There used to be a pool table too but some fool tore the hell out of the baize so it's out of action.'

'Shame,' I said. 'I'd have taken one of you on if the price was right.'

'A betting guy, huh?' asked Hurwitz, the man who had recently been explaining to the others what anatomical acts of violence he was willing to visit on the man who owed him money.

'I like a flutter,' I agreed and laughed again, pretty much to see if they would all join in, which of course they did. Rapport is an easy thing to build if you keep your ears open and your pint glass filled. 'In fact I was hoping to meet a friend of mine here tonight.' I described Robie. 'He owes me twenty Deutsche Marks from a little horse race we had a bet on.' I turned away to collect my drinks from the disgusted-looking barman, letting the Americans think about the outstanding debt for a moment.

'I think I remember the guy you're talking about,' said Hurwitz. 'English feller, only seen him in here a couple of times.'

'The guy that ran off with Grauber?' asked Shepherd.

Hurwitz nodded, clearly put out to have his story hijacked. 'That's why I remember him. Anyone Grauber set his sights on. . .'

'Grauber's always in here,' said Franks, leaning in to me. 'Local guy, slimy as hell, drinks too much. Always causing trouble.'

'Yeah,' said Hurwitz, wrestling the conversation back, 'he sat down at your guy's table and we were all laughing because we know what Grauber's like. Then, all of a sudden, your man jumps to his feet and the two of them run out of here like they think the place is on fire.'

'Haven't seen Grauber since,' said Reynolds.

'I'll drink to that!' said Franks, going on to do so.

'I don't suppose you know where Grauber lives?' I asked. I was pushing my luck but they seemed onside enough to risk it.

'Got a place over in Kreuzberg, hasn't he?' Franks asked.

Shepherd nodded. 'Bunch of us went over there once, he said he had. . .' He fell quiet, suddenly realising he'd said too much.

Hurwitz wasn't going to spare his blushes. He put his fingers to his lips and mimed sucking the final dregs of a joint. The rest of them laughed, Shepherd just looked a bit, well, sheepish.

''Course, turned out he was full of shit,' he said, clearly wishing he hadn't brought the subject up.

'You remember the address?' I asked. 'I'd happily give him

a couple of my owed Deutsche Marks if he knows where I can collect the rest. Nothing worse than a guy who won't pay up.'

'Tell me about it,' agreed Hurwitz, who proceeded to not let me do so, repeating instead some of the card game conversation I'd eavesdropped earlier. 'Tell the man,' he said to Shepherd, having worked himself up into a righteous frenzy on the subject of debt collection.

Shepherd did so and, not wanting to seem suspicious, I called Engel over – introducing him as a trainee from my local office, which was more or less the truth – and we celebrated our new cross-Atlantic friendship with a couple more rounds of drinks.

TWELVE

Of all the areas of West Berlin wounded by war and separation, Kreuzberg bled the most. Hemmed in on three sides by the Wall, it had become a cheap residential area, filled with immigrants, artists and punk rockers. As will always be the case, while some looked down their noses at the area, others rejoiced in its diversity. In the last few years, music had brought a cultural validity to some of its concrete corners, Bowie and Iggy Pop giving their regal thumbs-up to the new wave of sounds bubbling up from the clubs and bars. Nothing breeds interesting culture more than decay.

Engel regaled me with band names that meant nothing to me as we made our way, ever so slightly more drunk than was strictly professional, towards Grauber's address. I think he was surprised at my enthusiasm for the music – I was English, in my forties and in the shadow of Battle (a man I imagined insisting that good music died alongside Vaughan Williams). I tried to explain I was also a Londoner who had relished diversity and change from the first moment my feet trod its ancient pavements.

The Wall loomed over us as we approached Grauber's block, lit by its constant arc lights. The snow was getting heavier, settling on the pavements and the top of the Wall, sharp white sparks coiling in the night sky.

Unlike the elaborate frescos for which the Wall itself would later be famous, the block's pale grey skin was tattooed with rough graffiti. Great whorls of green and red spray paint, the signatures of those who ran through these streets trying to leave their mark in the only way they knew how.

Engel and I walked up the short ramp to the block entrance. Sat on the adjoining wall, her legs swinging, heels pounding out a bored rhythm against the bricks, was a young girl. She looked to be about eight or so, her blonde hair pulled into pigtails, her face a rebellious sneer as she watched the two of us approach.

'Bit late for you to be out, isn't it?' asked Engel.

She smiled, the street lights only catching half of her exposed teeth.

'Do what I want,' she replied, rattling a box of matches at us as if to prove as much.

'Where do you live?' he asked.

She opened the box and plucked out a single match, which she lit and stared at as it crackled in the half-light. 'Wherever I want.'

She took the lit match and popped it into her mouth, the flame hissing out on her wet tongue.

Engel made to say something then thought better of it. What was there to say? Don't do that? It was done, and besides, the girl had made it quite clear how uninterested she was in our opinions. He shook his head and we continued on our way to the entrance.

Engel pressed the buzzer for Grauber's apartment. There was no answer. I pulled up the collar of my coat, but the chill of a Berlin winter cared little for my weak attempts to keep it from my bones. I looked to the young girl, meaning to block Engel from view as he forced the lock on the door, but she had jumped down from the wall and was dancing in the street, twirling around in the heavy snow.

Behind me, I heard the door open and Engel and I made our way inside and towards the building's elevator.

'Eighth floor,' he said, consulting the sign next to the graffiti-scrawled metal doors. Apparently Klaus was going to burn the world, or so he had promised in bright yellow spray paint.

Engel pressed the button calling the elevator and we waited a few moments, doing our best to appear utterly at home in the damp, tatty foyer.

On the wall there was a poster warning tenants not to dump their rubbish in the communal areas; another advertised the services of an affordable plumber; yet another invited callers to express their desires to Claudia over the phone. Premium rates would be charged but Claudia insisted it would be worth the caller's while. I wondered if Claudia was, in reality, a tired housewife doing her best to make ends meet. Did she moan her way through the tedium? Pouring impossible fantasies into the ears of the lonely as she dreamed of a burgeoning bank account?

The elevator arrived and Engel and I stepped inside. Engel pressed the button for the eighth floor and the elevator began to rise.

'Reminds me of the building where I grew up,' said Engel

as the cables creaked above us. 'I couldn't wait to get out of it.'

'It's not so bad,' I said. 'We're just seeing the shell. Home is what you make it.'

Engel shrugged but was clearly unconvinced. Having had the good fortune not to grow up in a divided city, I shut my mouth on the subject.

The elevator doors opened and we walked out into the cold once more. Up here, a wind forced a tunnel of snowflakes along the balcony before us. Looking down, I saw the young girl was still dancing in the road, now striking matches and flinging them into the air around her where they glowed orange for a second before winking out.

Arriving at number 114, I hung back as Engel knocked on the door. We had no idea about Grauber, he might be friendly enough, but an Intelligence officer always stacks the odds the best he can. People can react badly to strangers on the doorstep. They can react twice as badly when there are two of them. Guilty people might be tempted to run or fight (and in either case, the second man then comes into his own). In this case, it hardly mattered as nobody came to the door.

Engel knocked again. This time there was a noise from inside as someone sent something spilling with the shattering of glass.

'You think we're making Mr Grauber panic?' asked Engel.

'Always possible,' I agreed, 'or he's in terrible trouble and would very much like our assistance.'

Engel smiled. 'Either way. . .'

He once again took the opportunity to prove his skill with a locked door.

'You're worryingly good at that,' I said.

'A man needs a varied selection of skills in this business,' he agreed.

The door gave in and we stepped inside. We were immediately hit by the smell. Body odour and rot, food gone bad. Underneath that was another, more worrying smell: petrol.

Ahead of us, a hallway extended to the rear of the apartment, doors leading off from it. All was dark, the faint light from the open door behind us revealing the tatty state of the hallway wallpaper but little else.

'Mr Grauber?' I called. 'Are you all right? We just want to talk to you if that's OK?'

From further into the apartment came a wet slapping sound, like someone stepping out of the bath.

'Please don't tell me he was just in the shower,' moaned Engel.

'Better that than the possible alternative,' I said. 'Can't you smell it? The petrol fumes?'

'Stay back!' came a voice from one of the far rooms. 'You have to stay back. I can't . . . It won't let me. . .'

'Mr Grauber,' I said, 'please, there's no reason to be concerned. We just want to talk to you for a minute.'

'You don't understand,' he was crying. 'It won't allow it. . .'

'What won't allow it?' I asked but there was to be no answer. There was a deep pounding sound and an arc of orange light cut across the hallway.

'Oh God. . .' said Engel.

Grauber walked into the hallway – he didn't run, he walked – his entire body ablaze.

I looked around for something I could use to try to put him

out. I ran into the closest room, hoping it would be a bedroom – it wasn't. From the light of the burning Mr Grauber, I could see a ratty sofa, a television and a stack of discarded takeaway boxes. Then I noticed the window. In place of curtains, Grauber had hung a blanket. I snatched at it. Behind me, Engel screamed. I tore the blanket down, bringing the heavy pole it had been draped over along with it.

Entering the hallway, I was faced with the unbelievable sight of Engel being pinned against the wall, Grauber's flaming hands gripping him by the lapels of his jacket.

I lifted the blanket, meaning to throw it over both of them. Engel's shirt was already alight, the flames from Grauber's arms licking upwards towards the young man's face, singeing his hair and searing his cheeks. Grauber had other ideas. He threw Engel towards me and continued on his way out of the door.

I beat at Engel's chest with the blanket. The young man hadn't suffered any major injury, though he'd be sore for a while.

'Go!' Engel shouted. 'Get after him!'

I did as I was told, stepping out onto the balcony where Grauber was stood looking out into the snow-filled night. How could he still be moving? Surely the shock of the flames should have killed him by now? I could smell his meat burning, hear his skin and muscle crackle and pop as it constricted around his bones.

I raised the blanket but there was no time. Grauber climbed on to the edge of the balcony and jumped out into the Berlin night.

I watched as his flaming body toppled towards the snow-covered ground below, the flames whipping behind him in the updraft. Then he hit the ground with a dull crack, splayed out on the ground. He looked uncomfortably like a flaming swastika, the snow hissing around him.

THIRTEEN

'You expect me to believe that?' Ryska asked, tapping at the table in irritation. 'That a man can set himself on fire and then just walk around?'

Shining watched her fingers, the short nails striking out an irregular rhythm on the surface of the table. He tried to decide if she was just angry or whether the irritation was covering something deeper. He realised he was overthinking matters, always a failing of his. Ryska was simply expressing the incredulity everyone always did when faced with the business of Section 37. No doubt she was conflicted, on one hand relishing the fact that she might be on the front line against a possible rogue agent, on the other cursing the fact that said agent was clearly mad.

'You've read my file, yes?' he said.

She looked at it and snorted.

He did his best to remain calm. 'A common reaction,' he admitted, 'though, forgive me, a stupid one. Do you really think someone like me gets to exist if everything he files is fantasy? Does that sound possible to you? That our masters would continue to fund – however poorly – my department, provide me with staff, a level of authority . . . Do you really think they would do that if I was just wasting everyone's time?'

Her derision possessed a little less conviction. 'It's absurd.'

'Of course it is. Deeply absurd. That anyone with half a mind could look at the evidence, and there's plenty of it, and still scoff. Whatever your logic tells you, whatever your preconceptions, once presented with contrary information you have no choice but to alter your world view. Nobody likes doing that. We like to cling to our beliefs, they're our security. But once someone categorically proves you wrong, you simply have to. To do otherwise would be idiotic. And, as I seem to need to remind you regularly, I don't believe you're an idiot. Please prove as much and think for a moment before you take the stupid way out again.'

Ryska stared at him. 'But if all this was real, people would know, we'd all be discussing it.'

'Remind yourself what it is we do for a living and then think again, you're nearly there.'

'Don't patronise me. . .'

'After a career of banging my head against a brick wall, it's either that or screaming. And considering the situation I currently find myself in, you will forgive me if I'm a little less easy-going on the subject than normal. Question my story all you like, that's your job, I have faith that we'll get to the end of it and we'll all walk away satisfied. But don't question my job – it's no doubt saved your life in the past and probably will do again. Be clever, or this situation isn't going to just be annoying, it's going to be completely intolerable.'

'Fine, I'll suspend judgement.'

'You're too kind. So, where we? Grauber – or, more precisely, what was controlling him – had flung himself off the balcony of his apartment block. Young Engel wasn't badly hurt, luckily, but we were left with a mess to clean up. Luckily, cleaning up messes is something the British secret service is used to. It causes enough of them after all. We finally called it a night and I returned to the questionable comforts of Frau Schwarz's guest house. . .'

FOURTEEN

I woke up to a cricked neck from Frau Schwarz's pillows. I'd discussed matters with them during the night, explaining the basic principles of softness balanced with support, but they'd remained dogged in their refusal to concur. I'd tried punching them but, like all forms of violent coercion, this had resulted in little but battered pillows and increased resentment.

I put on my dressing gown and made my way down the corridor to the bathroom, rolling my head all the way. If that didn't help loosen my neck muscles then a hot shower surely would. I had no desire to stare at my second day in Berlin from a pained angle of forty-five degrees.

The bathroom had the sort of functional, aggressive air one expects from military establishments or expensive English boarding schools. It quite took me back.

The shower had the same personality as my pillows but was weaker-willed – within a few minutes it had agreed to pump out hot water and I took up a precarious position behind the glass partition and set to the soap with gusto.

I was, naturally, a blind mess of soap suds when I heard the door rattle.

'Occupied!' I shouted in the way of the Englishman abroad stating the obvious.

The door rattled again, a low scratching working its way beneath the rush of water as I worked faster to rinse my hair.

I alternated between swearing and washing away soap, straddling that middle line between someone who wants the situation to end and yet refuses to be altogether hurried in his simple business of washing.

There was silence and I relaxed, thankful to be able to go about my scrubbing in peace.

I was just considering another handful of shampoo (for fun rather than necessity) when an arm reached around my neck and pulled. My feet slipped immediately and my bodyweight collaborated with my attacker's attempt to choke the life out of me. I kicked out, trying to get purchase enough to wrest myself free. Wet feet pounded against the wall and the glass partition, neither achieving anything. I shot my head back, trying to catch the attacker's face but I'd slid down his body and all I was doing his banging my head against his chest. I decided to use my position better, throwing all my weight in the direction it had been going anyway: down.

He stooped slightly, struggling to keep his grip on my wet body. I planted my feet against the surface of the bath and kicked upwards. This time my head connected with his chin and I heard a satisfying, spluttered cry pre-empting the tip of his tongue falling into my wet hair. His grip loosened slightly, no doubt down to an involuntary desire to put his hands to his profusely bleeding mouth. This was the only opportunity I was likely to get, so I put all my strength into it, driving my elbows back into his belly and kicking back against the bath again to force myself free.

We both toppled over, hitting the floor with the sort of resounding crash you would really hope other people would hear (and take as their cue to come and help). I got to my feet but my attacker grabbed at my leg. That and the water spilled on to the tiled floor saw me fall backwards into the glass partition, which finally decided enough was enough, cracking behind me.

Now that I could finally get a good look at him, I wasn't all that impressed: he was middle-aged, slightly overweight and wearing a heavy postman's anorak. Still, it seemed churlish to be overly critical. He was, after all, doing a reasonable job of trying to kill me.

He ran at me, and our combined weight shattered the glass partition behind me. I grabbed on to its metal frame, desperate to avoid falling back on the exposed edge of the glass. I head-butted him a couple of times, partially sickened and partially relieved to feel his nose pop beneath my forehead. It didn't slow him down much. He lifted me up, turned me and slammed me against the wall. Definitely an amateur move and one that saved my life – if he'd had any sense he would have shoved me down onto the broken glass. I would have fallen into the bath and bled out. The cuts on my back were fairly severe as it was, making it hard to tell what was blood and what was water as I slid against the wall.

Reaching out for a shard of glass, I wrenched a piece from the frame and stabbed it into the side of his neck. It was an awful thing to do. Killing is something that disgusts me every time I'm forced to do it, just as it should, but my feelings on the subject don't extend to dying myself in order to avoid committing the act.

He staggered back, blood spurting from the hole I'd opened in his neck. Then, all of a sudden a look of absolute confusion settled on his face. You remember that trick mimes used to perform? Where they would pass their hand in front of their face, showing a seemingly instant switch from happiness to sadness with each pass. It was like that but without the hand. One minute he was snarling with a furious determination to kill me, the next he was a confused postman wondering why his blood supply was fast relocating onto the wall of a hotel bathroom.

'Who are you?' he croaked before dropping forward and landing face first on the bathroom floor. I slowly sank down to a sitting position, utterly drained.

'What is going on?' shouted Frau Schwarz, having finally had the good grace to investigate the sound of her guest's more than usually vigorous cleaning regime.

'Call Engel,' I told her. 'We need a clean-up team.' I tried to get to my feet but the pain from the cuts in my back knocked me back. 'And someone who can give me a once-over and some stitches.'

She stared at me.

'You have no clothes.'

'I'm fully aware of that, Frau Schwarz. I do apologise. Could you please be quick? I have no wish to embarrass you further by bleeding to death in your lovely bathroom.'

FIFTEEN

It took about twenty minutes for Engel to arrive, a small team in tow. By which point I had managed to drag myself out of the bathroom and tug on a pair of trousers. The wounds in my back needed a few stitches but were far from life-threatening.

While the team of officers worked quickly to clear the body out of the bathroom and tidy up after our little tussle, I lay face down on my bed and let a medic sort out my back.

'How lovely it is to have you with us,' said Engel. 'Two bodies to bury within the space of a few hours.'

'At least one of them isn't mine.'

'Yes,' admitted Engel, 'that is some small comfort. You do realise we don't have the staff for this sort of thing? The Berlin desk is now shouting at Battle and asking him angry questions.'

'All of which start with, "Now, this chap Shining. . ." I'm sure.'

'Oh they'll settle down soon enough. Last night was written off as an accident.'

'Quite an accident.'

'Kreuzberg man clumsy with a bottle of lighter fluid runs outside for help and keeps going.'

'And people will buy that?'

'Sad to say, Grauber wasn't a man much loved. He was a petty smuggler, got by trading in soft drugs mainly. No friends or family. Put simply: nobody cares enough about him to question it.'

'Well,' I told Engel, 'I care. We need to find out what interest he had in Robie, and who scared him enough that he would rather set fire to himself than talk to us.'

'"It",' said Engel. 'He said "it" wouldn't let him talk to us, not "who".'

'Yes,' I agreed, 'he did. Strange, wasn't it? A Russian soldier with a successful career ahead of him turns psychotic and gets mown down by his own men. A down-at-heel smuggler sets fire to himself and jumps to his death.'

'They're connected.' Engel was bright enough not to phrase it as a question.

'Too much of a coincidence not to be, I'd have thought, and Robie links them both.'

'And now we have a postman who decides that, rather than continue on his round, he'll try and murder someone in the shower.'

'What do we have on him?'

Engel shrugged. 'Nothing immediately obvious, though we'll dig into it. At the moment, from what we can tell he's exactly what he appears. Heinz Schumann, forty-five, father of two, no political associations – well, none that raise any red flags. There's no reason whatsoever to explain his behaviour. We're preparing a cover story.'

'What about the other guests?' I asked Engel, breaking off between words to offer a few English curses in response to the alcohol swabs being rooted around in the wounds on my back.

'There aren't any,' Engel replied. 'We pay Frau Schwarz for exclusive use of the place and, at the moment, you're the only one sleeping here.'

Aside from leaving me to wonder if this was the best room she had, this was a relief. The Intelligence service is not a police force, our response to acts of random violence is to make them vanish, not offer them increased attention. 'No witnesses' sounds chilling but, often, they're words we live by.

'So, working on the assumption that you don't turn up something terribly suspect in Herr Schumann's background, it's safe to say we've now had three people break out of their normal behaviour, becoming violent and out of control.' Out of control. That was the operative phrase and, as would soon prove to be the case, the heart of the matter.

'So where next?' Engel asked.

A local anaesthetic was now making my back feel dreamy, despite the fact that someone was repeatedly passing a needle through its flappy bits. 'Where else?' I said. 'I need to walk in Robie's footsteps. I need to pay a visit to our Eastern neighbours.'

SIXTEEN

According to the papers in my pocket, I was exactly what I had claimed to be in the American bar: a drinks importer. Not that the excuse would wash if I had to show them for a while; legitimate businessmen are not found conducting their business in the tunnels of the U-Bahn. Rats are not, I believe, great consumers of wine. They have little interest in the differences between a Riesling or a Chardonnay. Any East Berlin official I met down here would likely meet my cover story with disdain before proceeding to get very cross indeed.

Not that Engel had been exactly happy either.

'I told you we don't make a habit of using the tunnels,' he had said. 'It's a massive risk.'

'Given that we know I've been under observation since my arrival,' I had explained, 'do you really think I can pass through one of the checkpoints without bringing the whole weight of KGB scrutiny to bear? They'll let me through, of that we can be quite sure, they'll then follow my every move before picking me up for a chat so lengthy we may as well be honest and just call it a prison sentence. I'm too visible. The only way I can get to the East without bringing the whole operation down around our ears is to do so without anyone knowing I'm there.'

Engel had agreed, of course. Irritated he may have been but it didn't make him stupid. He'd tried to come up with some alternative plans, all of which would have taken time to arrange and brought their own share of risks. Finally, he'd relented and accepted my solution: a map, a torch and someone who might, at a glance, pass for me being driven to various, unimportant locations. Later, Engel was to drop my double off at the guest house and I could seem to be safely tucked away within the ignoble walls of my room. Spiegel may not fall for such theatrics of course – I probably wouldn't if I were in his place – but I could only hope that I wasn't deemed sufficiently interesting to worry about it in any great detail. All I needed was a short period of cover to allow me to enter East Berlin unnoticed.

The journey through the tunnels was long-winded but uneventful. The route on the map worked me around the various ghost stations, security blockades and bricked-up tunnels, leading me to a small chink in the network. Eventually, I came to an inspection entrance that opened out into the foreign world not a mile away from the relative security of West Berlin. In my pocket I had some East German marks, my ID papers and a crumpled sheet of paper that appeared like an innocuous till receipt but was actually my key to accessing Battle's network.

It had been a tiring few hours, cramming information on the identities of Battle's agents. It was worrying how readily such information had been given. Despite the network's fading reputation, I wouldn't have wanted to be an agent on Battle's books, having my name handed over to an interloper like me.

I knew *I* was trustworthy, but still . . . However difficult it may be for Intelligence officers, the people taking the real risks were often the little people, the embassy drivers, the clerks, the domestic staff, those vital people who sold secrets to the other side. Sometimes they did it for ideological reasons, sometimes just for the money (though they were the least reliable – never trust anyone who'll tell you anything if there's cash at the end of it, they'll soon realise lies can pay just as well as the truth). There was also something unnerving about containing the information, I felt like a stuffed wallet as I climbed out into the cold street, moving quickly so as not to embarrass myself by being caught halfway through a manhole opening.

We had timed things so as to see me arrive late at night, under the cover of darkness. I still confess to a feeling of abject terror as I walked down the street. I'd been intimidated by my position on arrival in Berlin, only too aware of being a fish out of water. That feeling was doubled now that I was strolling through the part of that city that could quite legitimately have me shot simply for being there. East Germany didn't look favourably on spies. Especially, I reflected, on those that might appear to have no great value. I had considered myself a prize for a few moments, a man who knew Battle's network, but if we considered that network of limited worth then certainly the GDR would as well. If caught, I was more likely to be thought of as the disposable spy, the head of a department that even my own country held in low esteem. Hadn't I said I was disposable when Battle first asked me to act on his behalf? With every step I took into truly enemy territory, the reality of that position grew heavier.

My first port of call had to be Robie's apartment. Engel had panicked, pointing out that it was probably being watched. I explained, with more confidence than I felt, that this was only the case if Robie had been caught.

Of course, this wasn't unlikely, so as I approached the small block he called his Eastern home, I was especially conscious of the street around me. The road was all but empty but brightly lit thanks to the increasing snow and I felt hopelessly exposed as I made my way up to the front door. I tried to reassure myself that, as far as anyone watching was concerned, I could be visiting any number of residents here. It was only me that seemed to think I was wearing a neon sign that flashed the word 'spy' at regular intervals.

It was standard practice for officers to deposit spare keys for their accommodation with the central office. This wasn't so we could feed the cat while they were away on business — though I had known a charming chap in Section 14 that frequently offered to do just that — rather it was a simple safety measure. As was the case with Robie, we needed the wherewithal to immediately access an officer's home should they go missing. After all, they might be dead in the bathtub.

Inside, I realised that now I was at my most vulnerable. If East German forces were monitoring the flat, they would likely be doing so from inside. I opened Robie's door quickly, stepping inside and closing the door behind me. I didn't turn on the light but I did immediately move to the far window, a sliding Arcadia door that led out onto a tiny balcony overlooking the East German Wall and the death strip beyond. Keeping back behind the curtain, I checked the set of keys and unlocked the sliding door. If someone did burst in, this was likely to my only escape route. Not that I fancied jumping down onto the death strip from three floors up – if I didn't break my legs, I'd certainly get shot at by the border guards.

I looked out of the window at the wide no-man's-land between the two walls and marvelled at the absurdity of it all. A line drawn in the sand for the last twenty years; was there no idiocy the human race was incapable of? From here I could see into the half of the city I had just left behind. I imagined Engel over there fretting. I wondered how often Robie had done the same, staring out at the safety he had temporarily abandoned.

I spent an hour searching the apartment but could have probably done it in less. It was as empty of character as a hotel room. There were a few tins and packets of dried food in the kitchen, enough plates, glasses and cups to handle two people, and no more.

In the bedroom I found a battered paperback novel stuffed under the mattress and I found that almost heartbreaking. It was nothing important, a cheap thriller, but the fact that it was in English had made Lucas consider it worth hiding from view. It was a sign of the everyday paranoia he must have had to live through and it put my little Wood Green world into sharp perspective.

I checked all the drawers and any other obvious hiding places I could think of, behind sofa cushions, under rugs. The place was empty, there was nothing helpful here.

Glad to be able to leave, I did so quickly, again deeply aware that a hand might fall on my shoulder at any moment as I descended to the ground floor and back onto the street.

Next was to contact the network, or at least, one member of it. Engel and I had discussed at length who to choose. The decision had balanced reliability against importance. A number of the network held light government positions and these were discounted right away. These were people whose safety relied on keeping their contact with the West minimal, it was hardly fair to roll up on their doorstep asking for a bed for the night. Put simply: I needed the least important member of the network, someone who was as far from GDR scrutiny as possible.

I crossed over the road and looked around for a public call box. At the end of the street a couple of policemen were making their slow way towards me, whiling away their shift in the empty streets. The emptiness of the street had felt comforting earlier; now I felt exposed by it. It was getting late, and I was the only other person in sight. Would they want to check my papers? If so, would they want to know why I was wandering around at such an hour? I adopted a slight lilt, affecting a moderate drunkenness.

The key to playing a drunk is simple enough but most people get it wrong. A sober man play-acting exaggerates the movements, plays up to the false alcohol in his system. Whereas a drunk man spends most of his time pretending to be sober, holding his limbs as straight as possible, walking rigid and heavy, refusing to give in to the booze that rages around his system. A true piece of theatre lies in the middle ground. I looked directly at the policemen, nodding at them in the sort of earnest manner I thought a wandering drunk would affect, hopeful – as indeed I was – of not getting questioned.

'Go home,' one of them said, 'sleep it off.'

I nodded and waved, allowing myself a little stumble with the extra movement but returning immediately to the imaginary tram tracks on the pavement before me, grinding forward with concentration and conviction.

I turned a corner and let the act drop, rubbing at my face nervously and shivering both at the freezing air and the fear that had threatened to take me over.

At the end of the street, the Wall stood, shining in the constant glare of the lights that surrounded it. A few feet away was a public telephone. I might have wished for somewhere a little less brightly lit, but the last thing I wanted to do was spend longer out here than necessary. The next time I chanced upon company, they might not be as easily fobbed off.

I stepped under the hood of the call box, pulled out some change and called the number created by combining the charges of the first couple of items on the false receipt in my pocket. Unsurprisingly, the phone rang for a while. I imagined the woman on the other end, slowly rising up from sleep, no doubt panicked by the sound of a phone in the night. Perhaps she would stare at it for a while, wondering what news the person on the other end might bring.

I looked around. The lights of the wall above me had the reverse effect of making the further end of the street seem all the darker. Try as I might, I couldn't quite dispel the thought of the two policeman I'd seen earlier. I imagined them having turned around, now heading towards me out of the darkness.

The phone answered, the tremulous voice of my contact crackling over the line. 'Who is this? Do you know what time this is?'

'I'm afraid I do. I'm a friend of your uncle and I need somewhere to stay. He told me you'd be happy to take in a clean guest.' This was prearranged code, an emergency message explaining that I was in trouble and needed protection. Unsurprisingly, the message wasn't well received. This was the sort of thing an officer cleared with his agents on the understanding on all sides that it was unlikely to happen. Now it had, and I imagined she was trying to get her head around it. There was a long pause. I imagine she was debating whether to put the phone down. She would have known that there was no easy way out of the situation. Anyone giving her that message must also know her address.

Finally she said, 'Come,' and the phone went dead.

The contact's name was Alexandra Hoss, and she was an actress. Her work had taken her all over the country. Her reputation and – a point that may have rankled – her looks had made her a regular attendee at many highbrow functions. People tell a beautiful face far too many things they shouldn't. Her career was, by all accounts, on the slide. Most of her work was now on the stage of the Brecht theatre and her film appearances few and far between. She no longer got the same invites – and indecent proposals – she once had.

She lived in an apartment an affordable distance off the Unter den Linden and I made my way towards it, having memorised the route earlier. Over the River Spree and past the State Opera House, I moved as quickly as I could without drawing too much attention to myself. At one point I made a show of walking up the entrance steps of an apartment block, jangling my keys, as another policeman walked by. He didn't so much as glance in my direction and, once he was out of sight, I backtracked and continued on my way.

Alexandra's apartment was part of a block that had probably once been desirable. Now the sheen had faded, the stone blackened and the fixtures grown tatty. She buzzed me in through the main door and I took the steps to the fourth floor rather than use the central cage elevator, as the idea of making so much noise in the quiet building set my nerves off.

'You should not be here,' she said as she opened the door to me, turning her back and walking off into the apartment, leaving me to follow on behind.

'Believe me,' I said, 'I'd rather not be.'

The apartment matched the rest of the building, expensive furniture a couple of years beyond the point at which it should have been replaced, framed posters of her movies and theatre appearances gathering dust on top of their thick veneer of nostalgia. The carpet was a light cream colour, turned beige from the smoke of cigarettes.

Hoss herself had taken up a hunched position on a large sofa, her legs pulled up beneath her chin, silk pyjamas glistening in the light of discreet lamps. Dyed-blonde hair was pulled back into a ponytail to reveal an unhappy face, worry lines she'd hard-earned deepening as she tried to resist chewing at the cuticles on a perfectly manicured hand. She resorted to tapping her teeth with the nail of her index finger, a nervous tic I felt guilty to have caused.

'Where is Robert?' she asked. This was Robie's cover. Robert Frick, a suitably European-sounding name that he worked under on this side of the Wall.

'I don't know,' I admitted. 'That's why I'm here.'

'You don't know?' Her voice crept towards hysteria. 'He's missing?'

I nodded.

'Then he's probably been caught!' She got to her feet, running out of momentum halfway out of the room, convinced she should run but unsure, now she'd set off, as to where.

'If he has, he certainly wouldn't reveal you, you're safe,' I said. I wished I sounded more convincing.

'How can you possibly know that?' she asked.

'Because I've known him for years,' I told her, 'and I trust him. He's also a good friend. That's why I'm here. To find him. To help him if he needs it.'

She didn't quite relax but I could tell she wanted to. When presented with two options: panic or calm, most people want to choose calm; they just have to be given enough of a reason to do so. I kept trying to find her one.

'You know how good Robert is,' I told her. 'He's a professional, and it's entirely possible that he's on the trail of something. We know he was following up some leads, he might just have had to keep his head down for a while. We shouldn't worry yet.'

'You are obviously worried or you wouldn't be here.'

'I'm here because I was sent,' I told her. 'Our people like to boss us around. It makes them feel important.'

'I know people like that,' she admitted. 'They make you work just because they can.'

'Precisely. Robert was looking into something on his own time, our employers don't like that sort of thing, so they throw me at him. But I know him and I'm just here to see whether I can be of any use. But I can't go wandering around the streets of East Berlin without somewhere to sleep, can I? Robert told me you were the most reliable of his friends so I came to you.' Now I was throwing flattery into the mix, shameless.

It worked. She offered a half smile and sat down again, this time on a rigid-looking armchair. I imagined she was the sort of woman who often found reasons to flit between the furniture, like an actor on a theatre set, shifting location with every damn line.

'I like working with him,' she said. 'He's a kind man.'

'He is,' I agreed, wondering quite how much Robie's influence had affected her. No doubt she was besotted with him, like everyone he came into contact with. 'So can I stay for a short while? I promise I'll be gone as soon as possible. Just a day, maybe two, so that I can look into things.'

She nodded. 'Of course. Robert would want me to look after a friend.'

'He would. How was he when you last saw him?'

She shrugged. 'The same.' Having given her automatic answer she then thought for a moment. 'Actually, no, he was excited. Normally he is very calm, gentle. He pays attention but nothing you say can ever really surprise him . . . not that I have had much to tell him for a long time. But that day he was full of energy, he was. . .' she clearly couldn't think of a better word than the first that had occurred to her, '. . .excited.'

'Did he give you any clue as to why?'

'He was talking about the soldier,' she said. 'You know the one? He went mad and shot some people.'

'I know the one.'

'I thought it was a strange thing to be excited about, it was so horrible, but Robert must have had his reasons, he wasn't someone who took pleasure in unpleasant things.'

'No,' I agreed, 'he wasn't. Did he give you any idea what he was doing about it? Anyone else he was talking to?' He shouldn't have done; an officer really shouldn't discuss anything with their agents other than the material the agents bring to them but I didn't know how closely Robie stuck to protocol. Given his advantage, the desire everyone had to please him, he may well have grown sloppy about certain aspects of his work.

'No,' she said. 'I don't think he was doing anything about it. What could he do? The subject just came up, everyone was talking about it.'

'Did you know the soldier?'

'No, he was only a lieutenant.'

The implicit snobbery was so natural she didn't even realise it was there, as if it was quite normal to dismiss someone because of their rank. That's the life of a movie star for you, even one on the downward escalator of her career.

'It's probably not important,' I said. 'I don't suppose I might have a drink?' Really I just wanted to change the subject and get her back on innocuous ground for a while. Not that I was opposed to something to settle my nerves.

'Gin?' she asked. 'Or vodka?'

'Vodka's fine,' I said. She paused for a moment, then realised I didn't know where she kept her liquor so could hardly help myself. She shuffled over to a cabinet in the corner and poured herself a gin and me a vodka. She stared at them for a moment, trying to remember what it was they might lack, then took both drinks out of the room and into the kitchen where I heard her ferret around in the freezer for some ice. She returned, still looking at the drinks.

'That one's yours,' she said, passing it to me.

'Thank you,' I took a sip and was grateful to note we paid her well enough to afford decent spirits. I drank it quickly. I wasn't tired – though I hoped the vodka would help – but I didn't want to talk to Alexandra Hoss any more for now. 'If you don't mind, I'd like to get some sleep.'

'Of course.' She still hadn't touched her drink but she used it to point out of the room. 'Right across the hall, spare room, bathroom's next door.'

There was nowhere obvious to place my glass so I took it with me into her kitchen, rinsed it under the tap and upended it onto the draining board.

I walked back through the lounge. Alexandra had drained her drink in my absence. I wondered about that – in my experience it was an alcoholic's habit, they always hide the act of drinking. I supposed it hardly mattered, this wasn't my network, and Alexandra Hoss was not my responsibility.

She walked behind me as I left the room, gesturing again towards the spare bedroom door and vanishing off into her own room without another word.

The spare bedroom was a forgotten room. Even the sheets had dust on them. On the wall was a picture of Alexandra taken, at a rough guess, at the age she'd been when she'd last entered the room. It was a cheesecake shot of the sort that pretended it was better than calendar fare simply because it didn't contain tyres. She was lying back on a stone bench, surrounded by moss-covered statuary. Several cherubs were as unmoved as I by the sight of her. It seemed strange to sleep beneath a life-size photograph of your host's exposed genitalia but I would do my best.

The bed was an improvement on the one at Frau Schwarz's but I was still too wired to sleep and I lay there staring at the window, waiting for the light of dawn to break.

Just as I thought I might drift off, I became aware of the

sound of talking from Alexandra's bedroom. Was there someone else in the apartment?

I slid out of bed and moved to the door. Wary of making a noise, I slowly pressed down the handle and was relieved it opened silently. It was pitch-black in the hallway but for a faint light from beneath her door. I tiptoed across to it and pressed my ear to her door. She was speaking quietly, and there was no audible reply so I decided she must either be losing her mind – a possibility I struggled to entirely dismiss – or, more likely, was talking on the phone.

'I'll do whatever I can,' she said. 'You know that. I just wish you were here. You'd be more comfortable here.'

A pause.

'I know, I know . . . but surely it would have been all right. He's a friend after all.'

Another pause.

'You know I don't mind the risk . . . I'm sure, if he's friend he'd also. . .'

How tempting it was simply to burst in and say 'For God's sake, just pass me the phone and let me talk to him.'

'All right, all right, I won't say anything. You know you can trust me. Wait. . .'

She shifted in bed and I stepped back, trying to decide whether it might, after all, be worthwhile brazening it out if she discovered my eavesdropping. Then she sat back down, the bed springs creaking, and I heard the sound of her cigarette lighter.

'I promised, didn't I?' she said. 'I'll be there.' The smell of cigarette smoke crept underneath the door. 'Yes, of course, as much as I can. . .'

There was another moment of silence then she began to speak. 'Darling, I. . .' then stopped. After a moment I heard her put the phone down. She'd obviously been cut off quicker than she might have liked. I snuck back to my room and carefully closed the door behind me.

So, I had discovered two things. Firstly, she was in contact with Lucas. This made life much easier, especially as she was clearly planning on meeting him. Secondly, given her little performance when I'd arrived, so shocked at the news of Robie's disappearance, she was a better actress than the current state of her career suggested.

Tomorrow I would follow her and see where she led me.

I moved over to the window and looked out. It was snowing again, adding to the layers I had walked through earlier, deepening and building up in drifts. In the middle of the street an old woman was dancing, spiralling around in the falling snow. I was reminded of the young girl Engel and I had seen outside Grauber's apartment. These Berliners do so love the snow, I thought, watching her spin and spin. Her head was upturned towards me, its sagging face pulled into a grin of joy. Suddenly she stopped and stared at me. The room was dark, there was no way she could be aware I was watching. I kept telling myself that as she stared directly at me. After a moment she hooked her index fingers into the corners of her mouth and pulled her face into a distorted mask, like a rude schoolchild pulling faces behind a teacher's back. Face distended, she hopped up and down on the spot, as if throwing the insult up at me. I continued to stare, trying to find reason and logic in her behaviour and coming up short. Finally she fell back into the road and lay still. I was just accepting that I would have to go down there and make sure she was all right when she slowly got to her feet, hands pressed to her left hip as if in pain. She looked around, seemingly confused to find herself there, and then limped away into the darkness.

SEVENTEEN

I had little choice but to sit by the window and wait for the new day. I couldn't risk Alexandra leaving the apartment without me. Of course, the sleep I had been so uninterested in earlier seemed far more attractive by the time the distant floodlights of the Wall were replaced by the encroaching dawn. Eventually I left the room in search of coffee and the opportunity to keep moving.

I finally found the things I needed in her lacklustre kitchen to put some caffeine in me and leaned out of the window to drink it, letting the cold of the morning shock me into wakefulness. The snow was thick now, the early morning traffic carving back ownership of the roads as pedestrians plodded up to their ankles in it on the pavement. It had stopped falling for now but the heavy clouds above us made it clear we could expect its return soon enough.

Alexandra woke late, damn her, and by the time she shuffled into the room I was on my third coffee and had searched the flat thoroughly just in case I stumbled on anything interesting. I hadn't, but I had given it a good tidy so at least one of us was up on the deal.

'It looks different in here,' she said, as she looked around the lounge.

'I couldn't sleep,' I told her, 'so I did some housework. I hope you don't mind.'

She shrugged and shuffled off into the kitchen. 'I haven't got much food in,' she shouted.

I already knew that, having tried to make myself some form of breakfast an hour or so earlier. I had come back with nothing but a working knowledge of how long tinned mushrooms thrived past their sell-by date. I followed her into the kitchen.

'I'll take you out for breakfast,' I told her, intentionally not phrasing it as a question, just to see how she would react.

The pause was brief. 'That would be lovely. We'll have to be quick, though, I'm meeting a producer in a couple of hours.'

'Then maybe you can suggest somewhere on the way. Get dressed as quick as you can and we can be off.'

She didn't argue, just took the small coffee she'd poured for herself and returned to her bedroom. After a moment I heard her turn on her en-suite shower and took the opportunity to jump into the bathroom. I hadn't wanted to shower myself in case she had crept out while I was otherwise distracted.

It was clear that, like the guest bedroom, the general bathroom had seen little recent use. The few bottles of toiletries were discoloured. A bar of soap turned the colour of a bruise on the edge of a cracked bath. The water worked, though, and the only thing that stopped me feeling suitably refreshed was the fact that I had no choice but to climb back into my old clothes once I'd finished.

'If you could fit a Chanel frock, darling,' she said when she emerged, considerably later, from her own preparations, 'I'd happily lend you one, but I think you might draw attention to yourself.'

This Alexandra Hoss was different to the woman I had met the night before. She had done her make-up and hair, selected her outfit and – like all performers in my experience – was now feeling more confident for having done so. Actors always thrive when given half an hour and years of experience in front of a mirror. Perhaps we're all characters we present to the world and they're just more honest about it.

We left her apartment and stepped out into the frozen streets. It served my stupid presumptions right to be presented with a thriving city, laughing and playing in the snow. Had I thought that everyone in East Berlin would be walking around sullen and fearful? Hanging their heads in case they drew the attention of the authorities? No, that was just me. As we drew close to the Wall I watched a group of children playing on it, hanging from the bricks and pelting it with snowballs that exploded in white stars against the concrete.

We breakfasted in a small cafe, Alexandra picking at a pastry as if it were made from something difficult to digest.

I tried to engage her in conversation about Lucas but she retreated into the safe ground of theatrical anecdotes, name-dropping and howling in fake amusement at stories she must have told a thousand times. So doing, she managed to block any attempts I made to get her to veer off-script until, finally, she got to her feet announcing that she had to go to her meeting.

'Spare key,' she said, placing a set of keys on the table. 'Make yourself comfortable and I'll be back later.'

I waved her off and watched her walk down Brückenstrasse,

doing her best to negotiate the icy pavement as if it were a catwalk.

I waited until she was a short distance away before picking up the keys and leaving money on the table for our breakfast. I followed after her.

She crossed the river then descended into the S-Bahn, heading south towards Plänterwald. I managed to keep track of her while maintaining my distance; she was, thankfully, far too self-obsessed to make a decent spy. Perhaps she was wary of being recognised by her fellow passengers but she kept her head down and turned away from the rest of the carriage. Alighting at Plänterwald, I followed her into the dense greenery of the park, the distant sound of the crowds and the whooping rides at the Kulturpark growing louder as we drew towards it.

In the years to come, the park would be one of Berlin's abandoned areas. Closed down due to bankruptcy, it would become a wired-off ghost of its former self, the large Ferris wheel towering above the rest of the attractions as the grass rose up to stifle them. Back then, the park was still in full swing, rich with the smell of the food stalls and the spin and grind of waltzers. The snow hadn't put people off from visiting, the staff working hard to ensure that everything was cleared so business could flourish despite the chill.

Alexandra sat down on a bench facing the Ferris wheel, and I hung back, only too aware that, while she might not be paying attention to her surroundings, the man she was coming to meet would be.

The cold winter sun did its best to shine on her before being choked off by the darkening clouds that threatened more snow. She checked her watch every few minutes, more with nerves than real impatience. No doubt she was also eager to be reunited with the man that held her under his spell. I must confess, I felt something similar.

I bought a hot dog and coffee, more to hide behind than through hunger or thirst and took up position on the opposite side of the wheel.

It was twenty minutes before Lucas appeared, and he was almost unrecognisable. He hadn't shaved or changed his clothes for days but even that surface dishevelment couldn't match the drawn look that hung around his eyes. All of his previous, easy-going nature had been buried by recent events; he had the look of a broken man. My immediate instinct was to walk straight over and demand that he let me help him. Which was idiotic – whatever my gut instinct said, I couldn't altogether be sure that he was to be trusted. Still, it was clear that this wasn't a man who had taken up with new masters; this was a man on the run, desperate and aged by it.

If I had been shocked by his appearance, Alexandra, who gave every indication of being a person to whom image was everything, didn't bat an eyelid. She responded to him with unrestrained enthusiasm, grabbing at him and pulling him down next to her on the bench. Robie snatched himself from her grip, putting his hand on hers and muttering something to her, looking around nervously. Clearly he wished to avoid any great show of affection in public. Either that or, as always, he found her subservience to him suffocating.

For a moment she looked distraught, upset at having her adoration refused. She recovered quickly, reaching into her coat to pull out an envelope, which she offered him. He opened it slightly and glanced at it, counting quickly. 'As much as I can,' she had said to him on the phone. He must have needed money. Slipping the envelope into his jacket, he patted her hands and, for the first time, smiled at her. The response from Alexandra was so ecstatic it was as if he'd offered his hand in marriage. When he looked away again, the pleasure continued to burn on her face, a look of warmth that all but melted the snow around them.

She continued to talk to him though he all but ignored her, alternating between rubbing at his tired face and watching the people around them. I wondered how much I featured as a topic in their conversation. Would he be pleased that I was here or resentful? I had never really cast myself in the role of mentor but it could be argued that he wouldn't have joined the service without my sponsorship. Mind you, given where that path had clearly taken him, perhaps he had reason to regret I had ever put his name forward. No doubt I would soon find out.

I had no wish to confront him just yet. It was only sensible to follow him for a while first, just to see where he would lead me, but I was quite convinced that he only represented a security risk were he to be caught and it would therefore be best for all were I to pick him up and do my best to ensure that didn't happen.

There was an explosion of laughter from behind them and Robie flinched, getting to his feet and turning to face the noise. In that moment, Alexandra's face suddenly went blank, as if all thought had emptied from her. She got up and walked over to the ticket booth of the Ferris wheel, reaching into her purse for change.

Robie turned back towards the bench and was momentarily confused until he spotted her passing through the barrier and climbing into a carriage. He watched her go, the confusion on his face slowly turning to panic. He ran towards the wheel but it was already climbing upwards and Alexandra was rising up into the air. He stood at its base, staring up at her, occasionally looking around, wary of making a scene but also desperate to do something.

A young boy, idly chewing on some candyfloss, tugged at his sleeve and he looked down, the two of them beginning to converse.

I looked back to Alexandra, the vacant expression on her face having now vanished to be replaced with bewilderment and a building sense of panic that rivalled Robie's.

I looked back to Robie. He appeared to be begging the young boy for something. I moved closer but couldn't hear their voices. I tried to decide if I should make my presence known; Robie was clearly panicking but I couldn't see why. I couldn't see what the problem was – as bizarre as it might have been for Alexandra to suddenly get it into her head to ride the wheel, it wasn't as if doing so put her in danger. How was she under threat? If someone had them in their sights, they could as easily have taken the shot when she was on the ground. And why would they send a child to deliver their threats? None of what I was seeing made sense. Of course, now I know exactly what was happening, but back then all I knew was what I saw.

I looked once more to the child. Robie's voice was getting louder and I could hear him begging the child not to do something. 'I can't,' he kept insisting, 'whatever you do, I can't. I won't. . .'

I noticed the child step away from Robie, looking up at him as if the man was mad. He certainly appeared so now, all attempts to maintain a low profile gone as he yelled at the boy. 'Don't do it!' he screamed. 'Please . . . just don't do it.'

Other people were beginning to stare at him now and a young man ran over to the boy, picking him up in his arms and shouting at Robie. What was his problem, the boy's father wanted to know, before suddenly breaking into a smile and talking to him as if he were an old friend. Robie's charm kicking in, I realised. Robie ignored him, his eyes rising up towards the Ferris wheel and Alexandra. Mine followed, and I saw that Alexandra was wriggling in her cabin. For a moment I wondered if there was something in there with her – a thought that was truer than I could yet have known – but then it became clear that she was trying to pull herself out from beneath the safety bar. Succeeding, she stood up, the cabin rocking, and, as Robie shouted one last plea, she launched herself forward as if diving into a swimming pool. Her face was blank as she sailed out into the air and then, as before, it suddenly filled with life and reason, her mouth pulled into a scream as if only just realising the situation she was in. Her head connected with one of the other cabins, flipping her backwards in mid-air with a terrible pounding sound. She fell the rest of the way to the ground, the crowd letting go a unified roar of shock as she hit the tarmac. Her limbs folded back on themselves, giving her a grotesque, crablike appearance, her head tipped back on a snapped neck, dead eyes staring up into dark clouds that chose that moment to finally make good on their promise of snow.

Robie's hands went to his face and he stared at her, unable to move even as others rushed forward.

I had to get him out of there. I ran over and grabbed his arm, pulling him away.

'Lucas,' I said, 'I'm sorry but we need to go.'

He looked at me but I don't think he really knew who I was as he hurried alongside me, too shocked to put up any resistance as I guided him through the drawing crowds and towards the exit of the park.

EIGHTEEN

Ryska was tapping on the table with her fingernails again.

'I'm making you uncomfortable?' Shining asked.

'She just jumped?' Ryska asked. 'For no reason?'

'There was a reason,' Shining said, 'but it wasn't her own.'

'That makes no sense.'

'I'm sure you realise by now that several people have been acting out of character, controlled somehow, driven to commit acts against both others and themselves. This was no different.'

'But why?'

'We're getting to that.'

'Well, can't you get there quicker? This isn't a bedtime story, I just need the facts.'

'The facts will sink in all the better if I take this at my own pace and tell it in my own way. You want to hear it, so shush and let me carry on.'

She tutted but nodded.

NINETEEN

By the time we had reached the exit, Robie was back in control, looking over his shoulder.

'We can't just leave her.'

'There's nothing else we can do. I'm afraid she's beyond help.'

'There was no need. . .' he said. 'It didn't have to. . .' He looked at me then, focusing on me properly for the first time. 'What are you doing here anyway?'

'When you dropped off the radar you sent Battle's heart aflutter. Battle then sent everyone else's hearts aflutter. Before you know it, I'm dragged out of my lovely, comfortable office and dumped into East Berlin. So, thank you for that.'

'They think I've switched sides?'

'They don't really know what to think and, for that matter, neither do I. I'm hoping that you're going to be able to help make things clearer.'

He tugged his arm out of mine. 'Nothing's clear.'

'Well, if *you* think that then we're really in trouble.'

He shook his head. 'There's no way I can explain. You wouldn't understand.'

'I'm sure that's not the case,' I told him. 'You know that I'm no stranger to things that are hard to explain.'

He stopped walking, gazing towards the sound of traffic on the nearby autobahn. 'It wouldn't be fair,' he said, 'especially not now. Now it's proven how far it's willing to. . .' He shook his head again. 'No.'

He looked at me and there was a sad smile on his face. 'Nice to see you, August,' he said, then glanced over his shoulder. I looked also. There was nobody near us; even the ticket collector had left his booth to see what was going on at the Ferris wheel. My attention elsewhere, the punch in my stomach caught me completely off guard.

'Sorry, August,' Robie said, running off the road and into the trees.

I supported myself with one hand on the road, trying to draw a breath, his punch having badly winded me. Through streaming eyes, I saw him vanish into the foliage and I fought to relax, to let the muscles unclench so that I could breathe again. Slowly, I drew a breath and stumbled into the woods after him, my diaphragm cramping as I forced myself to move and still breathe. I was stumbling through the undergrowth, my breath coming in short, barely sufficient gasps, light-headed from a lack of oxygen. Ahead I could hear Robie running, but there was no way I could match him. Falling forward, my knees sinking into wet leaves, I slowly regained control. Minutes passed, all the time the sound of Robie's movements growing fainter until I could no longer hear him. It was hopeless. I had lost him. If I'd known the area better then perhaps I could have tried to second-guess his direction. The only thing I could think was that he would try to work his way to the S-Bahn.

At a loss for an alternative, I returned to the train station and waited. It was soon clear that I was wasting my time. I'd lost him.

TWENTY

'I could do with stretching my legs, if you don't mind,' said Shining, standing up.

'Tough!' said Ryska. 'You can't just leave it there.'

'When you get to my age, my dear, your muscles are not content to be dumped on hard, wooden chairs for extended periods,' he told her. 'Unless you want me to start kicking the table and moaning about cramp, I suggest you let me move for a while. A pop to the loo wouldn't go amiss either. Or something to eat.' He looked at her. 'You did stock up with some food didn't you? I don't imagine we can exactly call for a pizza.'

'Mr Shining, do I have to remind you that you're here at our insistence? You break when I tell you you can break, you eat when food is offered.'

'Oh, do give it a rest. I've told you already, I'm only too happy to talk but my tolerance for bullying is perilously thin. Should you ever be in my situation – and let us hope you never are – I'm sure your attitude would be much the same. At this point you have no evidence to accuse me of anything, you're just shoving me around in that manner that we as a service do so well. I, on the other hand, refuse to be shoved, and unless you plan on beating me up, you'll just have to live with the fact. Toilet through here?'

He walked up to Jennings who, after a moment, stepped aside. 'Third door on the left,' Jennings said, turning back to Ryska as Shining passed. 'What?' he asked. 'The man's got a point.'

Shining relieved himself, realising that this was the first time since arrival that he'd actually been able to drop his guard and take a moment to think about what was happening to him. He'd made enemies in his career, but for the most part they were simply people who looked down their noses at the work he did. Not even Sir Robin was so spiteful as to try to close the department by branding him a traitor, surely? The call had come from him but the order certainly hadn't.

Try as he might, Shining also couldn't get his head around why this was happening to him now. What had turned an ancient case into a weapon to attack him with? There had been questions about his part in the mission at the time but, as always, most of them had surrounded his reliability or veracity. Nobody had ever suggested that his involvement with Lucas Robie might be evidence that he was untrustworthy. Now, thirty years later, someone had sanctioned the time and effort to drag him out here and cross-examine him as if it were of vital importance.

These days he wasn't even close to secrets his government considered sensitive, and he was no threat to anyone. Which left only one possibility: this was a personal attack using the only thing someone could find as viable ammunition against him.

But who? A friend of Fratfield's perhaps? Refusing to believe that the man had been a criminal?

He flushed the toilet and stared through the frosted glass window at the darkening sky outside. He's been here for hours, lost in his own reminiscences. He'd have to watch that, it was all too easy to go wandering in his own memories but someone was after him in the here and now.

Not that he had a better plan at the moment than playing for time. The longer he strung this process out for, the longer he allowed his opponent to show their hand. The longer also, for someone to come to his aid. Not that there were many options for that – after all, Toby and Tamar had problems of their own to contend with. Shining had been alone for so many years and it was amazing how quickly he'd come to rely on Toby since he'd been allocated to Section 37. Now, when he really needed him, he wasn't even in the same country.

TWENTY-ONE

April had left the office in the frustrated hands of the security officer, who was still trying – but thus far failing – to crack open its secrets. She didn't like doing so but was practical enough to think of the bigger picture. There were more important things at stake here than keeping an eye on August's files and his collection of *Pan Book of Horror* paperbacks.

She took up residence in the pizza restaurant across the road from the office, and began to make calls.

'All-you-can-eat buffet?' a singularly bored waiter asked her, staring out of the glass and into a world that didn't involve corporate uniforms and upselling meetings.

'Whatever,' April replied, working her way through the wallet she'd stolen from the security officer.

'Great,' the waiter replied, rewarding her with an empty plate that clanged on the table like a mournful dinner gong. 'Help yourself to the salad bar and drinks refills. Have a great lunch.' The words were there, even if the emotion behind them was not.

April all but ignored him until she noticed that the wallet

had a hundred quid in it, at which point she ran to the buffet bar, filling her plate while keeping a watch on the office door through the window. It was hardly the first time she'd helped strip a man of his clothes before letting him buy her lunch.

Within five minutes she was splattering her cheeks with Caesar salad dressing from an unreliable garlic bread stick and poking at crisp salad onions with a cautious fingernail.

She was also thinking very hard about what she should do next.

She tried to decide who she could trust to look into the security officer's background. The answer was infuriatingly slow in coming. It was hard to trust anyone that worked in their business. She would certainly never class herself as trustworthy. She'd just have to take the risk. Propping up his driver's licence on a glass shaker of chilli flakes, she rang an old friend in MI6 personnel.

'Valerie, you craggy old slut, how's tricks?'

'Presuming you mean Ms DeMarco, I can put you through. Might I ask who's calling?'

God save us from switchboards, April thought, forking some pepperoni into her mouth. 'April Shining. Another craggy old slut, in case you were wondering.'

'I'll see if she's available.'

April watched a group of kids in the street jumping up and down in front of Oman's shop window. They were offering all sorts of exciting hand gestures to accompany their opinion of his wares. After a moment she was treated to the sight of Oman's naked buttocks being pressed against the glass to form a white, hairy square. The kids laughed and ran away. April was pleased to see someone else shared her taste for frank expression in this modern world.

'April?'

'Hello, dear. I do hope I haven't made whoever answered the phone cry. I may have been a tad salty in my language.'

'I wondered why they were looking at me as if I'd just set fire to the stationery cupboard. Thanks for that.'

'Always a pleasure. Now listen, my darling, I have to make this quick as I'm running out of credit'– the most well-worn lie of the digital age, she supposed – 'can you look into the file of a chap called Hamish Bernstein?'

'Are you at a Glaswegian bar mitzvah?'

'I'm in charge of the canapés. One has to fill one's retirement somehow. I don't need any saucy details, just an idea of which department he answers to.'

There was the clattering of a keyboard on the other line that rather undercut Valerie's feigned reluctance. 'I can't just dish out that sort of thing to anyone who calls, you know.'

'I'm not anyone, sweetie, I'm me, you know I won't go blabbing. Anyway, it's not like I'm asking for his credit-card number.' I already have that, after all, she thought, fishing it out of the wallet.

'He's uniform,' by which Valerie meant military, 'currently seconded to Bertie's lot over at Section 12. Seen action in lots of our more tasty foreign fields.'

'Haven't we all,' April replied. 'Thank you, dear, it's much appreciated.'

'I don't suppose you intend to tell me why the interest?'

'Just wondering where to return his underwear. These boys will litter up the flat so.' April hung up and rewarded herself with a mouthful of pizza and a fizzy drink with too many flavours, none of them real.

'Bertie' was Albert Fisher, a particularly unpopular man, mainly due to the fact that, having hopped from one desk to another over his career at Six, his main duty these days was to investigate security risks within British Intelligence itself. Gone were the Cold War days when such things were a day-to-day concern, but his small section still monitored other officers for corruption or 'acting against home interests'. What on earth did he want with August? Her brother was an incorrigible pain in many a Whitehall arse but he'd certainly never been accused of disloyal activities.

April was positively livid as she hoovered up some jalapeño peppers.

Next to her she noticed a table full of young mothers busily stuffing napkin-wrapped pizza slices into carrier bags. Between them, they looked like they'd helped themselves to half of the buffet. That's tea for the kids sorted, April thought, and why not? She folded a couple of slices into her own handbag for a mid-afternoon snack.

Having stocked up, the table rose as one and dashed out of the door. The bored waiter appeared next to April, watching them go.

'They didn't pay,' he said. The fact seemed to sicken him, but not quite enough to give chase. He seemed a bystander to his own job. April felt rather sorry for him.

Out of the corner of her eye, she saw movement on the street outside. Bernstein was leaving the office.

'How much did this table of joy cost?' she asked.

'I'll get your bill,' he said, making no move to do so, still watching the retreating diners who had left without paying.

'Sorry, no time, I really have to dash.' She fished a twenty-pound note out of Bernstein's wallet. 'That do?'

'Too much,' he said. 'The buffet's only—'

'Then shove it in your pocket and pretend I did a runner too,' she suggested, pushing the note into his hand and dashing out of the door.

Bernstein was a little way up the street, heading in the direction of either the buses or the tube. She could only hope it would be the latter – surreptitiously tailing someone on a bus was all but impossible unless you could disguise yourself as used chewing gum.

As they both reached the top of the road, she was relieved to see Bernstein ignore the row of bus stops and make for the pedestrian crossing and the tube station beyond.

April put on an extra burst of speed so that she was only a short distance behind him. She watched as he discovered his wallet was missing. He hesitated, clearly wondering if he should go back. Then, deciding – quite rightly – that it must have been lifted rather than dropped accidentally, he cursed, pulled out his Oyster Card and carried on his way. She let him mount the escalator before darting through the ticket barrier, peering over the escalator to see which of the two platforms he aimed for. Once he'd stepped out of sight onto the westbound platform, she went down the escalator after him, hanging back from the platform. She waited for the train to arrive, watched him board and then dashed over and climbed into the next carriage.

Bernstein had clearly managed to break into the filing cabinets because under one arm he had a thick stack of cardboard files. He didn't look at them as the train headed towards Turnpike Lane; instead he picked up a copy of the *Metro* newspaper and began to flick through it. April perched in a seat with her back to him, only keeping an eye on him as the train stopped for a station. As they approached Finsbury Park, he got to his feet and she hung back as the passengers dismounted, waiting for him to walk past her on the platform before jumping up and getting off just before the doors closed.

Bernstein had wrapped the files in his copy of the *Metro* and made his way up the Seven Sisters Road towards the park, April keeping a safe distance behind him.

The park was quiet but for the odd determined cyclist and jogger, huffing great white clouds of condensation before them in the cold air. They reminded April of ailing locomotives, desperately trying to push their load up one more hill. In order not to be seen, she allowed Bernstein as much space as she dared, hanging right back as he sat down on a bench, placing the wrapped folders next to him. How she loved to watch people who weren't spies acting like spies. She just bet he had insisted on a code phrase.

He sat there for a few moments, quite failing to appear in the least bit relaxed and then, when he apparently couldn't take it any more, he jumped up and moved quickly back the way he had come, leaving the files on the bench. A drop then, she realised; he wasn't here to meet anyone, just to make a delivery.

She had little choice but to let him go, he wasn't important – it was whoever was pulling the strings she wanted to see.

It was cold, and April was struggling not to draw attention to herself by jogging on the spot, or beating her arms like an angry swan in an effort to keep her ailing circulation going. When you got to her age, there was only so much that could be achieved through the enthusiastic deployment of cardigans and scarves. She wondered if a cigarette would make her feel any warmer and decided, lacking the evidence to say either way, to give it a shot.

It was another half an hour before Bernstein's employer appeared, by which point April had seriously begun to consider climbing one of the trees in order to keep herself moving. When she saw who the man was, the flush of anger she felt all but undid her chill. It was Clive King, an ex-lover, now deputy business secretary and a man that owed Section 37 considerable thanks after they had salvaged an important set of diplomatic talks with the South Korean government. What the hell was he doing being involved in this? He wasn't part of the Intelligence community, had no links to Albert Fisher's department . . . April was as baffled as she was livid. She decided the only way forward was to stroll over there and give him a clip around the ear.

He sat down on the bench and was slipping the folders inside his coat when April dropped down next to him. She was only slightly mollified by the startled cry this brought from him.

'I hope you have a bloody good explanation for all this?' she demanded, refusing to grace him with a moment in which to recover. 'After everything August has done for you lately, I can't believe you're involved in this absurd business.'

He stared at her for a moment, regaining some of his composure. 'Hello April,' he said eventually. 'Lovely to see you, as always.'

'Don't give me that. Our days of being pleased to meet up on quiet park benches ended with the 1970s. Now, what's going on?'

King sighed. 'Your brother's in a great deal of trouble.'

'I wouldn't be freezing my particulars off out here if he wasn't,' she told him. 'What's your part in it?'

He shook his head. 'You're shouting at the wrong person,' he smiled, 'as always. He's being investigated by a man called Fisher. . .'

'Section 12, I know.'

'Fisher came to me, expecting me to offer evidence against August following the Lufford Hall business. Naturally I couldn't oblige. I had nothing but praise to heap on Section 37's shoulders – and you wouldn't believe how much vitriol that has caused in certain idiotic corners of the government. I told him there could be no question of August's loyalty, or indeed his importance to the security of our nation. I told him that we were damned lucky to have him and that we should count ourselves lucky that he was doing his job.'

April softened. 'That's terribly sweet, if it's true.'

'Of course it's true, April, you know me better than that. I'm not one of your two-faced lot, I'm just a politician. We're paragons of virtue and trust by comparison. Fisher was . . . I don't know how to describe it really: gleeful? He didn't care what I said, he was utterly convinced that he would break August. He relished the idea so much. He quite wrong-footed me. I don't think I'd ever seen someone so completely and utterly poisonous in his attitudes. He's a serious threat, April, deadly serious. . .'

'I can handle Fisher.'

King shook his head. 'I can't believe I'm saying this, knowing you as I do, but I really don't think you can. He hates August, I mean really . . . I know people bandy the word around, but the pleasure he was taking in his conviction that he would ruin your brother. What did August ever do to him? It was personal, that's for sure.'

'I don't think they've even met. Which, considering the time they've both spent in the service seems a feat in itself, but I'm sure there's no personal axe to grind.'

'You didn't see what he was like. He means to destroy him, April, utterly destroy him. I did my best to ask around, see if I couldn't pull a few strings to have the investigation stopped but I have no real influence, not in security. We pretend it's the politicians that have the power but you and I both know that's illusory when it comes to this sort of thing. I'm probably just another file somewhere in an MI6 office. So I decided to try something else. . .'

'Bernstein?'

'I know his father, he owed me a favour. Hamish is a career soldier, he does as he's told, as long as you're firm enough. Fisher had asked him to go through the Section 37 files. He wanted all the material he could find on Shining's time in Germany in the early Eighties.'

'He'd have had a job on. August doesn't keep the old stuff in the office, he hasn't got the space.'

'Then he's gone to Fisher empty-handed. Good.' King smiled. 'A small victory, but you take what you can get.'

April looked at the bundle of files on the bench. 'So what are these?'

'Take a look. I convinced Bernstein that, while he was there, he would be helping his country were he to select certain files and ensure they were removed from Shining's office.'

April opened the files and saw her own name. 'They're all about me?'

'I didn't want Fisher going after you next. I might not be able to help August but I could at least try to protect you.'

April put her hand on King's arm. 'Oh, you silly darling, I've got nothing to hide.'

'Fisher doesn't care. I told you, the man's a menace. He'd find something to twist against you, I'm sure.'

'But he's not interested in me, is he?'

King shrugged. 'He was interested in everything to do with August. He asked about you and Toby. Wanted to know what I knew about the both of you. I couldn't help Toby. . .'

'Nobody can at the moment,' April admitted. She patted the files on her lap, looking out across the park. In the distance a jogger in a hoodie was pounding his way across the grass towards them, his trainers beating at the ground. Beyond him a woman wrestled with two large dogs, neither inclined to walk in the same direction. In the far distance a group of school kids were laughing and shoving at one another, cutting through the park as a short cut home. Normal people, happy in their normal business.

'It was kind of you to think of me,' she said to King.

King shifted in his seat, slightly embarrassed. 'I often do,' he admitted.

She hugged his arm. 'Now, now, you're a happily married man these days, don't start digging all that up.'

'Just because the world moved on doesn't mean I don't still have feelings for you,' he said. 'They may not be the same feelings they once were. . .'

'Don't spoil it, darling.'

He laughed. 'You know what I mean, you're a great woman, April, and I'll always have your back when I can.'

'I can always depend on you, Clive, you gorgeous old sod.'

King coughed and April felt something spatter on her face. 'Clive!' she said, reaching for her cheek. Then she turned to look at him. It hadn't been a cough. There was a ragged hole where his left cheek had been, a thin trail of condensation rising from the small entry wound in the back of his skull. Her fingers touched the blood on her cheek even as she saw the spatter that had arced across her lap and the files her old friend had stolen in order to protect her. 'Clive!' she cried again, this time in shock and horror.

She ducked down and peered through the slats of the bench into the woods behind them. There was a flash of red moving between the trees towards her, the jogger from earlier, she realised, his hood pulled up over his head, his hands pressed deep into the pouch in the hoodie's front. One of which was almost certainly holding a gun.

She looked around, desperately trying to see a way out of her situation. If she ran, he would surely cut her down.

To her right a pair of cyclists appeared on the track through the park. In a few seconds they would be between her and the assassin – surely he wouldn't risk witnesses? It was her only chance: make as much noise as possible and hope that it made him back off for long enough that she could make her escape.

She looked to Clive as he slowly sagged forward, thick strings of blood dripping onto his crisp white shirt and the lapels of his expensive suit. Clive had always fussed about his suits. She thought back on their time together, mocking him from the bed as he slowly and methodically hung up his clothes. She had accused him of having no passion, no spontaneity. In a way it had been true, but she regretted every harsh word now.

We always remember our crimes against the dead, however small.

The cyclists drew closer, the assassin now aware of them too, halting in his advance and looking towards them, his face still hidden within his hoodie.

April jumped to her feet and waved her arms. 'Help!' she shouted, feeling absurdly pathetic. Pride be damned, she thought, continuing to shout. 'Please help me! This man is trying to kill me!'

The cyclists were both young men, students most likely, she decided. What happened to the good old days when students barely left the dope-tinged fug of their accommodation? It was broad daylight and here they were indulging in exercise.

The assassin didn't run as the cyclists reached them. They slammed on their brakes and one of them, a tall ginger-haired lad with calves you could have clubbed an ox to death with, started to dismount. 'There some sort of problem?' he asked.

'Watch it, Flinty,' said his friend, smaller and vainly attempting to grow a blond beard. 'They might be. . .' He suddenly realised he didn't know how to finish that sentence without causing offence.

'This man shot my friend!' April shouted, pointing at the assassin. Why was the man not just running away?

He turned to look at her and his face was shocked. 'I would never. . .' he said.

'Perhaps the old fucker deserved it?' suggested the ginger-haired cyclist, smiling at April. 'Had you thought of that?'

His friend stared at him. 'What are you on about, Flinty?' he asked. Flinty didn't seem at all sure, now looking baffled as to what was happening.

'You all deserve it,' said the jogger, no trace of shock on his face now as he pulled the silenced pistol from the pocket of his hoodie and smiled at April.

She kicked him has hard as she could between the legs, then ran.

'He's got a gun!' Flinty was shouting.

'Just get out of here!' she shouted over her shoulder, not daring to slow herself down by turning around. 'Just go!'

She heard the gun fire twice and the clatter of bicycles and bodies. All she'd done was get another couple of people killed.

She moved between the trees, heading towards the main road, knowing there was no way she could outpace the assassin but refusing not to give it a damn good try.

Ahead of her, the hiss of pneumatic brakes and the hum of car engines worked its way through the trees, the relative safety of the Seven Sisters Road so close at hand.

She could hear running feet behind her. He wasn't shooting, why wasn't he shooting? She had no wish to die but if that was how it had to be then let it at least be over and bloody done with.

She searched her handbag as she ran. Her phone was no use – why call anyone only to die down the line to them? A few years ago, she'd gone through a short phase of carrying pepper spray in her bag, not out of any general sense of vulnerability – she'd never been one for that – but an ex-boyfriend had made enough threats that she'd decided it might not have been a bad idea to be prepared in case he tried to follow through on them. Like all his promises, they'd turned out to be hollow and, after an awkward New Year's Eve when she'd blinded a fellow partygoer thinking it was a can of silly string, she'd made a point of dumping it in the bin. At the time she'd considered herself terribly sensible to have done so; now she wished she'd let it clutter up her bag like everything else she'd shoved in it over the years.

She threw the pizza slices over her shoulder. Maybe she'd get lucky and catch him in the eye with a stray jalapeño. There must be something she could use to defend herself?

'Shining,' hissed a voice behind her and her legs were cut out from beneath her by a kick. She toppled to the ground with a pained cry. Those old bones didn't fall as easily as they once had. In her hand she was gripping her keys and she folded them between her fingers as the jogger leaned down over her. There was no sign of the gun as he pushed his face towards hers. 'You're his sister, yes?'

'The fighter in the family,' she told him, punching him as hard as she could with the keys jutting out from her fist. They cut parallel lines across his cheek and he spun away, blood and spittle spraying from his mouth. She tried to press the slender advantage. Her hips were agony, hurt from her fall, and her back joined in as she pushed herself forward, punching again and again. She felt the keys cut into her own, thin fingers. As they connected with his cheekbone, the impact knocked them from her hand. She screamed in anger, punching him with both hands, blind in rage and fear and determination that no man would ever get the better of April Shining.

She suddenly thought of his gun. Was it still in his pocket? Could she snatch it?

She stopped punching him and tore at his hoodie.

She could feel the weight of it in the pouch, scrabbling at the openings to get her hands inside.

'You want my gun?' he asked, laughing. He gave he an open-handed slap across the face and shoved her backwards.

Lying back, staring up at the man that would certainly kill her, April was so angry she felt as if she could tear the world apart. He had just been playing with her! Patronising bastard! She'd never really had the upper hand.

'I like you,' he said, pulling the gun from his pocket and looking around. There was nobody within sight, they were all alone, free to let this play out however the killer wished. 'In fact,' he continued, 'I like you so much that maybe I should just be you.'

He turned the gun in his hands, offering it to her by the grip.

For a moment she was so determined not to be played for a fool again she just stared at it. Then, accepting that she would take any chance rather than go down without a fight, she reached for it. Her hand closed around the grip and he let it go, her finger curling around the trigger.

'Hang on,' he said, his face suddenly confused and panicked, 'what's going on? Who are you anyway?'

And that was all he said because then the woman that was no longer completely April Shining shot him in the head.

She got to her feet, picked up her handbag and dropped the gun into it.

She looked around, the coast was still clear.

She pulled a compact mirror out of the bag and checked her face, wiping away the blood with her scarf and rearranging her hair a little so that she wouldn't draw attention. Her hand was bleeding from where the keys had cut into her fingers so she wrapped the scarf neatly around it. Nobody would look twice, she felt sure. People moved through this city with their eyes closed, lost in their own, tiny little heads.

She walked past the dead jogger, now nothing but empty waste, and headed back towards the path that led out of the park. On the way she picked up the discarded pizza slices. They were covered in bits of grass and dead leaves but she ate them anyway.

TWENTY-TWO

Shining left the bathroom and decided he'd risk a wander. Stepping into the kitchen, he found Jennings removing the packaging from some ready meals.

'You're not vegetarian or anything?' he asked, noticing Shining behind him.

'No.'

'Not that it probably matters,' Jennings said looking at the packaging. '"Premium lasagne",' he quoted. 'I somehow doubt that's true. I hate eating this sort of rubbish. Fresh food, fresh ingredients, that's the way. People are so lazy these days.' He looked around. 'Not that we have any choice. This is all we have stocked – a freezer full of ancient crap.'

'You do this sort of thing a lot?' Shining asked. 'By which I mean interrogations, not food preparation.'

Jennings shrugged. 'A few. They always like a few forces boys around. You're a bit different. Usually it's terror suspects, you know the sort of thing, mouthy bloggers pretending they can build bombs in their bedroom.'

'I'm glad to be able to break the monotony.'

Jennings turned on the oven. 'It's a job. Someone has to do it. Doesn't sound as interesting as yours.'

'I've had my moments.'

'All that stuff true? The things you were saying in there?'

'Well, that's the most casual interrogation technique I've ever heard.'

'I'm not paid to do the talking, that's her job. Me and the boys are just security.'

'And where are they?'

'Outside.' Jennings looked at him. 'Why? You're not going to try and run are, you?'

'No, that would hardly solve anything, would it? I'll let this play out for as long as it lasts. I've nothing to hide.'

Jennings nodded. 'So is it?'

'Is it what? Oh . . . is it true? Yes. And believe me, it barely registers as weird on the scale of my usual investigations. My life has been a very interesting one.'

'I can believe it.'

'Well, as long as your colleague also can, this should be a walk in the park.'

'She's all right,' said Jennings, unpacking another meal and racking it up on the baking tray next to the lasagne. 'She tries too hard but you know what it's like. Even now, being a woman in the security service can be hard work. They preach equality but there'll always be some arseholes that make it difficult for 'em.'

'True enough,' Shining admitted.

'So she plays at being the hardest bastard of them all because that's the only way she's got anywhere.'

'Maybe.'

Jennings smiled. 'Yeah . . . maybe. Either that or she really is just a pain in the arse. You'd better get back in there and find out.'

'I suppose I should.'

'I'll bring some coffee in in a bit. No booze, I'm afraid. Standing orders.'

'Security and catering?'

Jennings put the food in the oven. 'Yeah, well, I'd rather keep busy, boring otherwise. And you're not trouble. You get to spot that in my job. You can tell the ones that are going to kick off. You're just doing your job, same as the rest of us.'

'I wish you were handling my interrogation, we could all have gone home hours ago.'

'Don't you believe it. If I was in her seat it would have been my job to be the arsehole, wouldn't it? We all play our roles.'

Shining nodded and returned to the dining room and Ryska.

Ryska was stood in front of the covered window, staring at it as if she could see through the cloth and out into the evening beyond.

'I hope I didn't keep you waiting too long,' said Shining. 'I was giving my compliments to the chef.'

She didn't turn around so he sat down at the table, unwilling to encourage her games of one-upmanship.

'The food won't be long, apparently,' he told her, 'but I'm happy to carry on for a little bit if you are?'

She turned around and inclined her head. It took Shining a second to realise he was no longer looking at his interrogator but rather at something that, for now, was wearing its body.

He found he wasn't surprised. After all, hadn't he been thinking about this force, this 'higher power' all day?

'How long have you been there?' he asked. 'Looking out through your stolen damned eyes.'

'I am not who you think,' Ryska replied and her voice was slightly different. Strangely, it was more natural, featuring traces of the Eastern European accent she'd worked hard to eradicate when at school. Gone also were her attempts to inject every syllable with cold professionalism. Shining only really noticed how much the officer had affected her abrasive personality now that it was gone. Her natural tone was lighter, it had a gentility to it. It was a voice that could offer kindness.

'I know exactly who you are,' Shining replied. 'Let's not play games, I've had quite enough of that.'

'I'm not who you think,' she said again. 'Is this the now? Is this right?'

Her face contorted. At first, Shining thought she was in pain, the essence of Ryska fighting back, perhaps. Then her expression continued to change, lips stretching, receding from her teeth and them pushing forward as if in a kiss. Ryska put her hands to her face and began to knead at the flesh there, moving her cheeks over the bone, pressing the tips of her fingers into every line and crease. 'This is . . . unusual.'

'I'd have thought you'd have got used to invading people by now,' said Shining. 'You have made something of a career of it.'

Ryska nodded, then shook her head. 'Which is it?' she wondered aloud. 'Which means no?'

Shining sighed. 'I mean it, my patience is thin. I have spent the last few hours being treated like a traitor. All the while being reminded, were it necessary – and it really, really wasn't – why I have reason to consider you the most insidious, vile and corrupt. . .' He sighed. 'I don't have the vocabulary. What are you? An entity? A consciousness? A thing? Whatever label I should choose, I don't suppose it matters. But let me be clear. I have lived a long life and I have managed to conduct myself through most of it with constraint, humanity and understanding. I have exercised grace, compassion and tolerance. I have, at all times, worked hard to avoid the pitfalls of narrow emotions. In particular, I have fought against the lazy, destructive emotion of hate. Everywhere you look in this world you see hate expressed, hate for another's politics, religion, sexuality or gender. Hate is terrible, it is weakness, it is failure. But when I look at you, whatever body you wear, whatever voice you use, all of that restraint counts for nothing. You are the one thing I cannot help but hate. You've ruined the lives of so many, including, were I to allow you the satisfaction, my own. So . . . I say again. No more games. What do you want?'

Throughout, Ryska had stared at Shining, her face showing none of the emotions felt by the consciousness inside her. After a moment, she replied, 'To help. I am not who you think I am. . .' She paused. 'The other, the rebel, the one who has worked against you. The one to whom you have promised flesh. I am not who you think. I am sent to find the other, to help, to guide you.'

Shining leaned back in his chair and rubbed at his tired face. His skin was clammy. He wanted fresh air, sunlight and freedom. Most of all, he wanted to believe what he was being told. But how could he?

'You expect me to believe you're another of the higher powers?'

'Higher powers?'

'It's what I call you. It.'

'We are not higher. We are just different. Reality is much more complex than you give it credit. An infinite number of layers. All with their own distinct breed of life. You know this but cannot comprehend it so you try to express it in terms of gods, heaven. . .'

'Hell?'

She nodded.

'You're learning,' he said, 'presuming you meant to agree?' He had intended sarcasm, still far from convinced he could believe a word he was hearing. She gave no sign of understanding it as such.

'The longer I inhabit this body, the more its intelligence leeches into mine. The more I understand. You know that your world is not all there is. You know that there is more. You feel this. You sense it. So you try to map the infinite with religion, philosophy, science. We were no different once. Trying to understand thoughts that were too much for us.'

'And did you?'

'No. We realised wisdom, real wisdom, is to accept your own reality and live it to the full.'

Shining couldn't help but scoff. 'Your own reality? Says the creature inhabiting someone else's body?'

'This is not normal. This is not who we are. I find it distasteful but there is no other way for us to be having this conversation. Of course there is one of us who does not find it distasteful. It relishes it. That is who I am here to discuss.'

'So discuss him.'

'It is not a "him" in the way you understand it.'

'He invades bodies without consent, causing destruction and misery wherever he goes. I can't help but think of it as "he". But arguing personal pronouns is a waste of time.'

Ryska nodded again. 'Very well. He. He is a rebel. A criminal.

'Your species dreams of the spirit, the soul, to be free from the flesh and to travel to other realities. To us that is normal. That is what we are. So some . . . he . . . dreams of the reverse. He wants flesh. The solid. The dirt.'

'Now you're being insulting.'

'I do not mean to be, it's just . . . to most of us his desires are abhorrent. He is unnatural.'

Shining was struggling. He had spent his entire life coming face to face with the abnormal, of doing what he had insisted Ryska should do earlier: accepting the evidence and rearranging his beliefs around it. But this? For some reason this felt a step too far. He had known the higher power for thirty years and in that time it had moved in and out of his life, playing its games, vying for deals, making threats. He had grown to accept it. Why then was it so strange to imagine it wasn't alone? That there were more of them? That he was talking to one of them right now?

'You had, I think, almost come to believe that the rebel was a spirit?' said Ryska. 'A . . . devil? Because that made sense to you?'

Shining shook his head. He had always denied that, had insisted to Toby that it wasn't the case, but maybe. . .

'I don't really know what I thought,' he admitted. 'Perhaps I tried not to think about it at all.'

'But it wants you, it is your enemy.'

'Then it can join the queue. Besides, when I made our deal I was a young man. I've avoided it this long. I think . . . thought . . . that I would always stay one step ahead.'

'You're not. It's a point of principle to him now. He will have his way. He will win. It's important to him.'

'Then I suppose he's not so different to us, is he?'

Ryska nearly shrugged. It was slightly over the top, unnatural, but the emotion was conveyed. 'He wants to be no different at all. He wants to be just like you. To be you.'

'Which never did make any sense, to be so powerful, to possess the abilities he does and want to restrict himself. The things he can do! Flesh is just clay to him, he can heal mortal wounds, he can even duplicate it, and the consciousness inside it.'

Shining was thinking of Fratfield again, who had escaped Section 37 only by accepting what the higher power had called a 'doppelgänger contract', doubling himself up into two distinct Fratfields. One had been killed, the other. . .

'Flesh is easy to us,' she agreed. 'Externally at least. It is all just matter. We can rearrange it, manipulate it, build with it. But he wants to wear it, to feel the sensations that come with it. He doesn't want to play with clay, he wants to know what being clay is really like. Power is something that only makes sense by comparison. To you, the things he can do, the mental gifts he possesses, that is power because it's something you don't have. To him, you are powerful. You feel, you taste, you grow, you die. Your bodies thrive and rot. You're solid, packed full of animal strength. You can break things. He does like to break things.'

'You're telling me.' Shining looked at her. 'Why are you telling me? You say you want to help? Then get rid of him. Take him back to wherever it is you come from and leave us alone.'

'But that's precisely the point. I can't, because I don't have the power. How can I force him to do anything? We're not like you. We're. . .'

'Insubstantial?'

'Consciousness. Just that. We're thought. We're mind. To force something is the province of flesh. Thought cannot fight, it can only question.'

'But I can't fight him either. If I attack him while he's in possession of someone else, all I'm doing is attacking the host, not the consciousness, all he has to do is leave. I thought that when he really inhabited someone, took full possession . . . You said, "Is this the now?" What did you mean?'

The sudden change of subject seemed to confuse her for a moment. She stared at him for a couple of seconds before answering.

'Moving from my plane to yours, it's hard to be precise. Time is not so linear to us. I have found you before but it was never the right time. Sometimes you were younger, sometimes it was too late.'

'Too late? That's reassuring.'

'You must make it that he can't leave. You must give him what he wants.'

'I don't understand.'

Ryska began tapping her nails on the table. That nervous twitch of hers. 'Understand what?' she asked.

'I don't understand what you. . .' Shining looked at her hand, her tapping fingers. The other presence was gone. 'It doesn't matter.'

She shook her head. 'Are you ready to carry on? That old body of yours stretched its legs enough?'

He smiled. Wasn't that the important question? When would he finally let this old body give up stretching its legs?

'What's funny?' she asked.

'Nothing really,' he admitted. 'Far from it, but sometimes you have to smile, don't you? The alternative's much worse.'

TWENTY-THREE

I decided there was little I could do but go back to Alexandra's flat. I needed to think, to try to decide what my next step should be. I could just return to West Berlin, but that would be giving up and what would I have achieved? I'd seen Robie, yes, and there was no evidence to support his being a traitor. But there was little evidence of anything else either. To my unblinkered eyes, it seemed clear that something was possessing people, making them act against their wishes. The Russian soldier, Grauber, my would-be postman assassin. Finally, of course, poor Alexandra, throwing herself to her death even though she had no idea why. But there was no way any of my superiors were going to accept a report about that.

Perhaps they were right. Sometimes, accepting the preternatural is no help at all. Yes, I could accept the notion of these people being possessed but by what and why? Expressing an opinion about it at this stage would get me nowhere – I just didn't know enough.

What could I tell them about Robie? That he was on the run,

afraid for his life. He clearly believed that whatever it was that was possessing people had him in its sights. It was all nonsense. It was as insubstantial as air. They would send me back to England in disgrace, and Robie would be no better off than he had been before I came.

I had to stay, I had to find out more. I had to find *him.* Nothing else would do.

I stopped off to buy a change of clothes. When the shop assistant seemed suspicious, I spun him a tale about the border control having confiscated my bag for no reason. That seemed to work: he shook his head sadly as if it was the most common thing in the world. 'They are a disgrace sometimes,' he said, clearly deciding that, as a foreigner – and one who had not had enough clout with the authorities to even maintain ownership of a spare shirt – I was unlikely to cause trouble over him expressing such opinions. 'They do as they please. They take your money, your belongings. I think they share it between themselves.'

'Well, I don't imagine they'll be fighting over my socks,' I told him. 'They were nothing special.'

He laughed and bagged up my purchases. On the spur of the moment, I dashed away again to look at their winter coats, adding a padded parka and a pair of gloves to my order.

'More snow soon,' he said, by way of endorsing my decision. 'They say it's going to get much colder in the next couple of days.'

'I don't suppose you sell brandy as well?' I joked.

He laughed. I was doing a marvellous job of making friends with him. 'Nature's thermal vest, eh?' he suggested.

I took my bags and walked the rest of the way to Alexandra's flat. At least she had given me a spare set of keys. Without Engel around to negotiate locked doors, I would have been stuck out in the cold without them.

Upstairs, I dumped my bags and took another shower, as much to warm myself as anything else. My stomach was still tender from where Robie had punched me, and I tenderly soaped the bruise he'd left me with. I tried to be angry at him for it but, in truth, I couldn't manage it. It had hurt like hell – still did – but despite his panicked and confused state, I still trusted Robie enough to believe he had done only what he had thought was necessary. I just hoped I could track him down and point out how wrong he was.

I put on my new clothes, trying to convince myself that jeans and a heavy jumper were extremely practical and, after all, what better way to stay undercover than for August Shining to walk the street in denim? I raided Alexandra's drinks cabinet and sat down to sip at vodka and think.

Where would Robie hide? He knew the city but was clearly trying to avoid his normal haunts. Alexandra had given him money, probably not a great deal, she was clearly not as solvent as she once was. A rich person doesn't say 'as much as I can' when discussing funds. She had given him as much as she had to hand, most likely whatever had been in her purse. Probably not enough for a hotel. But then I was jumping to conclusions . . . grasping at straws. Stick to the facts, let the wild supposition come in its own time.

He hadn't shaved. He'd been wearing the same clothes for some time. This wasn't in itself surprising, as he'd clearly dropped everything and run. This wasn't a man who'd packed a toiletry bag before going off the grid. Except. . .

Except Lucas Robie had always fallen on his feet for one simple reason: he had a gift that enabled him to do so. He charmed his way out of every problem. So why was he in such dire straits? If he wanted a bed for the night then all he had to do was ask for one. If he wanted a change of clothes then he need do no more than walk into a clothing store and lift one off the peg. Money? Money wasn't the vital commodity for Lucas it was for the rest of us. His belly need never go empty, his throat never dry. So why had he wanted money? Because he was trying to avoid using his gift? It wasn't something he could turn on and off; that was, after all, what had driven him close to suicide all those years ago. So why the money?

I didn't know.

Lucas's gift. Why had he even asked Alexandra for help? He didn't need her. He'd clearly gone to every effort to avoid being close to her at the park, had all but ignored her. Why? He had been desperate to avoid me too. Because I might otherwise have shared her fate? 'It wouldn't be fair,' he'd said. 'Especially after it's proven how far it's willing to. . .' Willing to go? It – whatever 'it' was – had killed Alexandra, that was clearly the assumption, despite his begging it not to do so.

Lucas's gift.

I couldn't tear my thoughts away from it but I was going around in circles. I topped up my glass and tried to clarify my thoughts.

Lucas was avoiding using his gift. The only way he could do that was . . . There *was* no way he could avoid it; whenever he met someone (bar the odd exception like me, but we really were few and far between) they found themselves devoted to him.

The only way Lucas could avoid using his gift was. . .

By not being near people. By avoiding people altogether. But he'd agreed to meet Alexandra in the crowded park . . . so did that wash? It still might have done. Lucas had avoided direct contact with anyone, keeping his head down, withdrawn. A crowded place was beneficial if he hadn't wanted to draw attention to their meeting: basic spycraft.

East Berlin was full of crowded places. He could have met her at any of them.

I was getting there, piece by piece, question by counter-question.

Lucas was avoiding people. But to meet Alexandra he had to select a busy location. East Berlin was full of crowded places. So there was another reason why he'd chosen the park. He'd chosen the park because. . .

Lucas was living rough somewhere.

Lucas was avoiding people.

Lucas had lost me in the forest around the Kulturpark.

The forest next to the Kulturpark.

The forest that was isolated despite being close to the city.

Lucas was living rough in the forest.

It was a guess, but it worked. It matched with the facts. Frankly it was better than nothing.

As to why he was avoiding using his gift, I could find that out once I found him.

I decided to put some food in me before returning to the

Plänterwald forest. I had no idea how long I'd be searching and the snow was continuing to fall as I stepped out of Alexandra's apartment block onto the street outside. There was a little bar at the end of the—

TWENTY-FOUR

'Ah!' Shining recoiled from the table, nearly tumbling out of his chair.

'What?' Ryska jumped to her feet in surprise, looking around and reaching for a weapon she immediately realised she wasn't wearing.

'Can't you see him?'

Ryska looked around her. There was nothing. They were alone in the room.

'What are you talking about?' she shouted.

'He's right. . .' Shining stared just beyond Ryska at the figure hanging a foot or so above the floor. The man was screaming at him, as if desperate for Shining to hear him. His face was distorted, the air around him rippling. It was like looking at your reflection in a pond after a stone had hit the water. Still, he recognised the face, yes, it was clearing. . .

'Jamie?' Shining asked. 'Jamie is that you?'

And then the figure vanished and Shining was left staring at thin air.

'Is this supposed to help your story seem more convincing?' Ryska asked, her voice heavy with sarcasm, 'because I hate to tell you but right now I'm thinking you're completely off your head.'

The door opened and Jennings stepped in.

'Food's up,' he announced. He looked at Shining, still staring at nothing, his face agonised, then to Ryska who appeared to be a hair's breadth from beating the old man. 'Just in time too by the looks of it.'

TWENTY-FIVE

Cassandra Grace tugged the rubber head off her shoulders and flung it in the general direction of the director. She couldn't be certain of her aim because she hadn't been able to wear her glasses under the costume, but the head certainly hit someone because she heard a cry of pain. 'Now you know how heavy it is!' she shouted. 'Full of the memories of war and the misery of being unable to spawn on our home world and forced to come to Earth for sex slaves! I mean . . . Earth! Have you actually tried to get a decent boyfriend on this planet? No wonder the Xtraxillons are killing everybody!'

She stormed off, ignoring the angry shouting behind her. If they couldn't take her truth then they could just piss off and find someone else for the part. It was their loss.

She picked up her bag from the dressing room, just managing to catch a bus back towards town by running hell for leather out of the quarry and towards the main road. She was damned if she was going to sit in the minibus and wait for the rest of the cast to come in and tell her what trouble she'd caused.

They didn't understand her either. They were only here to cash a cheque. Were there no real artists left these days?

'What are you supposed to be?' asked the old man sat next to her on the bus, prodding at her latex belly. She probably should have taken the time to change out of the bodysuit, but when you've decided to storm out you just have to stick to your guns.

'I'm Queen of the Xtraxillons,' she told him, 'on Earth to gather breeding stock.'

'Oh aye.' He thought about this for a moment. 'Is there a medical exam?'

'Not really. By all accounts we just go for brainless cheesecake, especially if they've had a guest role in *Hollyoaks*.'

'You want to be careful,' he told her. 'You'll get nowhere if you're not selective. Don't want to end up with a load of deformed babies, do you?'

'Are you an expert on breeding, then?' she asked him, peering over the wide neck of the bodysuit.

His face took on a wistful air and he scratched at his thinning scalp. 'Not these days, the wife has issues. It makes her feel "proximity-challenged". I used to breed spaniels, though.'

'Good for you. I like spaniels.'

The bus eventually pulled into Brentford and she left her new best friend and spaniel expert and caught a train to Ealing Broadway. On the train she finally had the space to strip off the hot, claustrophobic body of Queen Cthar of the Xtraxillons and put on her normal clothes. There were a few complaints from the fellow passengers but she explained that her body was just one of the tools of her craft and therefore couldn't be deemed offensive when exhibited on public transport and besides, these pants were new.

Dragging the bodysuit all the way home was annoying but these things were expensive and she had every intention of repainting it and wearing it the next time she put on one of her theatrical evenings.

'Hello house,' she shouted, as she clambered through the front door and up the stairs to her flat. There was a low murmur from the couple that rented downstairs. They were so impolite. She bet they wouldn't be so shy once she was famous – they'd soon be returning her greetings then.

She finally got the suit through her front door and sat it down in the bathroom. It would get in the way when she wanted a shower – and having sweated in it for hours she wanted one now – but there was nowhere else it could possibly fit.

First there must be a glass of wine. Life could not possibly continue without one. She turned on her phone and scrolled through the several angry texts, emails and voicemails, lost in threats, insults and demands as she shuffled into the kitchen and scrabbled around in the fridge for the bottle she knew should be in there. Still staring at the screen, her hand waved unproductively around in the largely empty space, singularly failing to fall on anything wine-shaped. She borrowed it back for a minute to wipe at her eyes – why did people always have to be so horrible? Finally, she stopped looking at the awful, mean words and stared into the fridge. The wine wasn't there. She stamped her foot and wailed in frustration at her day. She'd bought a bottle, thinking it would be a well-earned treat after a hard day being all successful finally in an actual, proper movie for which she was being paid and everything. So why was it not there?

'Are you looking for this?'

Grace gave a squeal of surprise and nearly fell backwards into the fridge.

There was an old woman in her kitchen. Why on earth was there an old woman in her kitchen? An old woman that appeared to be drinking her bloody wine.

The old woman raised the bottle towards Grace by way of a toast, then took a large swig out of it. 'I hope you don't mind me letting myself in. Spare key on the door jamb really isn't a terribly clever hiding place.'

'I keep losing . . . What are you doing in my house?'

'Shush, darling,' said the woman that still was not altogether April Shining. 'We don't want to disturb the neighbours.'

'Fuck the neigh—' But she didn't say any more because that was when the woman turned the bottle around and smacked her in the face with it.

Grace stumbled backwards, her foot slipping in the trail of spilled cheap hock, and crashed back into the open fridge.

'I told you!' the old woman hissed. 'Shush!' And she continued to pound at Grace's head with the bottle until there was nothing left but a shattered stub of its glass neck.

Sighing with the exertion, she stepped back, took April Shining's phone out of her handbag and took a photo of Cassandra Grace's ruined face.

'I never quite know how to work these things,' she explained as Cassandra tried to draw a liquid breath. 'Is it better to email or text? Hang on. . .'

Cassandra slipped down out of the fridge, half-eaten goods spilling on her from the collapsed shelves.

'Email, I think,' the old woman said. 'Yes. That's it. August Shining. Yes. Send. Sending . . . still sending . . . Sent!'

As Cassandra tried to get to her feet, blind from the blood in her eyes, a question seemed important to her. 'Woo Gers Hiny?'

'Who's August Shining? Oh, my poor lovely, he probably didn't give you his real name, but according to his files you've worked as an agent for him several times. Expert on curses? I'm sure you were very helpful.'

Cassandra tried to make a run for the front door but, still blind, she collided with the wall, leaving a crimson splash on the white paintwork that looked like a child's painting of a butterfly. Behind her she heard the old woman rifling through her cutlery drawer. 'Don't run off, darling,' she said. 'Aunty April hasn't quite finished with you yet.'

Derek Lime dumped his toolbox in the back of the van and made a pretence at wiping the dirt of the Victoria Line off his face with a piece of paper towel.

'We all square, Derek?'

Derek looked over at Faraday, his boss, and nodded. 'Reckon so. Just needed to re-channel some of the output through—'

'Good lad,' Faraday interrupted. 'You know me, always get confuddled with the technical stuff.'

Lad? Confuddled? Derek didn't know what TfL was coming to these days. And to think the man was named after a genius.

'So we all good to go, then?' Faraday asked, offering him a weak smile as if that made all the difference when repeating yourself.

'Yes,' Derek said. 'Good to go.'

'Poptastic. I'll pass on the good news upstairs.'

'You do that,' agreed Derek. And go away now, he managed not to add.

Thankfully it proved unnecessary as he was immediately left to pack up the rest of his stuff while his boss dashed away to explain how brilliant he was to someone who earned more than both of them put together.

Some days Derek wished he was back on the wrestling circuit. At least then he had been allowed to roar at his opponent from time to time. He imagined rebounding off the ropes and launching himself onto Faraday, perhaps forgetting to take his weight on his arms as he dropped, just slapping right down on him, gravity and gut in perfect symphony. He liked to think Faraday might end up several inches thinner and a foot taller.

Still, with his heart, the wrestling had had to go. It was one thing loving your job, it was quite another dying over it.

Van packed, Derek made to get in the driver's seat when he saw something that stopped him dead in his tracks. On the other side of the car park was an old Mini. Poking out beyond it, only just visible in the amber glow of the street lights, was a pair of legs.

Oh Lord, Derek thought. What's happened here then?

'Hello there!' he called, jogging towards the car. 'Are you all right?'

He rounded the car and saw it was an elderly woman, lying face down on the tarmac.

'Christ on a bike,' Derek muttered, trying to remember his first-aid training.

He quickly checked her for signs of bleeding but she seemed

safe to move. He took hold of her shoulders and gently made to turn her over.

'Watch it, porky,' the old woman said, spinning around and punching him in his stomach. 'Keep your hands to yourself.'

She kept punching at him and he stumbled back, only realising as he tried to stand up that she had a knife in her hand. She wasn't punching, she was stabbing.

'What you doing that for?' he said, falling back onto his considerable behind, looking down at his dark jersey. It hid any sign of damage in the low light. It was only by touching it, by the spreading sensation of heat that crept over him, that he really appreciated the trouble he was in. He sighed, his head spinning as the blood loss brought him close to fainting. Only now did he begin to panic, that unreliable heart of his clattering around. It'll be the death of me one day, he'd always thought. Sooner or later that damn thing's just going to stop. He was partially right.

'Let's see if you can't lose a little weight,' the woman said, as he lay back on the ground, his last short breaths pumping out of him. She straddled him and began to carve.

A few minutes later, the car park was briefly lit by the white burst of a camera-phone flash.

'I have just checked,' said Jamie Goss, pouring himself another vodka and coke, 'and I am entirely full of mimsy.'

'Shush,' said his partner, Alasdair, staring intently at the television. 'Why do you always have to kick up a fuss when I choose the film?'

'Mimsy levels reaching critical in fact,' Goss replied.

'Mimseygeddon mere seconds away. And you always choose the bloody films, ever since we first met. The last time I had full control of my LoveFilm account, my bed had a man called Enrique living in it.'

'Shush! You're spoiling it!'

On the screen, a young man fell to the floor of his artist's garret and wept about his AIDS.

'I think you'll find it was spoiled long before I caught a glimpse of it,' said Goss. 'I may have to go into the bedroom now before I'm forced to smash the television.'

'Good. Go away.'

'You won't say that when you come in later, you changeable cow.' As Goss shuffled out of the room with his drink, the young man on the screen was talking to God. God was played by Tilda Swinton.

Deciding to postpone his visit to the bedroom for a few practical minutes, Goss took his drink into the bathroom, dropped his trousers and took up a relaxed position on the toilet, sipping his vodka and coke and perusing the bookshelf for something jolly.

The doorbell rang. From the lounge there was nothing but the sound of an old Eurythmics song being sung a cappella.

The doorbell rang again.

'Well, get the bloody door, then!' Goss shouted, selecting a tourist guide to Greece.

'You get it!' Alasdair replied.

'I am without trousers,' Goss replied, 'and if you make me go I'll explain to whoever it is that the reason they are staring at my balls is entirely due to the indolence of my boyfriend. "The one with no taste in films?" they'll ask. "That's him," I'll reply. They will pity me.'

The sound of the film ceased just as Tilda prepared to sing about how noble and brutal love was.

'I hope it's another boyfriend being delivered,' Alasdair muttered as he walked past the bathroom door.

Goss took another sip of his drink and looked at pictures of waiters.

He heard the door open and Alasdair say hello.

'Hello, dear,' came an elderly woman's voice. 'Are you Jamie Goss, by any chance?'

'He's otherwise engaged at the moment,' Alasdair replied. 'Can I help you?'

'Oh, it's all gravy as far as I'm concerned,' the old woman said and there was a popping sound followed by a crash.

What the bloody hell had Alasdair done? Goss wondered, putting his drink behind him on the cistern and pulling up his trousers.

'Have you actually managed to fall over just by answering the door?' he shouted. 'That's genuinely amazing.'

He opened the bathroom door to see Alasdair lying in the hallway with a hole in the middle of his forehead. A few feet away, an old woman with a gun in her hand was pushing the front door closed and turning the lock. 'In all fairness,' she said, 'I did help a bit.'

She pointed the gun at Goss, who darted back into the bathroom, slamming and locking the door behind him.

'Fuck, fuck fuck. . .' he whispered, his brain spasming all over the place in shock. That can't have really been . . . Old women didn't just come into your house and . . . Alasdair couldn't really be. . .

The silenced handgun popped a couple more times and a

pair of holes appeared in the door; behind Goss, there was the sound of cracking bathroom tiles.

He gave a wail of panic and utter disbelief. What was going on? Why was this woman. . .?

He fell back into the bath and his body shook a couple of times before going completely still.

Goss was out, his mind lifted from his body and into that other place, the other plane he occasionally travelled to. He had, to use the term he favoured when leaving messages for Alasdair, *gone fishing*. It was this skill, remote viewing, astral projection, spirit walking, call it what you like, that August Shining had found occasionally useful. Nothing beat an agent that could leave their body behind and observe the world around them. Not that the plane Goss went to was the world he had left. It was always distorted, shifted, a nightmare place. But he had frequently picked up messages, translated what he had seen into something that was useful to Section 37. Now, of course, he was just running scared and, as much as his rational mind knew it was useless – there was a limit to what you could do when you'd given up on the benefits of a body – he couldn't bear the thought of trapping himself back inside it. He had to run, get away from mad women and their guns.

He opened the door – the door in the other plane, the real one would stay resolutely closed – and stepped out into this plane's version of his hallway. On the floor was the shadow of his dead boyfriend. Lovely Alasdair. Brilliant Alasdair. Poor, long-suffering bloody Alasdair. He was facing towards the ceiling, his face a corruption, an exaggeration of death, a bloated thing of moss and rot. Goss looked away. He couldn't bear the idea that that would be the last image he would have of the man he loved.

Then he saw the woman, the woman as this plane presented her. She stood a few feet away, and she had become a swirling mass of movement. At the heart of the swirling shape the old woman appeared just as she had in the brief glimpse Goss had had when he'd opened the door. Normal, recognisable, human. But around her the darkness moved, long tendrils of it slapping against the walls, ceilings and floor. It looked like ink in water, dissipating and reforming, as if it were not quite a part of this world but moving in and out of it.

'Hello, darling,' it said, and surged towards him with a dull screech like wet skin pulled across glass.

Goss ran, hurling himself at his front door, not bothering to try to open it, just passing right through and falling to the blackened stone of the balcony outside. He got to his feet and kept running, heading for the stairs. He half jumped, half floated down them.

He'd never allowed himself to be so fluid before, the panic teaching him skills he didn't know he'd been missing. Before he had always navigated this world as you would any other, treating his surroundings as physical. Now he was almost flying as he burst out into the central courtyard of the block and towards the main gate.

He looked over his shoulder to see the thing that had killed Alasdair blossom against the front of the building. It rose from the balcony, the old woman still at its centre but unmoving as the black tendrils pushed off against the walls of his home and sailed through the air towards him.

There was no way he could outrun this, no way he could escape it.

There was also no way he wasn't going to try.

In his times here in the other plane he had often seen creatures lurking at the edges, shadows in the sky, presences in the walls, pushing their way through this reality. When asked for his opinion on these creatures, he would say that they were, like him, passing through from another world, one that was different again from the one we were used to. Was the thing that hunted him one of those creatures? It certainly seemed more than the shadow versions of real people he met here. They were distorted avatars, the psyches of people in the real world extending out into this realm, exaggerated into something grotesque. This creature was more proactive, clearly as comfortable negotiating its way along the twisted streets as he was.

As it sailed through the air it made a squealing sound, as if it caused the air pain to have such an abomination tear through it. In its wake, the buildings rippled, affected by the proximity of it.

Panic lent him a new-found speed. Just as he had managed to half glide his way down the steps from his apartment, his feet now seemed to gain extra traction on the road beneath him, the street streaking past him as he pulled his way forwards. It was as if he was tugging the world past him like a theatrical backcloth yanked hard on its pulley.

He reached the shadow version St Pancras in seconds, bursting through the glass frontage in a sudden icy moment of transition. He lost his momentum on the concourse, distracted by again having passed through something that should have been solid. He rolled along the stone floor, his hands partially dipping into its surface. He yanked them free, terrified of what might happen if the ground hardened once more. The last thing he needed was to trap himself up to the wrist.

He looked around but there was no sign of his pursuer, just the faceless crowds of shadow passengers, flickering and blurring as they dashed to and from the platforms. Could he hide here? Lose himself amongst these ghost crowds? He looked up towards the next level, running and flinging himself towards it, pulling himself up through the air. He came to land by the champagne bar, surrounded by people with hollow faces, golden sparks fizzing and crackling in the off-white hole where their features should be. One of them raised a glass towards him and its fiery contents popped and burst like a firework. God, he could do with a drink, even one that looked as if it might burn its way right through him.

He moved towards the trains, howling beasts of metal and glass that moved like a piece of speeded-up film, ebbing and flowing on the platforms. Could he get on one? Might it steal him away from the reach of his pursuer? At the speed they were moving he could be in the shadow version of Carlisle in a matter of moments. Surely that was a better option than just waiting here?

He ran towards them, wondering if he might be able to time it precisely enough to leap from the track and inside one of the carriages.

Above him the ceiling shattered like ceramic and glass, and the air was once more filled with that squealing sound that heralded the movement of the creature. It was too late. It had found him.

He couldn't manage this on his own. Where was Tim when he was needed? This was the sort of thing he dealt with, weird monsters, impossible threats.

'Tim?' the creature asked. Not even his thoughts could remain hidden it seemed.

When it spoke it was partly with the lady's voice but beneath it, just slightly out of sync, was a deeper tone, a drone that reverberated through him. 'Oh . . . you mean Shining? He has so many names with so many people. Such a duplicitous boy.'

It sailed down towards Goss and he closed his eyes, unable to bear the thought of running any further. It was hopeless. Let this thing just do its worst.

'I'll be seeing him soon,' the creature continued. 'I'll be sure to give him your love. No doubt it will break his tiny, ageing heart. . .'

Shining, Goss thought. It had called him Shining. It was an apt name. For all his feigned cynicism, Goss had loved helping the old man, had enjoyed the thought that his skills were being put to good use. A drunk dreamer helping to save the world: it wasn't a bad legacy. Though he'd give it all up to not be here now, to be back in his flat with Alasdair, sat in front of an awful damn movie.

Shining. If only he could have found Shining. Maybe, between the two of them, they could have stood a chance.

Shining. . .

Goss suddenly felt himself dragged along the floor, the creature bouncing back off the spot where he had just been lying, dissipating and losing form for a moment as the impact shook it apart. What was happening? Where was he. . .?

The world blurred around him and he couldn't focus on the streaking lights and buildings. Up in the air where great edifices of cloud rose up before a liquid moon. Beyond that: the stars, pinpricks that burned in the darkness.

Shining.

They began to vanish in the distance, the creature following him still, its bloated body blocking out the night sky.

He felt himself falling, passing through trees, whipped by branches before colliding with the wall of a small house. Where was he? How had he been drawn here? To think, all of the things he could achieve in this plane and he had only just discovered the gift now when his time to appreciate it had grown so horribly short.

He pressed his hands against the bricks of the house and felt a charge of energy pass through him. He pushed through and there, right in front of him was Tim – Shining – sat at a bare table talking to a severe-looking woman. These were not shadow people – Goss was somehow pushing back into the real world. He screamed at Shining, desperate to get his attention. Could he not hear him? Behind him, there was the squealing sound that meant his hunter had found him. Already it was too late. He had to make himself heard!

Goss screamed again, focusing all his strength towards the man at the table. Shining suddenly looked up and stumbled back from the table. He could see him! He'd done it!

'Help me!' Goss shouted. 'It's right behind me! It killed Alasdair and it's right—'

It grew dark and it took Goss a second to realise it was because the creature's black tendrils were wrapping around him.

'Hello, gorgeous,' it whispered in his ear and he felt the

warmth of the old lady's breath. He could smell her perfume, so real, so solid in this insubstantial world. 'You are a darling, you've found him for me. Aren't you clever? I'll be sure to tell him how much you helped as I crush him.'

The light was gone now, cold, back smoke surrounding him, passing into him through his nose and mouth. He could feel it move into him, a chill more real to him than the ghost of his body.

'Maybe you can even watch,' it continued, 'from here. . .' There was a tearing sound and Goss faintly became aware that his body was lost to him. This thing wasn't going to kill him, it was worse than that, it was abandoning him. He felt the darkness withdraw and he floated up through the air. When travelling here, there had always been the distant sense of his body left in the real word, the anchor that held him fast, a home to return to. Not any more. Now he was just thought. He tried to move but even that seemed beyond him now; he was just a thought, rising forever up into an impossible sky.

In the bathtub, Goss's body twitched once, then again and then remained still.

The bathroom door burst open and the woman who was partially April Shining stepped inside.

'Empty,' she said, 'just meat and bone.'

She had an idea, retreating from the bathroom and wandering around the flat. She found what she wanted in a kitchen cupboard and returned to the lifeless body in the bathtub.

'Best to be tidy,' she said, pouring the contents of the bottle of paraffin over Goss's body, letting it soak into his clothes and his hair. 'No point in leaving it hanging around now there's nobody using it.' She lit a match and threw it onto the body, stepping back as it burst into flames.

'Lovely,' she said as she took her photos. 'Lovely, lovely, lovely. . .'

TWENTY-SIX

Toby and Tamar passed over a narrow bridge and on towards St Mark's square.

Venice in winter seemed a haunted place, not the romantic paradise of holiday brochures and paperback novels, but a sinking city of old stone and ghosts. In the light of a street lamp, a young woman played a sorrowful lament on a violin. Toby put a euro in her violin case but she didn't seem to notice, lost in the key of D.

'Who is this man?' Tamar asked as Toby checked the street signs against his map. He passed her the small black notebook Shining had given him, the collection of contacts and friendly faces around the world.

'He's under "V" for Venice,' Toby told her.

She flicked to the page and began to read. 'Giovanni, carpenter and seer.' She pronounced the latter as see-er, which was accurate enough. 'I wonder what he sees?' she asked.

'Fratfield, we hope.'

'It says "Carl" after it.'

'That's the name August uses with him. He changes his name more often than his socks.'

Toby and Tamar had left Mexico following the trail of an aeroplane ticket booked in the name of Jim Lufford, an alias, they were sure, of Fratfield's. After a few days, the trail had grown cold in Padua so Toby had checked the book in the hope of finding someone close by that could help them heat it back up again. Venice being a short drive away, they had booked a night in the cheapest hotel they could find.

They had needed a rest anyway, as difficult as it was to relax knowing their target still roamed free. Their travels from one country to another had sent their body clocks into meltdown and, after a breakfast that felt like dinner, they had gone to their room – a graveyard of ostentatious furniture and gilt grown tatty by neglect – and slept through the day.

After making a phone call to arrange a meeting with Giovanni, they were now on the hunt for both his workshop and dinner.

'There it is,' Toby said, pointing to a small shop at the end of the street. A wooden sign featuring an embossed harlequin's mask hung above a window filled with doll's houses, puppet theatres and carnival masks.

Toby looked at his watch. 'We've got an hour and a half to kill, let's find some food.'

Grabbing a table at a nearby pizzeria, they looked at the menu and tried to pretend they were normal tourists.

'I've always wanted to see Venice,' Tamar admitted, having made her choice of pizza.

'Horse meat pizza,' Toby tutted. 'Who wants to eat a horse?

Let alone put it on a pizza?' He looked up at her. 'I'm glad we came, then.'

'It is a place you hear about,' she said, 'a place you are supposed to go.'

'True enough, to ride the gondolas and eat expensive ice cream. Or, alternatively, stalk an assassin with magical powers. Both are popular.'

They looked at one another for a moment then, as one:

'Sorry.'

'You've got nothing to be sorry about!' said Toby. 'All of this is my fault. Fratfield did this to get at me, not you.'

Tamar shrugged. 'It is what it is. I do not blame you. You did nothing wrong. But now I am a burden. I am weak. I do not like to be weak.'

'How can you say you're weak? You're the strongest person I know.'

'I am the accident waiting to happen. Where I go, people get hurt. I cannot fight him. I have to let you fight for me. I do not like letting others fight for me.'

'I know you don't,' Toby admitted. 'But you're right, if you get too close, others will get hurt. We have to be careful. You're our early warning system. Our tracker. That's not weakness. You're still taking a hell of a risk.' He hesitated then decided to carry on. 'You know I wish you'd just go back to England.'

She looked at him with unrestrained anger. 'You do not say that. It is bad enough I cannot fight. I will not run as well.'

'I know,' Toby sighed. 'I know you won't.'

The waiter appeared and they ordered their food and a bottle of wine. For a while they were silent. Their wine came. Toby poured and then they continued to stare at the street around them. Then, if only to break the mood, Toby spoke.

'We'll catch him soon.'

Tamar made a dismissive clicking sound with her tongue. 'You are so sure?'

'Yes,' said Toby, 'because he can't hide for ever. He won't want to. He's an assassin. He relies on invisibility, on being able to do his work unnoticed. The more pressure we put on him, the harder that will be. Eventually he'll come for us, he'll have to.'

'I suppose that is true,' Tamar agreed, 'and however that ends, I look forward to it.' She took his hand. 'I married you because you are a good man. And because I knew that together we would be better than we had been before. That is what marriage is for. It is to make people better than they were when they were apart. He is not letting us do that, so let him come. I want our future, not this.'

Toby leaned over and kissed her.

'One day it'll all be done,' he said, 'but tonight we drink wine and eat horse pizza.'

'You order the horse pizza?'

'He took me by surprise. I panicked.'

They stayed in the restaurant until just before their arranged meeting, ordering another bottle of wine and allowing themselves the indulgence of being drunk. For weeks now they had always had to be on guard, to be ready for the worst. It was a wonderful relief to know that, tonight at least, they were unlikely to die.

Giovanni's shop was dark. Toby rang the small bell hung by the door and they waited by the window, Tamar pulling faces at the grotesque masks and Toby giggling in that way that only a drop too much wine allows.

After a minute, a light switched on at the rear of the shop and they saw a white-haired man weaving his way through the shop towards them.

'It's Pinocchio's bloody father,' Toby whispered and Tamar nudged him in the ribs.

'Do not be rude, he is a friend of August.'

'Everyone's a friend of August.'

The door opened and Giovanni greeted them with the sort of exuberance English people only ever find abroad.

'My friends,' he said, his Italian accent thick enough to spread on ciabatta and garnish with olives. 'It is good to see you.'

He led them inside, closing the door behind them. 'And how is my wonderful friend, Carl? It has been too long since I saw him, much too long. It must have been. . .' He stopped, placed his finger on his chin and looked towards the sky, the most perfect mime for 'Giovanni thinks' that could be imagined. '1998, yes . . . the problem of the singing fish.'

'Singing fish?' asked Tamar.

Giovanni immediately burst into 'O Sole Mio!' while weaving between them like a fish, his hands as flippers, his eyes wide, lips pursed.

'Singing fish,' Toby repeated and laughed.

Giovanni stopped singing and continued to lead them towards the back of the shop.

Toby stumbled slightly and nearly poked his eye out on a carnival mask. 'Hell of a nose on him,' he muttered, ducking beneath it.

'It is the plague doctor, no?' explained Giovanni, miming

the long nose. 'They wear herbs in their beak. They think it will stop the plague. It did not!' He laughed and, pulling back a black curtain, ushered them through into his workshop.

Everywhere they looked, surfaces were covered in half-finished toys and puppets.

'It is beautiful,' said Tamar, squatting down to appreciate a highly polished rocking horse.

'It needs a saddle,' said Giovanni, cantering around as if on horseback, 'otherwise the little people will not be able to ride him.'

He pointed towards the far end of the workshop. In the corner was a large puppet theatre. The stage was about a metre square, ornately painted, decorated with pieces of wooden scenery, trees, bushes and a sea broken down into white-crested waves. Golden-painted wings jutted out from it and the whole was surrounded by a cubicle draped in heavy purple cloth. The puppeteer would stand inside the cubicle, invisible to the audience as he enacted the play.

'I have a story for you, I think!' said Giovanni, pointing to a couple of fold-out chairs that were placed in front of the theatre. 'Since your call, I have been talking to my friends' – he mimed being a string puppet – 'and they have something they want to show you.'

Toby and Tamar looked at one another and began to laugh. 'Why not?' Toby said.

'Excellent!' Giovanni gave them a little round of applause, bowed and then disappeared behind the purple drapes.

'I like him,' whispered Tamar. 'He is mad, but a nice mad.'

All around them, the lights turned off until only the stage was visible in a single narrow spot.

A puppet trotted on from downstage left. It was a man dressed in a suit. It's face bore a large smile as it approached centre stage.

'Good evening, my friends,' it appeared to say. 'I am a spy from fair London town and I am hunting a bad man.'

'It's you!' laughed Tamar, tapping Toby on the arm.

'Looks nothing like me,' said Toby, laughing along.

'If you see the bad man,' the spy puppet said, 'you will be sure to tell me, won't you?'

Toby and Tamar didn't reply.

'I said,' the puppet repeated, a slightly angry edge to its voice, 'you will be sure to tell me, won't you?'

Toby and Tamar looked at one another before both shouting 'Yes!'

The spy puppet gave a bow. 'Thank you. Though I ask you to remember an important thing. Sometimes we do not see what is real. Sometimes, what we think has played out before us is not as we perceive it. Our eyes cheat. Our hearts lie. Sometimes it is necessary to make. . .' It stretched out its arms, 'a little theatre.'

It bowed once more.

'So, I am looking for a bad man. I must catch him because he wishes to harm the ones I love. I will do whatever it takes to make sure he is stopped.'

Behind the spy puppet, another appeared. This man was dressed all in black. It stopped, half on, half off the stage, peering around the curtain. Then, from the other side of the stage, another creation appeared. This was not human: it appeared like a dark cloud, streamers billowing from it thanks to some unseen updraft.

'It's Fratfield and the curse demon,' said Toby.

'The bad man is there!' shouted Tamar. 'Look behind you.'

'I can feel it coming,' the spy puppet agreed, 'and I thank you.' But it did not turn around, even though the other two puppets now began to creep towards it. 'I will not run. Because sometimes running is not the way.'

The other puppets continued to draw closer, the spy puppet placed one wooden hand to its temple as if in pain.

'You will have no choice but where to go,' it said. 'I do not need to tell you. Everything falls into place. Everything falls.'

And closer.

'And you must remember, sometimes it is all just theatre.'

The cloud puppet pounced on the spy puppet and it gave a piercing scream that made Toby flinch in his seat.

'And sometimes,' the puppet continued, as the cloud began to obscure it from view, 'it is death.'

The Fratfield puppet extended its arm and in its hand it held a gun. There was a loud pop and the smell of gunpowder filled the air.

The cloud suddenly vanished upwards revealing the spy puppet once more, a red streamer dangling from its temple. The Fratfield puppet extended its other hand, and this one held a pair of scissors. It extended the scissors towards the puppet's strings and, one by one, they appeared to snap until the spy puppet toppled to the stage.

'Was that helpful?' asked Giovanni from behind them, his voice making them jump. He presented them with a tray. On it were two small glasses of limoncello.

'How did you. . .?' Toby stared at him, the question hanging unfinished, then looked back at the stage where the Fratfield puppet was slowly walking offstage.

Suddenly there was another bang and this time both Toby and Tamar nearly jumped out of their seats. A thin cloud of smoke worked its way across the stage, dissipating into the air.

'I thought I would get us all a drink while my friends told their story,' said Giovanni, standing up and turning on the lights. 'I don't always like to see what they do.'

'I can't say I enjoyed it much either,' Toby admitted. 'But how did you operate them if you were. . .?'

Giovanni put his finger to his lips. 'Hush, my friend. Sometimes you do not ask questions, no? I am sure Carl has told you that. Now, drink. . .'

He handed each of them their limoncello, pouring a third for himself.

'Sometimes,' he said, 'the meaning is not always clear. Sometimes it only becomes so later once it has time to make sense in your head.'

'Maybe,' said Toby.

'It was clear,' said Tamar, 'and I do not like it. You died!'

Toby sipped his drink. 'It's just a puppet show.'

Giovanni laughed. 'So is life, my friend, so is life!'

They left Giovanni's as quickly as politeness allowed, their earlier good humour thoroughly trashed by the old man's bizarre little play.

'It's just like I said earlier,' Toby insisted, 'in order to catch him we'll have to let him come to us.'

'I do not want him coming so close you are dead.'

'Well, no, neither do I.' He put his arm around her shoulders as they worked their way back through the narrow streets to their hotel. 'But we'll worry about that when it happens. I won't die easily, I know that for a fact.'

'How can you know?'

He squeezed her tightly. 'Because I have you to look after me, don't I?'

They stopped and kissed. Somewhere in the distance a catfight erupted followed by the sound of shattered glass. A voice cried out in anger. Somewhere else a violin played, its high, beautiful note cutting through the Venetian night. Beyond that a crowd of people laughed and burst into song, a raucous, brutal thing filled with notes that no musician had ever written.

Toby's phone rang. They broke their kiss so he could answer it. He was on the phone for no more than a few seconds.

'It was April,' he told Tamar. 'August is in trouble. We have to go back.'

Two hours later they were on a plane back to London.

TWENTY-SEVEN

April was sat behind the wheel of her old Mini. She hadn't the first idea of how she'd got there. The last thing she could remember was the jogger in the park. He had offered her the gun . . . had she taken it? She just couldn't remember. Her head was aching and she made to press her hands to her temples but discovered that they were fixed to the steering wheel with plastic cable ties.

'I'm afraid I couldn't risk you running off,' said a voice from the back seat.

She looked up and saw Oman's face looking back at her from the rear-view mirror. She tried to turn around, but her fixed arms held her in place. She looked through the car windows. She was parked just around the corner from the Section 37 office.

'Oman?' she asked. 'What the bloody hell are you playing at?'

'Oman . . . Oh man!' He laughed. 'I'm just giving you a little rest. You can only bear to have me inside you for so long.'

'You're not getting inside me for one second, you filthy git!'

she replied and then gave a pained sigh – shouting made her head hurt all the more.

'The connection gets . . . painful,' he continued. 'For both of us actually. I don't mind so much. I quite like pain. It's better than nothing.'

'Cut me free and I'll give you all the pain you could want.'

'No, no. You have to rest a little more yet. Just a few hours. Just until you're better. You need to eat and drink too. I can force you if you make me but you're not stupid, I think you'll just do it. After all, I just bet your little mind is ticking over with ways you might be able to overpower me, isn't it?'

'It might be,' she admitted.

He nodded. 'And of course, your best bet is to bide your time, wait until I do cut you free so you can drive. Yes. That will be your best chance. You'll have to be quick, though. Alert. So a little sustenance won't go amiss. I bet you're hungry.'

She was. Starving, in fact, though she couldn't for the life of her figure out why. It wasn't usually her first concern when she found she'd been made a captive – dear Lord, she thought, you just know you've lived a full old life when you can talk from jaded experience about being someone's prisoner.

'Thirsty too,' said Oman. 'You've had a busy night and having me on board can really drain some people. I wonder why that is? Because it's forced perhaps? Like a virus? Is the body constantly fighting me off? Who knows?'

April certainly didn't. 'I haven't the first idea what you're talking about,' she admitted. 'Or why you're doing this. You're our friend, Oman.'

'Really? The funny little foreign man who runs the shop downstairs? A friend? How often did you invite him out for a drink? Dinner? He was just useful to you. He was a commodity. That's fine, I'm no different, but at least be honest about it.'

'Why are you saying "he"?'

'Hmm?' Oman was staring out of the window, watching a group of girls stumbling out of the local pub in a burst of raucous laughter. 'Obviously I'm not Oman,' he replied, offhandedly, still staring at the girls. 'You'd think I'd tire of it, wouldn't you?' he said. 'The flesh. But I never do. I don't know how you people restrain yourselves. I'm never sated. Never. Look at them.' He stroked the glass with his finger, following the route of the girls as they walked past. 'How can you see that and not want to pounce? Why are they not just torn apart the minute they appear? It's almost more than I can bear to let them go. I want to fuck them, kill them, bite them, eat them. I want to bury myself in the meat of them. I want to drown in meat.'

April looked at the girls and wished they'd hurry up and leave. They had no idea what was being thought about them as they laughed and joked with one another.

'What are they for except to play with?' Oman – or the thing that looked like Oman – said. 'There's no other point to them.'

'What do you mean there's no other point? They're people!'

'What's that even mean? They're people? They're not me, that's all that's important. Inside me there's real thought. I exist.'

'So do they.'

He shrugged. 'So you say. I can't tell from here, I can't feel their thoughts, can I? Why should I believe they even have any? I look at them and their insides are silent. They're just moving meat. In their heads there's nothing unless I go there and then I'm just wearing the meat sack. Eventually, April, you realise you're the only real thing left in existence. Everything else is just empty.' He smiled and touched her on the shoulder, making her recoil. 'Including you, of course, so it's no wonder you don't understand.' He sat back again. 'I was too careful in the past. Why didn't I just have more fun? Lesson learned. If I didn't have to keep an eye on you, I'd go and have fun now, just jump from one to another, over and over again, feel all their flesh. Give them all meaning. Boys, girls, old, young, I'd turn this whole street into an orgy. The gutters would run thick. But no, I have to stay here.' He sighed. 'And soon, of course, I'll have a permanent home. Well, semi-permanent. I have plans about that . . . Who wants to be an old man for ever? Principle is one thing but I'm not stupid.'

'You know I don't have the first idea what you're on about?' April asked, relieved to see the girls turn the corner and vanish from sight.

'Your brother,' he said, 'made me a promise a long time ago and promises have to be kept. Of course, he's done all right out of the deal. When I made the bargain he was young, fit, handsome. Now what have I been left with, eh? The last bloody chicken in the shop. Still, I can do a few things to improve on that. Flesh is so easy to manipulate, you're all just base matter. On the subject of which, I did a little work on your hips and had a general tidy.'

April had no idea what she was supposed to say about that.

'It's a freebie,' he continued. 'Don't mention it. I just needed to be a bit more agile, it was getting tiresome lugging your old bones around. Still, Shining. . .it's about principle. He made a promise and he has to deliver on it. He's done well out of it, for a long time I was. . .' He looked uncomfortable. 'I wasn't together. I wasn't myself. But I will have him, I will use him, and, after that, there's always Fratfield, another debt owed. . .Or. . .' He leaned forward again. 'Do you find Toby attractive?'

'What?'

'Just wondering. Strikes me he would be a good choice. Easy to convince too. All I'd have to do would be to threaten to cut the throat of that new wife of his. She's lovely. He'd do whatever I wanted if he thought he was saving her.' He laughed. 'Of course, in the end I'd do what I wanted to her anyway! But he'd be too panicked to think about that.'

'She'd break your legs if you so much as put your hand on her.'

'Possibly,' he nodded. 'Anyway, there's more to life than sex and death. I can't quite think what at the moment, but I'm sure there is. You'll have to forgive me, I'm in an . . . earthy mood.' He looked up the street, remembering the girls. 'All I want to do is fuck!' He laughed.

He rubbed at his face as if trying to shake himself out of it. 'I think flesh is addictive. I think I'm in danger of becoming a little too single-minded. I blame this obsession with your brother. I should have left him alone, I'd probably have had a better time of it.' He grinned. 'I don't know, though, it has been fun. Ah. . .' He waved his hands in the air like a giddy schoolchild. 'I'm all conflicted tonight, aren't I? I don't know what I'm thinking. Just ignore me.'

'Chance would be a fine thing,' she told him.

'Right, I'm going to get us something to eat and drink,' he said. 'Any preferences?'

'Couldn't care less.'

He shook his head. 'Such a waste. To have taste and not revel in it. I'll get you something nice.' He started to climb out of the car before leaning back in. 'Oh, and I really don't think you'd be able to get free in the time I'll be gone, those ties are tough to break. Still, I suppose you might be able to attract someone's attention so. . .' He reached forward and placed his hand over her mouth, pinching her nose closed with his fingers. 'I'll make you a little promise. If you try anything, if you involve someone else, I'll kill them in front of you, OK? I'll paint you with them until you can't breathe for the smell. So, for their sake more than yours, be a good girl, yes?'

He let go of her and got out of the car. As he walked past, he gave her a little wave and then jogged away.

She watched him go and then, just because she wasn't a woman who would ever give up easily, spent a few minutes trying to free her hands. He was right, she couldn't, not without something to cut them free. So did she call his bluff? Did she beat on the horn until someone came running? She glanced at the clock, it was approaching midnight. How long could you sound a horn in Wood Green before someone came running? She was rather afraid you could probably work your way through a lengthy symphony before getting someone to brave taking a look. London was a place of noise and disturbance, alarms rang out ignored all the time. This would hardly be any different. She stayed quiet and waited to see what would happen next.

TWENTY-EIGHT

It was hard to tell from the way that Jennings was staring at the remains of his vegetarian cannelloni whether he was disgusted at the food or himself for having eaten it.

Ryska had barely touched her own meal, though Shining got the impression that this wasn't about the food so much as her inability to relax in front of them. She'd made a point of getting up from the table and moving several feet away, leaning against the worktop and watching them finish eating. An observer, never a participant.

'Well,' she said, 'this has been charming. Might we get on with the reason we're here now?' She gave them a look that suggested she was the only one in the room that remained aware of their business in the cottage. 'Or is there pudding and coffee?'

'You need to relax,' Jennings told her, earning himself an angry stare. It clearly didn't bother him. 'You know as well as I do that Mr Shining's not a traitor.'

'On what do you base this instant judgement call?' she asked, moving her gaze from Jennings to Shining.

'I've read his file and shared a meal with him,' Jennings

replied, pushing his plate away, 'in the loosest definition of the word. Whoever's feathers he's ruffled to get himself here is neither here nor there, this whole thing's a farce. Digging over a thirty-year-old mission as if it holds any relevance to today? Someone's just giving him a poke in the eye and they're using your finger to do it. Hardly the first time.'

'If I may,' said Shining, 'it wouldn't even be the first time for me. That said, I'm not sure you're quite right when you say that what happened between myself and Lucas all those years ago is irrelevant to today. These things have a habit of coming back to bite you.'

'What in life doesn't?' Jennings replied. He got up from the table. 'Anyway, before I earn myself an even filthier stare for breaking with protocol, I'd better let the boys have a break.'

He began to leave before remembering something.

'Your phone,' he said to Shining. 'You've had a load of messages from your sister. Do you want to check them?'

'Jennings!' Ryska shouted. 'Why not just ask if he fancies renting a movie while you're at it?'

Jennings shrugged. 'Just thought they might be important.'

'She'll just be wondering where I am,' Shining replied, 'and as I can't tell her it can wait.'

Nodding, Jennings walked out to relieve the guards, leaving Shining alone with Ryska.

'Well, how lovely that you've made a friend,' she sneered.

'Only one,' Shining smiled. 'He's just bored with having to jump through hoops he considers pointless. We've all had moments like that, haven't we?'

'I'll decide whether this is pointless or not.'

'Of course you will, and quite right too. After all, you don't want to go to Bertie with anything other than a full report, do you?' He watched to see if the name had struck home. 'I presume you are Section 12?'

She was silent for a moment before deciding that it was an obvious enough conclusion and hardly important. 'Yes.'

'Who watches the watchmen, eh? It must be a miserable department to work for. A shame. I hope someone has the decency to transfer you somewhere more fulfilling soon.'

'We do important work.'

'Maybe that used to be true, but these days it's all fudged expense claims and botched paperwork, isn't it? When was the last time we had a really fruity defection? Your last real troublemaker was Bill Fratfield but it wasn't you that caught him, was it?' He smiled. 'Bring back the old days when people were hopping from one side to the other, eh? Say what you like about the Cold War, at least it made things more interesting.'

'I don't believe in nostalgia.'

'Oh, neither do I, not really, you've got to look to the future, haven't you? Even when you get to my age and can, quite reasonably, wonder how much of one you have.' He got up. 'Still, if you're willing to traipse around in the past a little longer, so am I. Do you want to continue?'

He made for the door to the kitchen, intending to lead her back into the interrogation room. At least if you walked in front you felt you had a modicum of control. When Ryska didn't reply he paused and turned back. She was looking at him with a quizzical expression that he recognised as a sign that Ryska's consciousness was no longer in residence.

'You again, is it?' he asked.

She nodded. 'Have you thought about what you mean to do?'

'About the rebel?'

She nodded.

He leaned back in the doorway, checking briefly that the others were out of earshot. He could hear them faintly outside, chatting in the porch.

'You're the same as him?' he asked. 'By which I mean you can do everything he can?'

She nodded.

'Then, yes, I know what I mean to do, as much as the idea terrifies me. You said it yourself, I have to give him what he wants.'

'Tell me your plan.'

So he did.

TWENTY-NINE

On the hill above the safe house, the Watcher brushed the remains of a sandwich from his fingers, raised a pair of night-vision binoculars to his eyes and followed Jennings as he stepped out of the cottage and made his way over to the two other security officers.

The Watcher had been in position for several hours now, had monitored the movements of the security officers as they took it in turns to make circuits of the building, plodding through their duty in the thorough manner only ex-military could really manage.

You learned a great deal training in the army but he often thought one of the most impressive skills you inherited was an ability to do the mundane without going mad with boredom. For himself, as important as his supervision was, he had found himself begging for something to happen within a couple of hours of setting up position. Waiting wouldn't kill him, he knew, but there were times it felt like it would.

He reached for his phone, checking for messages. Nothing. This was no great surprise. The Assassin was waiting on his orders like the good professional he was. The Watcher wondered when those orders would be given. He trained his glasses on the blank window of the interrogation room, picturing the target beyond the drapes. He wondered when it would be time for August Shining to die.

In his hotel room, some distance away, the Assassin tried to relax. He was quite used to waiting on jobs. It was always part of the game, your client frequently wanting a kill to happen at a specific moment (usually so they could ensure they were some distance away at the time, working on an unassailable alibi). That was less common with Intelligence cases like this, but he had long given up on questioning the rationale of those that paid him. Over time he had developed an ability to compartmentalise his thinking to the degree that the waiting passed more easily. You ensured all of your preparation was in place, that you were ready to move at a moment's notice, but then you switched that part of you off. You put him away in your pocket with the phone that would reactivate him when needed. You got on with pretending to be a normal human being for a while. You ate meals, read a book, watched the television. All of the things normal people did with their spare time. Tonight, try as he might, he couldn't manage it.

Shining.

That was the problem, the target. His impatience to see the job done was overriding his usual state of mind.

Several times he had pulled on his coat, meaning to leave the room and find the man. Even if he couldn't kill him, he could at least watch. He could monitor his movements, even imagine the impending pull of the trigger. The instant shock hit that his client was demanding. It was a fascinating thought when looking at one's victim, seeing them move around, smile, laugh, busy with their life, not knowing that with the click of your fingers that would be gone. Who didn't like to feel powerful?

Each time he had made to leave he had hesitated in the doorway then turned around and sat back down on the bed. He just wasn't sure that he could have Shining in his cross hairs and not pull the trigger. His enthusiasm for the job was too strong. Better to spare himself the temptation. Better to stay away.

Soon, he assured himself. It was bound to be soon.

THIRTY

Shining and Ryska were back in the interrogation room, the latter having no idea of the strange conversation her lips had just been part of. If she had been aware of it, if she could have heard the words said, she would have dismissed them in an instant. She had difficulty enough believing the comparatively simple story he had already been telling her, though if she were honest with herself, believe it she did.

'So,' she said, 'Robie was sleeping rough in the park, avoiding whatever it was that was controlling people and making them kill themselves.'

'Or others,' Shining added. 'Don't forget the people mown down by Anosov. Or the man that tried to kill me in the shower.'

'What was it?' she asked. 'Some sort of brainwashing program? A drug?'

'I wish I could say it was, you'd probably have an easier time accepting it. Though how you could possibly administer a drug that instantly made the recipient do a set of preprogrammed acts is beyond me. We're clever in our methods for killing but that's still beyond us.'

'What was it, then?'

'Something far more simple in a way. It was a consciousness. A self-aware presence that invaded the victim, controlled them like a puppet and then vacated the body once its aim was achieved.'

'Simple?' she laughed. 'They were possessed.'

'I dare say you imagine that to be completely impossible. Which, in the circumstances is almost funny. . .'

'Funny?'

He shook his head then glanced at the video camera. 'Doesn't matter for now. Shall I continue from where we left off?'

THIRTY-ONE

Heading back to Plänterwald, the snow was now so thick that it was getting hard to see more than a few feet ahead of me. I could only hope that within the shelter of the forest visibility would be better; in the open I could barely see the faces of the people around me.

The S-Bahn was crowded with people trying to get home. Nobody wanted to drive in weather like that.

By the time I arrived, the streets were all but empty. I had this cold world to myself.

The Kulturpark was closed, of course. I imagined the inevitable brightly coloured police tape that would mark out the red concrete where Alexandra Hoss had fallen. Would her past glories achieve a new audience now? Old movies achieving a new, bittersweet edge of notoriety thanks to the apparent suicide of their star. I suspected she'd see that as some consolation, even if I didn't.

The idea of scouring the entire forest seemed impossible now I was faced with it. I even began questioning the train of thought that led me to believe Robie was there. Still, as it was the only route left open to me – if he wasn't here I couldn't begin to guess where he might be – I retraced his steps from earlier, avoiding the footpaths and entering the trees.

The cover offered by the foliage immediately made moving forward easier, the dense leaves above keeping much of the snow out. What filtered through fell in a soft, dreamy fashion around me. I imagined the forest viewed from above, the snow accumulating on the tops of the trees, sealing the forest off, a hidden world.

Forests can be terrifying places. They make me think of the grave. It's the way they seal you off from the outside world. They muffle and distort sound, imposing their own dull silence, broken in this case only by drips of water and the almost nautical creak of straining branches. People talk about getting lost in forests, I feel lost the minute I enter one.

I knew it was important to try to be organised, I had brought a pack of brightly coloured ribbon that I'd found in Alexandra's apartment and I used short lengths of it, tied on to low branches to mark out my way as I zigzagged through the trees. It was hardly Ariadne's thread, offering a safe return path through the labyrinth, but it did at least mean that I was unlikely to double back on myself without noticing. There were enough paths that I could never truly be lost, but I could walk right past Robie without noticing him unless I made a concerted effort to quarter the forest, covering it as methodically as I could.

I'd been walking for about an hour when I began to hear voices ahead of me. As I drew closer I heard the crackle of a fire, the smell of wood smoke cutting through the clean, chill air.

It was a little group of homeless men and women. Five in all. They had constructed makeshift tents between the trees, lengths of sheeting strung up between the trunks. In the centre of their camp a small fire smouldered. On seeing me, one of them, no more than eighteen, jumped to his feet in surprise. I couldn't tell whether he meant to run or attack. Either way, I held up my hands and hastily explained I meant no harm.

'I'm not police,' I explained. 'I'm just trying to find a friend.'

'In this weather?' one of the others laughed. She no doubt appeared older than she actually was, her lank blonde hair having formed ringlets around her ruddy face. 'One for you, eh, Jan?'

Jan was clearly the young man who had jumped up. He was also clearly embarrassed at the woman's suggestion. 'Fuck you, Karin,' he said, kicking some wet leaves at her.

'The man I'm after really is a friend,' I explained. 'I think he's been staying out here for the last few nights.'

One of the others, a man all but hidden by his bushy beard, was quick to answer. 'Don't know anyone else out here,' he said. 'Keep ourselves to ourselves.' He lay on a park bench, no doubt dragged in here from one of the more public spaces. He looked curiously like a Roman Emperor, propped up on one elbow, as if waiting for grapes to be delivered to him.

'You haven't seen anyone else around?' I asked again, suspicious, but not altogether surprised at the speed with which he had denied knowing anything. 'He's a bit younger than me, thinning hair. It's his eyes you'd have noticed, they're each a different colour. I'd happily pay you for information.'

'I could take your money,' he said, 'spend it on something

to keep me warm. But I don't know anyone, none of us do, so we can't help you.'

He glanced around at the rest of them, most likely making it clear they should keep their mouths shut too. Frustrating but, conversely, hopeful. I doubted he'd be so adamant unless he was hiding something.

'Fair enough,' I said, reaching into my wallet and pulling out a few Deutsche Marks for them anyway. My conscience wouldn't allow me to walk off without giving them something.

I left them to their fire and continued to weave between the trees, and soon all around me was silent once more. Enough so that when Jan suddenly appeared ahead of me, peering out from behind a tree, I nearly cried out, embarrassing both of us.

'Hello Jan,' I said. 'You nearly frightened me to death.'

He grinned. 'I move quietly.'

'You certainly do. Have you remembered something?'

He nodded, glancing over his shoulder. 'Kurt doesn't want us to say anything so if anyone asks I just offered you a blow job, OK?'

I wasn't sure what to say to that. I just nodded in what I hoped was a suitably casual manner.

'The man you're after is that way,' he pointed off to my left. 'He uses one of the shelters. We used to but they kick you out after a while. Easier to build your own.'

'Will you show me?' I asked. 'I'll make it worth your while.'

He shook his head. 'I can't be gone too long, Kurt will know. You'll find it, just keep straight through the trees towards the river. You cross the path and then into the trees again. He is English.'

The sudden change in subject almost threw me. 'I know,' I agreed. 'He really is my friend.'

Jan shrugged. 'People say that, but they don't always mean it. He gives me money sometimes.'

I must have given him a funny look because he immediately became defensive. 'He gets me to buy him food,' he explained. 'He doesn't like to go himself. He doesn't like people.'

And people like him too much, I thought. I nodded. 'He likes to keep his own company.'

'I hope you are his friend,' Jan said, perhaps wondering whether he'd done the right thing talking to me. 'He's a good man.'

'I am,' I promised. 'I'm here to help. He's in a bit of trouble.'

Jan laughed. 'Of course he is. You don't live out here if you're not.'

I pulled out some money for him and he ran back to the camp, leaving me to hope Robie's shelter was as easy to find as he'd claimed it to be.

After about ten minutes, I stepped out of the forest into the open air again. As Jan had promised, I'd reached one of the footpaths. The snow had lessened slightly and I could just see the shadow of the Ferris wheel to my left, a vague grey arc in the white sky. I crossed the path and entered the trees on the opposite side.

A few more minutes and I saw the shelter. It was a small wooden cabin, open at the front. In the corner sat a bundle of blankets with a head poking out of them. I'd found him.

I advanced quietly. He seemed to be sleeping and I didn't want to give him enough warning that he could make a break for it. Hopefully, this time he'd refrain from punching me too.

I was about ten feet away when he spoke.

'Hello, August. There's no need to creep.'

Obviously he hadn't been asleep after all.

'Lucas.' I joined him in the shelter, sitting down in the opposite corner. 'Lovely place you've got here.'

'It's quiet,' he replied, 'usually. I hoped you'd stay away, August.'

'How could I? You're in trouble. I wasn't going to just abandon you.'

'No,' he tugged off one of his blankets and threw it at me. 'It's been some time since we shared bedclothes but you'll be glad of it after you've been sat still for a minute.'

I pulled it around me. 'What's going on, Lucas?'

He was silent for a while, then, 'How much do you know already?'

I told him my suspicions, that something was controlling people, making them commit violent acts. I told him about the postman that had attacked me, and about Grauber.

'Who?' he asked.

'You talked to him in the bar, he told you something and you went off with him.'

He nodded, remembering. 'He wasn't Grauber.'

'He was according to the soldiers I talked to. And it was certainly Grauber who flung himself off his balcony while I watched.'

'You misunderstand me. I mean it wasn't Grauber when I talked to him. It was the thing inside. The puppeteer.'

'The thing that killed him.'

He nodded. 'I don't have a name for it. I don't know what it is. All I know is what it wants. It wants me.'

'For what?'

'To wear. To be. . .' He rubbed at his unshaven face. 'It can borrow people, for want of a better term, wear them for a while. Then it has to leave them again. There's a time limit.'

'How long?' Trust me to be thinking in such practical terms already.

'I don't know,' he snapped. 'It's not important. But it wants a more permanent host. For that it can't just take you, you have to allow it. Like selling your soul to the devil. You have to agree.'

'And you haven't?'

'Of course I bloody haven't. Can you imagine the trouble it would cause inside me? You've seen what it's like, what it does. It's psychotic. Imagine if it had my skills.'

'Your charm. Yes. Which is why you've been doing everything you can not to let it see what you're capable of.'

He looked at me in suspicion. 'August?'

'Yes.'

'How do I know, though?' he asked. 'How do I really know?'

I told him of one of the more memorable things he'd done on our first night together. Immediately the suspicion dropped away and he laughed, his voice echoing between the trees. 'Oh Christ . . . August, love, trust you to think of that.'

'I often do,' I admitted. 'It's me. You can trust me.'

'I know,' he nodded. 'But you've no idea what it's been like. Ever since it found me, I haven't known what to do. I keep thinking I should just kill myself, that would be the sensible thing to do, the fair thing.'

'Nothing fair about it.'

'You know what I mean, How can I risk it taking control of me? How can I allow that? It's selfish of me to put my own welfare first.'

'But you have to allow it. It can't just take you. Not permanently anyway.'

'And you've seen what it's willing to do to try to convince me.'

'Alexandra.'

He nodded. 'Her death's on me. No two ways about it, if I was dead then Alexandra wouldn't be. And now you're here.'

'It already knows about me anyway,' I reminded him, 'after Grauber. It's been watching me.' Perhaps it had even been watching me before then. I thought about the little girl outside Grauber's block, the old woman in the street beneath Alexandra's apartment. 'It's tried to kill me once. If it does it again then it's not your fault.'

He shook his head. 'OK, maybe it's not my fault, but killing myself is still my only option. I was ready to do it, you know, just as you turned up. You annoying, lovely man.'

'Then I'm glad I came when I did.' I took his hand. 'There has to be another way, Lucas. Together we'll find one.'

'You can't stop it, August. It's nothing. It's a thought, an idea. How do you fight ideas? Look at this bloody city for proof of that. Millions of people kept apart, not by a wall, that's just bricks, anyone can kick down bricks. They're kept apart by thoughts and ideas.'

'It can't just possess you permanently, that means it does have weaknesses. Anything with weaknesses can be fought. You just have to figure out how.'

'Weakness, singular. We don't know of any others. And while we're busy trying to figure things out, more people will die. The next one probably you. Can't you see I don't want that? Enough is enough.'

There was a cracking sound from in the trees and I looked towards it. I wondered if it was Jan having decided to come and find us anyway.

Then, behind me, there was the sound of a revolver cocking and I turned to see Lucas had pulled a gun from beneath his blanket and had pressed the barrel to his temple.

'No, Lucas.' I reached for it and then time seemed to jump. The very next thing I knew, I was stood several feet away from the shelter, Lucas lying in the snow just in front of me. For a moment I thought he'd succeeded in shooting himself, blood trickling down the side of his face. Then he looked up at me, a terrified look in his eyes.

'What. . .?' I looked around, trying to understand what had just happened. 'How did we get out here?'

'It's here,' he said, pushing himself up to his knees. 'It took you over.'

'I don't. . .' I looked towards the shelter. Was it possible? Had I just lost a section of time because I'd no longer been conscious in my own body? I looked down at my hands. One of them was holding the gun by the barrel, the grip was wet with blood.

'It expressed its distaste for the idea of my killing myself,' said Lucas, dabbing at his wounded head. 'In no uncertain terms.'

'Where is it?' I asked, looking around.

'Who knows where it goes between hosts? Is it in the air? Has it jumped hundreds of miles away to someone else? Do you get it now, August? Do you see what we're dealing with?'

'There has to be something we can do.'

He suddenly charged at me, laughing maniacally. I was so surprised I didn't even raise my hands to defend myself as he jumped on me, our momentum sending us tumbling backwards. I crashed to the wet ground, the gun falling from my hand as Lucas – or the thing that was now wearing him – jumped up and down on my chest like a small child demanding to play.

'You could both blow each other's heads out?' he said. 'Or, and here's an idea. . .' He pressed his face close into mine, Lucas's lips against my cheek. 'How about you just try to kill everyone in the world? Every. Single. One.' He poked my chest with each word. 'That would fix me, wouldn't it?'

Then time jumped again and I found myself back in the shelter, pinning Lucas up against the wall.

I immediately let go of him and he slumped to the ground.

'It happened again,' I said, rather redundantly. 'Did I hurt you?'

'Not as much as he'll hurt you!' Lucas replied, laughing and kicking my legs out from underneath me.

As I fell back into his nest of blankets, he ran out into the snow, picking up the dropped handgun and turning to face me. 'I think it's time to teach Lucas another lesson, don't you?' he shouted, firing into the wood a few inches above my head. 'Why don't you run?'

'What would be the point? You can find me anywhere I go.'

'True,' he said, 'but why would I want to be you any more? This one's got the gun!'

As if to prove the point he fired again, this time into the wood at my feet.

'So run!'

When he put it like that, I didn't see that I had much choice.

THIRTY-TWO

As I burst out onto the path, I considered running along it. Even with the snow underfoot, I would certainly be able to move faster. I would also make a much easier target.

Snap decision. I retraced my steps from earlier, ducking back between the trees and weaving between them as much as I could, hoping they would take a bullet in my place should the need arise.

Behind me, Lucas whooped like a child playing Cowboys and Indians. 'Run! Run! Run!' he shouted.

Of course I bloody would.

And as I did so, I tried to think about what I could do in the long-term. Ultimately, beyond staying alive for the next few minutes, running was getting me nowhere. Lucas had been right: how did you fight something that was only a thought? What could I threaten it with? How could I attack it?

It wanted a more permanent host. For now, it had decided that would be Lucas. I was sure that, were Lucas to die, it would only choose someone else. His death would achieve nothing in the long run. Though, as he had rightly said, if it possessed someone else it would, at least, not have access to Lucas's powers. Had he been right that it was worth doing anything to ensure that didn't happen?

A shot rang out, clipping the tree next to me and I veered away, losing my footing and crashing to the ground.

'Nearly!' he shouted and I could tell he was close behind me. Dare I stand up or would he shoot me the minute I presented him with a target?

I decided to lie still. I thought it was unlikely he'd just walk up behind me and put a bullet in my head, since everything he'd done up until that point relied on the same twisted need for the dramatic. Frankly, killing a man who's lying flat on his belly is dull.

Of course, as I heard him step behind me, his borrowed feet crunching in the undergrowth, it occurred to me that the real drama in this situation would be letting Lucas see what he had done. For a moment I was convinced that I had misjudged the situation.

'Get up,' he said, nudging me with his feet. 'Come on. Get up.'

I was, for the most part, completely still. The only thing that moved was my right hand. I was lying on it, and the short branch it was holding.

'I said get up!' he shouted, stooping down and tugging at my coat to flip me over. I moved a little more easily than he would have expected, spinning around, the branch in my fist. I beat at his hand, sending the gun flying into the dirt. He was quick to respond, grabbing the branch and kicking out at me. I'd expected that and pushed the branch away, kicking at the leg he was using to balance himself. He fell backwards and I got up, looking around for the gun.

I saw it, perfect black in a small mound of snow and made for it even as he got up and threw himself at me. We both toppled to the ground, the gun still out of reach.

Again I tried to use our momentum to my advantage, continuing the roll in the earth rather than fighting against it so I ended up on top. I headbutted him in the face and brought my knee up between his legs. I felt sure poor Lucas would forgive me; after all, he'd intended visiting worse on himself.

I got to my feet, just managing to evade his grasp, and grabbed the gun, turning to point it at him.

'And what are you going to do with that?' he asked, chuckling. I'd broken his nose I think, blood dripping off his face to patter on the ground beneath him. 'You've made it quite clear you have no intention of killing Mr Robie. Only one of us is willing to murder to get what they want, I think.'

After the fact, when that day in Berlin was long behind me, I thought of lots of things I could, and should, have done. Isn't that always the way? Going over and over missions, especially the ones that didn't go our way, and seeing the alternatives that didn't occur to us at the time. If we didn't do it then our superiors certainly would, because it's easy to plot a perfect mission from behind your desk, when the adrenalin's not making your brain scream and you're not shaking with fear and anger. When you know all the facts, can look at everything in a cold and analytical manner, the best route is simple. When you're in the thick of it, it's often a case of doing the first thing to pop into your head.

I punched him as hard as I could, knocking him out, slung him over my shoulder and carried on the way I had been running.

I figured that if the host was unconscious then the problem was – at least for the moment – solved.

But of course, the forest was filled with potential hosts. It could have chosen that moment to leap back into me, surely the simplest response. Perhaps, like me, it was wired and high on the chase. Perhaps it just decided the alternative was more fun.

'Hey!' shouted Jan as I approached the homeless camp. 'You found him, then?'

Kurt stared at him, clearly having his suspicions proved with regards to how Jan had really earned his money from me.

'I did,' I replied, stumbling into the camp and dropping Lucas to the ground, 'and I'm still trying to help him. I need something to tie him up.'

'Why bother?' said one of the other homeless, a young woman, head shaved but for a thin strip of bleached stubble that ran down the centre. 'I'll only untie him.

'Or I will,' laughed Karin.

'Or me,' said another, a cheap tattoo of a rose blooming across his cheek.

'Maybe I'll do it,' admitted Kurt.

'And if they don't,' added Jan, 'then I certainly will.'

It was leaping from one of them to the next, hopping between host bodies at the speed of thought. I had surrounded myself with potential enemies.

I held up the gun.

'Again?' Karin laughed, though the rest looked frightened. 'Even if I thought you would be willing to shoot an innocent, you'll have to ask them nicely to line up. You only have three bullets left.'

'And I can move like lightning!' said Jan, hopping into the air like a ballerina, much to the surprise of the others.

'And you'll always be too slow,' said Rose Tattoo, snatching at the gun with his left hand and punching me with his right. I fought him off but only because the controlling power had already moved on to the skinhead, who was now behind me, choking me with her arm. I dropped forward and threw her over my shoulder, straightening up just in time to receive a kick to the cheek from Karin. This time I did lose the gun, my head sparking with white light as her boot connected with my face.

'And I'll always win,' said Lucas, awake now and picking up the gun. He dug into the pocket of his jeans and pulled out more cartridges, reloading the pistol.

'Because. . .' shouted Jan.

'I. . .' added Karin.

'Am. . .' said the skinhead.

'Better. . .' said Kurt.

'Than. . .' offered Rose Tattoo.

'You,' finished Lucas, turning the gun on each of them in turn.

He shot Jan, then Rose Tattoo. The skinhead tried to run but she got hers in the back, crashing face down into the fire. Karin wailed, stumbling back over her small pile of belongings before a bullet took out one of her few remaining teeth en route to more vital areas. Kurt just stared, old and weary enough to see there was no point in running. He sat back on his bench and awaited the inevitable. But it didn't come, because then Lucas turned the gun on me and pressed the trigger.

THIRTY-THREE

I lost consciousness again for a while, coming around to a blurred vision of the trees above me. All black. Jagged lines and shadow. A searing glimpse of white poking through, tiny pinpricks of light.

My belly felt cold and, when I tried to sit up, I found it impossible.

Slowly, I touched my stomach and felt the wet blood from the stomach wound. Touching it was remote and confusing, as if it couldn't possibly be me that was lying on his back in the snow, dying by degrees. It was, of course. A part of me knew that, but the rest of me couldn't countenance it. It couldn't accept that all this would finish with Lucas running away and me a freezing corpse beneath East Berlin trees.

Had Lucas run? I tried to look but I could barely move. The most I could manage was to turn my head a few degrees to either side. One way, there lay Jan, his young face a dumb model of vacancy, spittle on his lips and nothing behind the eyes. Looking the other way, I saw Kurt, sitting on his bench drinking from a bottle of vodka. I wished he'd share.

'He's gone,' Kurt said, answering my question. 'Took off into the trees. Laughing. Bastard.' He took another drink. 'I don't think much of that friend of yours. Knew he was trouble.'

'Not my friend,' I said, my voice barely more than a whisper. 'Just someone wearing his body.'

Kurt stared at me for a moment then shook his head. 'And I thought I'd seen some crazy shit.' He looked at his bottle. 'See all manner of things when the drink's on me.'

'I don't suppose. . .' I stared at the bottle. He looked at it, judging how much he had left. He sighed, not really wanting to part with it but not willing to refuse the last wish of a dying man either. He nodded, moved over to me, lifted my head slightly and poured some into my mouth. 'Cheap shit,' he said. 'That's the best in this weather.'

The alcohol tore through me and I coughed, dimly aware of a pounding response in my stomach. Kurt stared at the wound and I realised it had probably spurted as I'd coughed.

'Maybe that's not a good idea,' he said, with an element of relief. He returned to his bench, wiped the neck of the bottle with his filthy hand – the absurdity of which was not beyond me, even then – and took another good mouthful himself. He didn't cough – Kurt was immune to the fiery ravages of cheap vodka.

'I won't lie to you,' he said, 'but I don't think you're going to be leaving this place.'

'No,' I agreed, 'I think you're probably right.'

'Sorry about that, but you'll not die alone. It's a crowd of you that are taking the trip today.' He looked around at the dead bodies of his friends. 'I didn't like them much but they were better than nothing. Sleeping out here on your own is no good, no good at all.' He took another drink.

I may have passed out again then. My memory is vague, I wasn't at my best. The next thing I knew was that Kurt was smiling at me. Except, of course, it wasn't Kurt.

'Just thought I'd see how you're doing,' he said. 'Still with us, then?'

'Shouldn't you be keeping your eye on Lucas?' I asked.

'Where's he going to go that I won't find him? I have plans for Mr Robie but they can wait a few minutes.'

'Just long enough for you to watch me die. How nice.'

'I enjoy it,' he admitted, scratching at his beard. 'This one is full of life. He has whole nations thriving on him.' He tried the vodka and smiled. 'I see why he drinks. You nearly dead?'

I couldn't really see the point in replying, but then half an idea occurred to me.

I said before how the really good ideas often never occur to you in time to be of much use. I've had my moments, I certainly wouldn't still be here otherwise, and some of my ideas can be very good indeed. This wasn't one of them. It was, however, better than nothing, though I've come to wonder about that since. I think, on balance, what I did was for the best, however much I've since regretted it.

'Of course,' I said, 'you could probably stop me dying.'

'Really? How do you figure that?'

'Just a guess. You obviously have a degree of control over your hosts. Grauber should never have been able to stay alive as long as he did, his body a ball of flame. And how about Anosov? How many bullets did it take to finally drop him? Too many. I think it more likely that he went down only because you were happy to allow it.'

He nodded. 'Meat is easy,' he admitted. 'I have my limits:

I can't raise the dead, but I can fix a fair bit. Yes, you're probably right. I probably could heal you. Here's the more important question though: why would I want to?'

'Because only an idiot doesn't have a backup plan,' I said. 'You're pinning all your hopes on Lucas, but what if he never agrees to let you have his body?'

'He will.'

'But what if he won't? Why take the risk?'

'Be clear. What are you proposing? You don't have long enough to be long-winded.'

'Heal me,' I said. 'Make me live, and I'll promise you my body.'

'Just like that? What would be in it for you?'

'Well, obviously, you couldn't have it straight away; we'd have to come to an agreement as to when you could take it. Let's say the next time I'm mortally wounded.'

'Make a habit of that, do you?'

'I do enjoy a risky lifestyle. I'm not fixing a time on it – you'll have to take the gamble. But the next time I'm in this position, with no more chance of survival . . . well, I'm going to die anyway, so why not? You can jump in, make me better and keep the body for your trouble. What have I got to lose?'

'Not much,' he admitted. 'It's not a great deal for me.'

'No, I don't suppose it is. But it's a gamble, isn't it? I could be on the brink of death this time tomorrow or years from now, who's to say? Why not? It's not like you're losing on the deal, either. You have a guaranteed body at some point in the future: mine. Considering Lucas has flat-out refused you, it's the best offer you've had so far. And if you do possess Lucas then. . .'

It was getting difficult to speak now, the cold seeping into me and making my teeth chatter. 'Well, if you do, you do. You still win.' I decided there was no harm in pandering to his ego. 'Of course, if you're worried that I'm a threat?'

'A threat?' he laughed.

'Well, that's the only reason I can think of for why you'd refuse. You must think that if you let me live I'll be able to stop you. Perhaps I will. Yes . . . I suppose that's what it is. You want me out of your way.'

'Out of my way?' He was suddenly furious. 'You? You're nothing to me! Any of you! How can you even dream of being better than me?'

Well, I might have said, you do seem to be going to a lot of effort to become like us. But that would hardly have helped my cause. I remained silent.

'Fine,' he said, crouching down next to me, 'I'll take your deal. But a deal is a deal, understand that, yes? This is not something you go back on. I will have you one day. I will wear your body as my own. That is the agreement.'

'Yes.' I could no longer say any more than that, I was fading now. If he wasn't quick about it then the whole conversation was going to be redundant.

'And if you think you've got what it takes,' he said, and, in the disorientation, focusing on his words made the world spin, 'come and find me later. We'll be at home.'

I closed my eyes and I felt the cold become total. First the darkness, then nothing. In that moment I believed he had left it too late. I honestly thought that my fading consciousness was death. But then life returned, and by God it hurt. I couldn't imagine what the sensation would have been like had I been in my body when he'd worked his magic – this was the aftershock, the tail-end of creation, and it was more than I thought I could bear. Nerves firing in confusion, rebelling at the new flesh.

I screamed and screamed until my throat was so hoarse all I could do was push out pained air.

I felt someone grabbing me and I realised it was Kurt when he spoke.

'Just go!' he was shouting, assuming I was in the middle of a death agony. 'Christ Jesus, let him just go!'

I managed to open my eyes a fraction, just in time to see him pick up a rock. Dear God, he meant to try to put me out of my misery. With considerable effort, I forced out words: 'No! Wait. . .' Extending my hand towards him, not able to fight him off but hopefully enough to give him pause.

Suddenly the pain became nausea and I found I was able to move, rolling in the dirt and vomiting. Time and again my guts rebelled, contorting and spewing bile into the leaves beside me. Then, finally, it passed and I was left, utterly exhausted, drained but alive.

I lay there for a few minutes more then found the strength to sit up, if only to make sure Kurt didn't try to brain me with a rock again.

He was sat on his bench, crossing himself.

'Drink?' I said, wiping my mouth.

He tipped the empty bottle up. 'You kidding? You made me drink it all.'

I made him. Yes. Just by having the audacity to survive.

'Wait a minute,' he said, getting up and moving over to where Karin lay dead amongst her belongings. 'Maybe she had. . .' He moved her out of the way and began ferreting through her possessions, rising triumphantly with a small bottle of whisky.

I suppose, for Kurt, principles were all well and good until you got really thirsty. He took a long drink and then offered the bottle to me, at which point I proved myself as bad as him by taking it.

The whisky was foul but, conversely, one of the best drinks I'd ever had. Kurt, having now realised the potential upside to a reduction in camp numbers, was checking everyone else's stuff, so I took another drink. It cleaned my mouth and I felt the heat of it sink all the way down to my impossible, intact belly where the burning sensation expanded. I can't really tell you how reassuring that felt. To know that the part of me that had been destroyed was now whole again and filled with heat.

Kurt returned with an opened can of beer and a third of a bottle of vodka.

Part of me wanted to do no more than stay there and share the lot with him if he'd allow it. Hell, if not, I'd have suggested we go to the nearest off-licence and buy more. But, of course, I had something far more important to do. If you're going to make a deal with the devil then you damn well need to make it count for something.

I got to my feet.

'You going?' he asked, not without a hint of hope.

'Yeah,' I replied, steadying myself against one of the trees for a moment, my legs quivering beneath me. Slowly I managed to get them moving. 'I need to find my friend.'

'We'll be at home,' the presence had said. I could only think of one place it could have meant. Lucas's apartment. Why there? Time would have to tell.

I cut across to the closest path and headed straight out towards the road and civilisation. I didn't know how much of a head-start Lucas had on me, but my body still felt weak and unresponsive. As fast as I tried to move, it took me longer than I would have liked to escape the forest. I began to speed up a little once I was on Dammweg and en-route to the S-Bahn. Moving, as painful as it was, seemed to help. Every now and then my muscles would spasm and cramp, responding to alien signals, but the further I walked the more my body felt my own again.

I was crossing over towards the station when a familiar car pulled up alongside me and my heart sank. I really didn't have time for this. The driver wound down his window and leaned out, a smile sitting strangely on his cauliflower face.

'Good afternoon, Herr Shining,' said Ernst Spiegel, the KGB officer who had followed me from my arrival at Gatow. 'I've been looking for you all over the place. How good to have finally found you.'

Behind him a car beeped its horn. He showed no anger, just waved at it to drive past, never taking his eyes off me.

'Get in,' he said. 'We can have a nice long talk.'

THIRTY-FOUR

I considered making a break for it. I really didn't have the time to delay. It showed on my face.

'Don't run, Herr Shining,' he said. 'I have no wish for this to be uncomfortable. Besides, you may be surprised to hear what I have to say.'

I didn't see that I had much choice. It was unlikely that I'd be able to outrun him. At least he was on his own, so I didn't discount the possibility of being able to overpower him and take his car.

I climbed into the passenger seat.

'Good man,' he said. 'Which way were you aiming?'

'Mitte,' I told him, which was true but general enough to give me some leeway as and when I made a break for it.

He nodded and headed north.

I stayed silent. If he wanted to talk it was up to him to pick the subject. Apparently, it was to be my potted history.

'August Shining,' he began. 'Brought into the secret service direct from Cambridge University. Eventually given control of

Section 37, a department whose reputation could hardly be more of a joke.'

'Break it to me gently, why don't you?'

He laughed. 'It is the truth. I know all about it from Gavrill, a friend of mine. He is in the same business as you.'

Gavrill Leonin, my Russian counterpart. In a few years I would handle his defection to the UK, his department having been pulled out from underneath him. Back then he was still in operation, albeit in an even more limited capacity than Section 37. The KGB simply didn't have any interest in his work.

'And just as respected,' I told Spiegel.

'Just as respected!' Spiegel laughed again. 'Because nobody likes to believe in such things, is that not so? Even when they find one of their own men going mad and shooting his fellows. Or a petty smuggler setting fire to himself and jumping off a balcony.' He looked at me and winked. 'Or an old film star jumping to her death from the Ferris wheel.'

'You sound like you have lots of problems,' I replied, refusing to be led.

'Problems shared, I think. And problems that my bosses are not willing to consider. They do not listen to me. They ignore what is happening because it does not make sense to them.'

'And it makes sense to you?'

'No,' he admitted, 'but I am not a man who believes in ignoring what he does not understand. It is not a risk to security, I think. These are not people with access to important information.'

'You can add four homeless to your list of deaths. They weren't in possession of state secrets either.'

He shook his head sadly. 'People are dying and I do not know how to stop it. Do you?'

I decided to take a risk. 'If I did, what would you want to do about that?'

'I would find a way of letting you do so that did not betray my country. You are not important to us, Herr Shining. Your government doesn't want you and neither does mine. I could take you in, but for what? They would laugh at me as if I'd brought home a stray dog. "It can't stay here!" they'd say. "Put it back where you found it."'

'Or have it put to sleep?'

Spiegel shrugged. 'I would rather not. I am not a monster, Herr Shining. I am not someone who kills another for the sake of it.'

'But the thing that's causing us both trouble is.'

'And you can make it stop? Because Gavrill, he talks of you in a most unpatriotic manner. He thinks you are a very special man.'

'If I send him a Christmas card, will it get him shot?'

'I do not think he gets post in his little Moscow basement,' Spiegel laughed. Then he looked at me seriously. 'You do not answer me. Can you make it stop?'

'I mean to try.'

'Then tell me where you are going and I will let you do so.'

'Isn't that traitorous? I had it on good authority you were rather loyal.'

'I am loyal to my people. If I suspected you meant my country harm, you would be in the trunk of the car not the passenger seat. I do not believe you wish harm. At least not today.' He laughed. 'Tomorrow is always another day for us, no? But if you can help in this, then today I will ignore you. I will, in fact, pretend you were never in this car. Let tomorrow be another story.'

I gave him Robie's address.

THIRTY-FIVE

That night was much talked about on both sides of the Wall. Few knew the real cause of the chaos that was to come, of course – though Ernst Spiegel may have made some educated guesses – only those who later read my report (and believed it). It was a night referred to in sad, horrified whispers by all of those who saw it. Even when the Wall fell and Berlin made its valiant effort to memorialise the past but move on from it, the story of the crossings survived. It existed not on official accounts but in the horror stories told by those who had been there: the soldiers, the witnesses, the families who lost their loved ones.

When you visit Berlin now, Checkpoint Charlie exists as a museum, a place to reflect on times that the young are lucky enough to struggle to imagine. People stand next to it and smile into digital cameras. They laugh and smile and wave at the photographer. Look where we are! It's that place from those old movies! How cool is that? Back then, it was an unremarkable structure that signified so much more. Much like the Wall itself, a simple, grey functionalist thing that towered higher in its ideology than it ever could in the flesh. Charlie was not just a set of prefab structures, barriers and signs, it was – like all the crossing points in the city – a focal point of the absurdity that Berlin lived through, a city divided. A city possessed.

I didn't see much, I knew only my own small part of it, but I picked up enough of the details from talking to people later.

The first to run was a young woman. Her name was Heidi Ackermann and people said that, like many others, she must have hankered for what she believed would be a better life in the West. The fact that she was leaving behind her husband and an ailing mother was glossed over. 'It was the child,' they said. 'She was doing it for the child'.

Certainly she was holding the baby, screaming in her arms, as she jumped over the Wall. Its cries carried even over the sound of her own laughter, the shouts of the guards and the eventual gunfire that cut her down in the snow, mere feet from the other side.

Then there was Franz Brand, a watchmaker from Pankow. He'd shown no interest in crossing before then, by all accounts having accepted his place in the East. He had focused on the intricate cogs and gears of his craft rather than the metaphorical ones that ground around him. Nonetheless, while Heidi Ackermann was still bleeding into the snow, her baby howling in pain and terror next to her, Herr Brand followed her example, running out into the no-man's-land of the death strip. The guards, already on edge thanks to Ms Ackermann, were quicker to respond. Brand didn't even make it halfway towards the West; a single pistol shot brought him down. According to eyewitnesses, he was giggling at the time.

There was some discussion about that single shot, Western

news agencies debating how that proved the lie with regards to the GDR's claim that, while it had issued orders to border guards encouraging them to use their weapons in the event of an illegal crossing, it had not issued 'shoot to kill' orders. If the so-called 'traitor' was killed with a single shot, the commentators said, the guard holding the gun was either extraordinarily unlucky or in no uncertain terms as to both his literal and figurative aim. No doubt this commentary was well meant, yet to me it was another example of people focusing on the detail in order to avoid the atrocity as a whole. Franz Brand was only one of many who was to die – what did the number of shots matter?

Herbert Feldt came next, pulling his wife behind him. She begged him to stop, yanking him back towards the border but he cuffed her around the head until she was barely conscious as she was dragged through the snow, her feet leaving a deep pair of tracks behind them.

Then there was Helmut Fuchs, Claudia Gott, Hans Kahler, Werner Jund, Maria Hoefler, Gert and Sofie Hermann . . . Am I boring you? Do you find this list of names hard to process? I'm sorry but the list goes on. Friedrich Gross, Veronika Forst, Anneke Derrick (she was only twelve years old and was performing a cartwheel through the death strip when she was cut down).

The guards had lost their minds by then, calling for reinforcements, convinced they were about to be overrun by rebellious citizens. They were panicked. It's easy to paint them as the villains, isn't it? To consider them ruthless killers with happy trigger fingers, cutting down men, women and children. But they were blind to rational thought by then; they thought the balloon was going up and their turn would be next. One even fired into the crowd, convinced they were about to charge. Of course they weren't – everyone was in shock and afraid for their lives. The crossings came from up and down the strip. Some as far as a couple of hundred metres away, some from within the crowd itself.

At one point, one of the border guards even made a run for the West. Lieutenant Heinz Dreher. He acted like he was charging an opposing trench, running towards the crowds building on the Western side, spraying them with bullets from his machine gun. It was the Western border guards that killed him. What choice did they have?

Are you still trying to find a villain in all of this? Still trying to rationalise the dead? The names on a page, on a tombstone? Of course, there was one, and I was running as fast as I could up the stairs to Robie's apartment, desperate to stop him.

THIRTY-SIX

Robie had been tied to the balcony railing facing the death strip. It was his private box for an evening of cruel theatre, watching each and every one of the innocents forced across the line by the thing that wanted his body. 'How many?' it had no doubt asked him. 'How many before you just say yes?'

Lucas was a pragmatist. You have to be, in our world. He knew that the deaths would not stop if he gave in, they would just stop *for now*. He knew that, but still he couldn't hold out for ever.

By the time I'd made it up the stairs and through the open door of his apartment, he was begging for it to stop. He would do anything, he told it, just let the killing stop.

The stairs had exhausted me and I all but fell into the room, Robie framed by the open arcadia door that led out onto the balcony. He was thrashing against the balcony wall and I could see that the rope tying him to the rail had torn his wrists open.

I had no plan, no idea how I was to stop what was happening. I just knew that I had to be there, to try anything, for Lucas's sake as well as everything else.

'Do it!' he screamed. 'Do it! Just make it stop!'

He thrashed one more time and then slumped down, his legs giving out beneath him.

I was too late. Lucas was no more. Now there was only what was wearing his body.

'Is that the little man?' he said, turning slightly to peer under his new arm. 'Come to prove he's better than me?'

'To try,' I admitted.

'What's your plan?' he asked.

I didn't reply.

'Then maybe you could come over here and cut me lose?' he asked. 'You'll find a decent knife in the kitchen.'

I was on my way back with the knife before I'd even realised what had happened. Hadn't I always been immune to Lucas's charm? I was sure that had been the case, and yet now, at the slightest suggestion I had been about to do as I was told. I stopped in the middle of the living room, staring at the dangling body, the knife in my hand.

'Well?' he asked. 'Cut me free.'

I took another step forward before managing to stop myself.

'You didn't think this through, did you?' I said, fighting hard to focus on the situation, to push away the urge to help him. 'You've taken him over and now you're trapped.'

'I could just possess you and do it myself.'

'If you could do that, why haven't you? I think you're bound to him. Is that how it works? Are you now fixed in one body?'

'Of course not.'

'You don't know, do you? You don't know how this works any more than I do.'

'Just get over here and cut me loose!'

This time I actually had the knife pressed against the rope before I regained control. Was Lucas's power somehow stronger now?

'Do it!' he shouted.

I squatted down behind him, holding on to him and thinking of the man he used to be. Then I cut his throat.

I held him as he choked and swore and bled and thrashed and remembered that first night I'd met him, that brilliant night of laughter that had led to this.

THIRTY-SEVEN

'So you stopped it,' Ryska asked. 'You killed it?

She stared at Shining and noticed he was crying. She didn't know how to handle that.

'I'm sorry,' he said, wiping at his eyes. 'I think maybe you were right after all. I did love him rather.'

'You had to do it,' she said, falling back on clumsy attempts to reassure him over his actions.

'Of course I did,' he replied. 'What else could I do? I couldn't let him go.'

'And it was worth it,' she said, 'wasn't it? You stopped it.'

Shining rubbed his face, trying to shake off a sadness that had clung to him for thirty years. 'So you believe me now, then?' he asked. 'It wasn't so long ago that you were hinting that everything I said was make-believe. Aren't you going to try to suggest that it was all just an implausible cover-up? That I'm a traitor who assassinated Lucas Robie? Surely that's your job.'

'My job was to interview you,' she said, 'and draw conclusions from that.'

'And the conclusion you're supposed to draw is that I'm at best a lunatic, at worst a traitor.'

'Are you?'

'That's up to you to decide, isn't it? I'm tired of trying to preach my corner, to hell with it. People can believe the evidence or not.' He looked at the camera. If she reviewed the footage, she'd see for herself the truth of what he was telling her, she'd see herself possessed. He thought about mentioning it and then decided he couldn't be bothered. No more begging for belief. 'I'm sick of holding everyone's hand. And as for whether I stopped it, no, I didn't. I thought I had, for many years I thought I had, but then it reappeared. Brief visits at first, the sort of thing you could write off as paranoia. An overheard phrase, a smile in a crowd. But then, recently . . . it's been getting stronger.'

Ryska didn't reply and, for a moment, he thought she'd been possessed again, then he realised she just didn't know what to say. He could hardly blame her.

'It's coming for me,' he said, 'and those around me. In fact I wouldn't be surprised if this whole business is one of its games. How difficult would it be to take over Albert Fisher for a few minutes and set the ball rolling? You've heard what it can do. I've been tucked away in a box, removed from play, forced to relive the time I first met it. It's exactly the sort of twisted, stupid thing it loves to do.'

She stared at him for a moment and then made her choice. She decided, against all her better judgement, against all her training, to trust August Shining. She decided to believe.

'But how can it be stopped? If killing its host didn't work then what else is there?'

'Killing its host *will* work. I have it on excellent authority.'

'Whose authority?'

He smiled but decided not to explain it was hers, or the entity that had been speaking through her. He was still digesting the details of their last conversation together and didn't think trying to explain them to Ryska would help.

'The process takes time,' he said, 'for the two to become fully bonded. I was too quick. It was only damaged, terribly so, that's why it took so long to build its strength back up. But next time. . .'

'Next time? How will you know who it means to possess?'

'Oh, sorry, I thought that was obvious. It's going to be me.'

THIRTY-EIGHT

Albert Fisher was telling a young woman who worked in PR how terribly important he was. He gave no details, naturally, but had become an old hand at communicating in a series of knowing winks and half sentences, giving just enough information to make him sound all the flavours of brilliant. She seemed impressed, but then he'd had so much gin and tonic that his ability to read people – or stand up straight – was not at optimum.

Paramount was the perfect place to get drunk if you liked pissing away money looking at a good view. Situated at the top of London's Centre Point, the glass windows offered a panorama of most of the city. Naturally this attracted a certain amount of people who wanted to look at it and imagine owning it all.

Fisher was not one of those people. What he did like, though, was rubbing shoulders with those he considered less important than himself. Fortunately for him, this was pretty much everyone. He drank alongside businessmen and media figures, all the while basking in the warm glow of superiority and overpriced, imported gin. The overpriced, imported gin tasted like normal gin but with just a hint of bank balance. He thought it quite delicious. He had another mouthful of it while watching the distant lights of a jumbo jet pass over the city.

'Of course,' he said, turning back to the woman who worked in PR, 'I can't really talk about it.'

This wasn't going to be a problem because she had wandered off. He could see her black hair bobbing away towards the opposite end of the bar.

'Terribly rude,' said a man next to him, 'she obviously doesn't realise how important you are.'

Fisher turned to look at the man. He was in his early thirties, his suit was shiny and, while his white shirt was buttoned up to the neck, he'd forgotten to put on a tie.

'Do I know you?' Fisher asked.

'We've worked together a fair bit over the last few weeks,' the man said. 'Though you weren't aware of it.'

'How could I possibly be unaware of working with you?' asked Fisher, concerned that his professionalism was being questioned.

'What?' the man asked, staring at him in confusion. 'Sorry, mate, do I know you?'

But the man who was no longer entirely Albert Fisher didn't reply. He simply walked away.

'Nutter,' the man said, forgetting him instantly.

At the other end of the bar, the woman from PR finally relaxed having managed to extricate herself from Fisher's conversation.

'You all right?' asked her friend, smiling in that way a friend does when secretly taking pleasure in someone's embarrassment.

'I thought I was going to be stuck with him all night. You could have come and rescued me.'

Her friend shrugged. 'I didn't want to cramp your style. Not planning on seeing him later, then?'

'I hope I never see the boring old sod again!'

She wasn't to get her wish. She saw Albert Fisher again only a few minutes later. She was, at least, saved his conversation this time. He didn't say a word as he sailed past her on the other side of the window.

April had been tempted to refuse the food Oman had offered her, the idea of having a Peking duck wrap hand-fed to her by a psycho having almost entirely robbed her of her appetite. But only almost.

She took the food but struggled with the drink.

'What the hell is this?' she asked.

'Christmas-flavoured cola.'

'Did they not have any water?'

'What's the point of that? It doesn't taste of anything.'

It was like having a child choose the groceries.

She drank as much as she could stomach and then leaned back in her seat, wondering when the opportunity to break free might arrive.

They sat like that for three hours. At one point April even fell asleep.

She woke to feel Oman pulling at the bindings on her wrists. 'Time to go,' he said. 'Are you ready?'

She certainly was, tensed to move the minute she had her opportunity. He extended the blade of a craft knife, slipping it under the plastic of one of the ties.

'Any second now,' he said, chuckling to himself.

He cut the tie and handed her the knife. 'You finish off,' he said.

She grabbed it.

Oman screamed as the woman who was no longer entirely April Shining went to work.

Toby and Tamar ran through the labyrinthine halls of Gatwick Arrivals. Up stairs, down stairs, along motorised walkways, it sometimes seemed as if the plane had landed them at another airport altogether.

'Try the phone,' Toby said, weaving between a family grumpily returning from a fortnight in Crete.

'No reception,' Tamar replied.

Queueing to get through passport control was torturous, Tamar constantly checking the phone reception. They were, of course, surrounded by signs asking them to keep their phones switched off but, like every other passenger to ever get off a plane, she ignored them.

The phone beeped just as they reached the passport desk.

'Your phone's supposed to be switched off,' mentioned the customs official in the way of a person who simply has to say a thing, whether they believe it important or not.

'Sorry,' said Toby.

'No worries,' said the customs official.

As soon as they had passed through, they checked the phone.

'Text from April,' said Tamar, tilting the screen towards Toby.

'Map link,' Toby replied, tapping it so that it opened in the phone's map app.

'It is where we must go,' said Tamar. 'We should hire a car.'

They spent an irritating half an hour doing just that and were on the road three-quarters of an hour after having disembarked from their plane.

'I hope he's all right,' said Toby, not for the first time. 'Trust him to get in trouble when we're in another bloody country.'

'It is fine,' Tamar assured him. 'We have been as quick as we can. A few hours.'

'A lot can happen in a few hours,' Toby assured her, glancing down at the map on his phone before passing it to Tamar. 'Guide me.'

The phone beeped and the Assassin was tapping at it before the vibrate alert had even ceased. He had his location and a time: two hours from now. His client liked to cut things fine.

A calm descended over him at last, the agitation falling away to be replaced with a sense of purpose. Now it was all about the work. Now it was about what he did best.

He had no need to pack anything, having been so close to leaving several times already. He just picked up his coat and his bag and walked straight out of the door.

He would need a car. This wasn't a problem, in fact he had anticipated it. What he hadn't anticipated was the short length of time he had to secure one and reach his destination. It wasn't a problem but it was an irritation. After all the inactivity, he disliked the fact that he was now being made to rush.

He hailed a taxi and leaned through the window holding out four fifty-pound notes.

'This is to hire you for a couple of hours,' he said, dropping it onto the dashboard. He removed another note of the same value. 'And this is a bonus because it's government business and I need you to turn your radio off and not report your position.' Finally he showed the driver some ID. 'This is who I am and you'll be doing your country a great service if you help me.'

The taxi driver, a jovial man in a flat cap covered in metal badges, looked at the ID briefly and picked up the money. 'Get in,' he told the Assassin. 'But if you don't mind me saying so, there's a better way of vanishing from the control's radar for a bit than just switching the radio off.'

'Such as?' asked the Assassin, climbing into the passenger seat. The driver looked at him warily.

'You're supposed to be in the back.'

'I want to see where we're going. You don't mind, do you?'

The driver hesitated but the three hundred pounds had already made up his mind. 'Fair dos, sit where you like.'

'The radio?'

'Aye, hang on.'

The driver picked up his receiver and spoke into it. 'Debbie, my love, I've just had three buckets of pizza and Stella upchucked all over the back seat. I'm going to be out of action while I clean up.'

'I hope you charged 'em!' shouted Debbie through the speaker. 'Filthy toerags.'

'You bet I did, flower, you bet I did. Give you a shout when I'm free.' He put down the radio. 'And you're bloody lucky the GPS tracker's on the fritz as usual, otherwise they'd have known where we were going anyway.'

'Pleased to hear it.' He gave the driver the directions and they set off.

'You able to tell me anything about it?' the driver asked.

'Doesn't matter if you're not. This isn't the first time I've done government work.'

'Really?' the Assassin asked.

'Oh yeah, I've got up to all sorts in my time, don't you worry about that. I know the score. Discretion is my middle name. Bill Discretion Tanner. Pleased to meet you.'

'Likewise. How long do you think it's going to take to get there?'

'This time of night the traffic's not too bad. Jump on to the motorway. Bob's your uncle, Fanny, she'll be your aunt.' Bill Discretion Tanner thought for a moment. 'An hour and loose change?'

'That's fine, but less if you can manage it, the clock's ticking.'

'You leave it to me, son, I'll have you there before you can say Goldfinger.'

THIRTY-NINE

'What's the time?' Shining asked.

Ryska went outside and fetched him the box of his belongings. 'See for yourself.'

Shining glanced at his watch as he replaced it on his wrist. It was getting late, time to wrap things up. The first thing he wanted to do was ring April – no doubt she'd be close to blowing up the Houses of Parliament by now. If there was one thing you could rely on with April, it was that trouble would escalate around her if she didn't get her own way.

He picked up the phone, tapping the message alert to open her mails.

Then his world changed.

'Shining?' Ryska stared at him as he slowly slid down the wall behind him. 'What the hell's the matter with you?'

'All good?' asked Jennings, stepping from outside, the smell of a freshly smoked cigarette on his breath. He saw Shining, sat on the floor, staring at his phone. 'What's happened?'

'I haven't the first idea,' said Ryska, 'as usual. Shining, what's happening?'

He held out the phone to her, not saying a word.

She took it from him and looked at the photo he'd opened. 'Jesus. . .'

'There's more,' said Shining, his voice fragile and quiet as if he didn't want to wake someone.

Ryska scrolled through the emails, Jennings looking over her shoulder.

'Who are these people?' Jennings asked.

'Friends,' said Shining. 'More dead friends.'

'Who did this?' Jennings asked, tapping the screen. 'April . . . Your sister?'

'No,' said Ryska. 'It's him, isn't it? It. The thing that controlled Robie.'

Shining nodded. 'Tightening the screws. Making me bleed.'

The phone buzzed in Ryska's hand. She made to hand it back to him but he waved it away.

Ryska tapped the message to open it.

'"I'll be with you soon,"' she read aloud. '"Are you ready?"'

'No,' said Shining, 'I'm not.'

Ryska put the phone down on the table. 'But why doesn't it just, you know, appear?'

'Because it's in my sister and it wants to make me suffer. It wants to break every last part of me before we're done.' Shining was crying again. Nobody should have to see so many dead friends. 'It's enjoying itself.'

'What does it want?' asked Jennings.

'It wants him,' Ryska said, nodding at Shining.

'Well, we can't let it have him,' Jennings replied.

'That's exactly what you do,' Shining said. 'I need you all to leave now.'

'No way,' said Ryska. 'We can't just walk out of here and leave you sitting there.'

'Why not?' Shining shouted, accumulated fury spitting out of him like poison. 'Because I'm a security risk?'

'Of course not,' she said. 'Because we don't abandon one of our own.'

'Sorry,' he said, pushing himself up off the floor. 'I'm shouting at the wrong person, I know.'

'I understand,' said Ryska, 'but I mean what I say. We're not just leaving you.'

'Think about it,' he said to her. 'You can't help me. If you're here, you're just another weapon. I know what I have to do and I don't need your help to do it.' He thought for a moment. 'Actually that's not completely true, I need a gun.'

'But shooting at it won't stop it,' said Jennings, 'will it?'

'The gun's not for shooting it,' said Ryska, leaning back against the wall, her head in her hands. 'There has to be a way to fix this.'

'There is,' said Shining. 'I had a plan . . . but that was before I knew what it had done. Before I knew about April. Now I. . .' He shook his head. 'I need to think. I need to get this right. . .' He walked up and down, rubbing at his head as if trying to force his thoughts clear. 'At least Toby and Tamar aren't here. I haven't cause to be grateful for much but at least there is that. . .'

FORTY

'How much further?' Toby asked, checking the speedometer and risking another few miles an hour.

'I do not know,' said Tamar, 'half an hour, maybe? It is hard to tell.'

'I wish April had been clearer. Why wouldn't she explain? Why wouldn't she say?'

'We do not know. We will know in half an hour. I am sure August is all right, he is a brilliant man, a clever man.'

'He's the best man I've ever met,' admitted Toby and suddenly he was hit with a feeling he hadn't experienced in months. It welled up through him and he was forced to slam on the brakes. 'Christ,' he said, body shaking, 'not now, not now. . .'

When he had first met August Shining, dumped on Section 37's doorstep like an unwanted orphan, he had still been struggling with what he called the Fear. A terror so tangible, so all-encompassing, that when it fell on him he could barely breathe. The sensation was of a ceiling being lowered, the constant belief that you were about to smack your head on a world that was too close. He had hidden it as best he could, worked through it when possible, contrived an excuse to cover it when not. His file had shown a PTSD diagnosis after secondment to Basra, but he'd known how easily that could have been the kiss of death on his career so he'd done everything possible to deny it.

Of course, his career had hardly soared anyway.

Until he'd met August Shining.

Shining had trusted him. Shining had allowed him to grow strong, to be the man he'd always hoped he was capable of being.

The Fear hadn't vanished, not completely, but it had shrunk to a perfectly manageable level. It had become something he had controlled, something he could put inside a box when it threatened to take him over. He had beaten it. All thanks to Shining.

Tamar was holding him. 'Toby, it is OK. Just breathe.'

Now he was showing her how weak he really was, how pathetic. Why had she married him, anyway? He wasn't worth it. He was broken, stupid.. .

He gasped for air. He couldn't let it take him, not after everything he'd been through. He was better than that. He had to pull himself together. Had to put it back inside its box and fight. He had to make sure August was safe.

'Sorry,' he said, 'so sorry. It was just . . . I had a. . .' He shook his head. He'd never talked to Tamar about the Fear. Had always thought it would make him look less worthy. Ridiculous. He should give her more credit than that.

'After I was in the Middle East,' he said, 'I suffered a breakdown. Post-Traumatic Stress Disorder. Panic Attacks. When I first met August, I was still suffering. I could manage most days but . . . but sometimes it was hard. It was August that helped me deal with it. He made me stronger.'

'He made you the man you are?'

'Yes.'

'No. He let you be the man you always were. That is good, but he didn't change you. He showed you how to let the illness go.'

'Maybe. But I owe him a lot. He means a great deal to me. I couldn't bear it if he. . .'

'Of course you could. We can bear anything. We always think a thing will break us, then it happens and we do not break. We are strong. So strong we are scared to admit it to ourselves, I think.'

'But if he's. . .'

'We do not know what has happened to him. He may be all right. We will go, now, and we will find out. But you are strong, my love, you can do anything.' She smiled. 'And if you struggle, I will help you. Because I am strong too.'

'You are that,' he agreed, nodding. Slowly the Fear was receding, the ceiling raising a few inches. 'Sorry, it just hit me out of nowhere. I'm. . .' He rubbed at his eyes. 'Come on, this isn't helping any of us.'

He drove on.

FORTY-ONE

'Of course,' said the Assassin's cab driver, 'ideologically, most religion's on rocky ground, isn't it? You don't have to look overseas to see a text filled with stoning, bigotry and sexism. It was like I said to Justin Welby the other day. "Justin," I said, "it's all very well talking about reform and revisionist thinking but when your core text is built on outdated values you're building your house on sand."'

They were close to their target now, the Assassin watching the GPS marker on his phone, slowly edging towards the address he had been sent.

He tried to get a lay of the land through the window but it was next to impossible with the lack of lighting.

He checked his watch. They'd made bad time thanks to the congestion leaving the city but he still had plenty to spare.

As his phone told him they were almost on top of their target, he pointed towards a farm track that led off the main road.

'Pull in there,' he said. 'I don't want them to know I'm coming.'

'Fair enough,' the driver said, perhaps slightly aggrieved at having to halt his invective.

He pulled in and switched off the engine. Without the headlights all was dark around them.

'What's the plan then?' the driver asked. 'You want me to hang here while you do what you have to do?'

'Something like that.' The Assassin said, lifting his bag up from the footwell. 'I don't know how long I'm going to be.'

'Well, as long as you're not all night about it. I can't fob control off for ever.'

'That won't be a problem,' the Assassin replied, punching the driver in the throat. The man convulsed and the Assassin reached over, grabbed the man's head and wrenched it in a sharp turn. There was a crunch, the driver's legs kicking and thrashing for a few seconds then lying still.

The Assassin felt a sharp pain in his upper arm. One of the man's badges had come loose and embedded itself near his armpit. He plucked it out. It was from a caravan park in South Wales, a jolly sun offering an enamel smile. He pushed the badge into the dead man's chest and leaned over to disengage the safety lock on the driver's door and eject the man's seatbelt.

He reached up and deactivated the automatic light before opening his own door. He didn't want the sudden light to slow his night vision.

Climbing out, he moved around to the driver's side, opened the door and tipped the body onto the verge. It was an annoying few minutes, dragging the body out of plain sight but it will always be a killer's lot that fat people sometimes need to die too.

That done, he hoisted his bag over his shoulder and began to jog along the road.

It took him five more minutes to reach the house. At one point, he was forced to take cover as another car passed, a dark hatchback. Had they come from the house? Possibly, possibly not – who knew what else was around here?

Arriving at the cottage, he noted it was predominantly dark and there was no vehicle parked outside. This was no firm evidence of anything, though the part of his mind that constantly shifted and correlated the details around him, wondered if the car he had seen *had* come from here. Did that mean the house was now empty? Had he missed his target?

A small security light on the front porch was the only illumination. It revealed no sign of anyone but he made a wide circuit of the place just in case, moving carefully through the trees that surrounded it then returning to the front of the building.

He went back to the road and moved out of direct sight of the building. He withdrew his phone and sent a text to his client, letting him know that he was in position. A few minutes later a reply came: 'Your friend should be leaving shortly. Suggest you surprise him then.'

The advice was sound. The Assassin didn't know who might be in the house along with the target and, while he wasn't concerned about handling multiple aggressors, the neatest solution was always the best.

He put the phone away and unpacked his bag by moonlight. He lifted out what appeared to be an old laptop. In reality, its chunky casing cracked open to reveal a small battery that allowed it to give the illusion of functionality, the rest of the space taken up by a handful of polymer-framed components.

He didn't need to see to construct the pieces together, the process practised so repeatedly that it was automatic. Based on the popular Glock pistol, the gun had been further refined so as to make it lighter and invisible to metal detectors. It's capacity was smaller than the standard nine cartridges, but the five plastic rounds it held had always been enough. Choose your target with care and one bullet was all you'd ever need.

The Assassin moved back into the trees surrounding the house, took up a position with a direct line of sight on the front door and adopted a comfortable position. The minute August Shining stepped out of the door he would be dead.

FORTY-TWO

Convergence.

From his position on the hill, the Watcher saw it all come together.

He saw the car leave with the security officers inside it, bouncing its way out of the rough driveway, then speeding off along the road, its lights receding.

He saw the Assassin jogging along the road before making his cautious circuit of the house. He received the man's text message and replied accordingly. How strange it was to be sat here, orchestrating events from afar, pulling strings like a puppeteer.

Any moment now, he felt sure, August Shining would die and then the night's work would be all but over.

But plans are slippery things and, however much you may think you have anticipated all the possibilities, life invariably surprises you.

The first surprise of the night was the presence of another car on the road. This in itself was not worrying, it was an open road and, even at this time of night, traffic was hardly impossible.

When it pulled into the driveway of the cottage, however, the Watcher's plans began to fall apart.

Shining, finally alone with his thoughts, moved through the house, checking all the windows were closed and the back door firmly locked. Doors would not keep the higher power out, of course, but it would at least channel its host. He wanted the only point of access to be the front door.

He passed into the hallway, running his fingers along the wall, tapping gently at the door of the understairs storage cupboard before moving back into the interrogation room.

He was removing the covering from the window – revealing the best view of the front of the house – when he was suddenly blinded by a set of headlights. She was here.

The woman who was not quite April Shining had enjoyed a comical drive through the country lanes, constantly forcing the dead body of Oman out of her way as it kept toppling over whenever she hit a bump or a pothole. Finally it had folded on itself, its chubby, dead face wedged against the open glovebox. There it congealed against a battered A to Z and a box of tissues, no longer a problem.

She pulled into the driveway of the cottage and got out of the car.

She looked at the blade of the craft knife she had used on Oman and decided it was of no further use. She flung it into the grass and tried to remember where she had left the gun. Handbag.

She had to wrestle Oman's body out of the way, which took considerable effort. It eventually popped loose of its wedged position, its face blooming with stuck tissues and a torn close-up of Holborn Road. It hit the ground with a fart of dead air and she chuckled at the pantomime of it all as she dug her handbag out of the footwell. It was sticky with Oman's blood but she pulled out the gun and a glistening humbug that now tasted of copper and meat.

Time to call in all debts.

The Assassin had darted back into the trees when the Mini had appeared. He watched from cover as the driver got out and wrestled with a body on the passenger seat. He hoped this was not be a complication but, if need be, she would just be another target. Better to kill someone for free than leave witnesses.

As she got close to the door and the reach of the security light he recognised her face. August Shining's sister. Yes, he would have no reservations about killing her too.

She stepped inside the house and he moved closer. He glanced down at the body; in the low light it was difficult to tell but he didn't think it was anyone he knew. What had she been doing driving around with a corpse?

The open passenger door made suitable cover. He wound down the window so that he could rest his arms on the frame to steady his aim. Everything was tacky, he would have to check his appearance later, maybe even use the house facilities to wash. He had no problem getting blood on his hands either literally or figuratively, but he would need to ensure it didn't show before he returned to civilisation.

He took up position, partially aware that the wind was picking up around him. The empty branches of the trees were waving and creaking, the bushes around him bending and whispering gently.

He racked the gun, loading the first cartridge into place, and lined up his shot.

The wind continued to build, shaking the car door. At this rate it was more likely to harm his aim than help it. Realisation began to dawn. . .

From inside the house came the sound of a gunshot.

'Hello,' said August as his sister's body stepped through the front door.

'Hello,' she replied. 'Snap!'

They were both holding their guns to their heads.

'No more,' said August. 'I won't let you kill any more of them.'

'I can't imagine how you think you'll stop me,' she said. 'After all, once I have your body, I can do whatever I want, can't I?'

'If it's my body you're after, you'll have to be quick.' He pulled the trigger.

Toby wrestled with the steering wheel as the wind buffeted the car and nearly forced it off the road. He glanced at Tamar.

'Fratfield,' she said, and he couldn't help but notice the trace of excitement in her voice.

The wind came again and this time it was almost more than Toby could do to keep control. The car veered onto the verge, shaking both of them up and down in their seats.

'I have to turn around,' he said. 'He must be close.'

'If you turn around, we won't be able to help August,' she told him. 'Keep going.'

'You could get out.'

'Keep going!' she shouted.

In the glare of the headlights they both caught a glimpse of the fat, pale wind demon, appearing on the road ahead of them. The car sailed through it and began to spin, its wheels leaving the ground altogether for a moment before bouncing back down and breaking into a roll.

Fratfield heard the sound of a car crashing a short way up the road, the wind pressing him back against April's car. He wasn't prepared for this.

The passenger door blew back at him and it was only his quick reactions that enabled him to get his hand up in time to stop it hitting him.

He stepped out of the way, allowing the door to blow shut.

He wasn't going to walk away. Wind or no wind, he would get this job done. He would kill August Shining.

The entity was there in an instant. Leaping from April's body and into August's, spinning his head so that the bullet caught his jaw rather than his temple. The pain was exquisite, the old man's jawbone shattering, teeth flung loose.

'Now!' he heard someone shout, only partially aware of Ryska and Jennings bursting from the cupboard beneath the stairs and grabbing the body he had just vacated.

'What's happening?' April shouted, her mind reeling as they grabbed her and yanked her along the hallway.

'Quickly!' Ryska said, between them dragging April past Shining's fallen body and through into the kitchen.

'August!' she shouted.

'We have to move, Ms Shining,' Jennings insisted. 'He knows what he's doing.'

April's head was pounding even worse than it had earlier, the after-effects of the entity having possessed her for so long. Her vision was a mess of bright, flashing lights, nausea wracking her.

Ryska took hold of her as Jennings reached for the back door key, hidden on top of the lintel. He unlocked it and stepped out, gun moving through the darkness. The wind made it almost impossible to move, pressing him back against the wall of the house.

'I think we're clear!' he shouted, reaching back to help Ryska and April through the doorway.

'What the hell is going on?' April shouted, before convulsing and throwing up, Ryska stepping clear just in time.

'Help me,' she said to Jennings, the two of them lifting April between them and moving as quickly as they could away from the house, each step an effort against the wind.

The man that was no longer August Shining rolled on the floor, his jaw hanging loose and scraping against the ground.

'A deal is a deal,' he said, though the sound that came out wasn't recognisable, his bloodied tongue thrashing in the air.

He turned the gun on himself again and pulled the trigger. The bullet entered his stomach.

'Just like last time, eh?' he said. 'What goes around comes around, old man. The next time you're near death. . .'

He dropped the gun, blood oozing out of him as he slapped his way along the hallway floor.

His movements slowed, old hands pushing against the slimy floor, spreading the blood out in sharp arcs.

'Near death. . .'

The letter of the contract fulfilled, the entity went to work.

It wished Shining could feel the results as it knitted split flesh back together. It pushed its new jaw back into place, bone fusing with bone, teeth sprouting from roots that had once been dead. Skin stretched, nerves fired and it screamed in the most delirious pleasure as its new body healed around itself.

Toby pulled himself free of his seatbelt, falling on to the roof of the upturned car. 'Tamar?'

She grunted and he reached for her seatbelt even as the car began to spin again, turning on its roof.

'Oh God,' he moaned, 'Tamar. . .'

The car flipped again and he collided with the dashboard, losing consciousness.

The thing that was now August Shining stood up, straightened its tie and exercised its jaw. He still ached but that would pass, as would the burning sensation in his stomach. His essence oozed through the flesh, filling it with life and energy. Old? Not so much, not now. He ironed out some of the wrinkles, flexed the muscles, strengthened the bones. By the time he had finished he had knocked twenty years off the old bastard, not quite the man that had first made the deal, perhaps, but close enough.

He became aware of the wind raging outside. How suitably theatrical, he thought and decided to step out and see what it felt like on its face.

Walking towards the door he savoured every sensation, the clothes rubbing against his body, the gentle pounding of the floor against the soles of his feet, the tensing of every muscle as he moved.

Yes. This was life. This was flesh. This was real.

He turned the handle on the front door only for it to swing back on its hinges and knock him in the face. He laughed to feel the pain of it, stumbling back against the wind, delighting in the light-headed feeling caused by the blow from the door.

Everything was so strong! Everything felt so much!

He stepped outside and extended his arms in the wind, staggering slightly as it rocked him from side to side.

'Lovely,' he said, feeling the quiver in his throat and chest as he spoke. It had never been like this before; when he had taken temporary hosts, he had been insulated. The sensations had been remote. Pleasurable, yes, but not like this. It could feel *everything*.

A gunshot rang out and, for the briefest of seconds it felt that too, the bullet hitting him square on the bridge of the nose, plastic shattering on impact and exploding through his brand-new brain. A second shot was fired but unnecessary. By the time it entered August Shining's head, both the body and the creature now inhabiting it were dead.

FORTY-THREE

Bill Fratfield, the Assassin, worked at his belt and uncoupled himself from the tree he had strapped himself to. As he did so, the wind began to die down. Rather than curse the timing – thirty seconds earlier and he would have had a much easier shot – he chose to focus on the fact that this could only mean the demon had done its work. Tamar was dead and hopefully Greene had died with her.

He walked over to August Shining's dead body to admire his handiwork. He nudged it with his toe, taking a degree of professional and personal satisfaction in the limp, lifeless way the body moved.

He took his phone from his pocket and photographed the corpse, sending the image to his client. It was hardly a secure thing to do but he'd be ditching the SIM card shortly and was confident that it would never be traced back to him.

He went into the house to ensure he didn't look like a man who'd just killed someone. There was some blood on his palms from the woman's car but that was all. He scrubbed them clean and left again by the front door, taking one last look at the corpse of August Shining as he passed.

He picked up his belongings and made his way back up the road towards the abandoned taxi. He might have been inclined to use the old woman's car had it not been covered in blood. People would be looking for the taxi soon and, while the driver had assured him the GPS wasn't functioning, he would rather not be driving it. He would take it part-way there, he decided, and then switch to something else.

In the middle of the road was another car, upturned and dented.

He looked through the windows, hoping to see the dead bodies of Toby and Tamar, but it was empty. He looked around. Maybe they had been flung into the trees. He imagined the dawn falling on them in a few hours' time. Bad fruit.

Reaching the taxi, he climbed in and headed back towards London.

On hearing the final gunshots, April had tried to fight her way free of Jennings' grip but he had lain down on top of her, pinning her to the earth.

'We can't interfere,' Ryska shouted to her. 'He's doing what he has to do.'

'Says who?' April screamed.

'August,' Ryska replied. 'This is all him. He made us promise to help you but to keep right back. It's important. If we mess it up for him now, his sacrifice won't mean a thing.'

The wind had suddenly dropped, leaving her shouting for no reason.

'We can't leave him,' April was saying. 'I won't. We've fought through too much over the years, I'm damned if it's going to end up with me leaving him to rot in the middle of bloody nowhere.'

Ryska looked to Jennings. He nodded. It was silent now and neither of them truly believed there would be anything to go back for except a body.

Now that the wind had died down, it took only seconds to cover the ground that before had been the work of minutes.

April entered through the back door, slowing as she saw the body of her brother lying ahead of her on the front porch.

'Oh Christ,' she said. 'This is ridiculous. A man like August doesn't go down from a bloody gunshot. A monster, a demon, a stupid pissing vampire . . . that I can believe, but a bullet to the head?'

Ryska and Jennings stood behind her.

'Do you want me to look?' Ryska offered.

'Of course not, darling. I've been rolling corpses since before your daddy's balls had hair. Just give me a minute.'

Jennings whispered in Ryska's ear. 'Should I call back the other two?'

Ryska looked around for a moment then nodded. 'It's done, get them back here.'

He stepped to one side and called the two officers who had left earlier in the car.

April moved forward, shaking herself and walking with determination.

She squatted down next to August, turning away at the sight of his head. She pulled one of her scarves from around her neck and draped it over the worst.

'Ah fuck,' she sighed. 'You really are bloody dead, aren't you?'

She began to cry.

Tamar woke up, sitting upright in wild panic, and scrabbling at the grass beneath her. She was alone. She remembered the car tumbling, remembered the sound of metal and glass, the disorientation that had followed, a rush of colour and noise followed by blackness. She remembered hands reaching for her, the tight grip of the seatbelt then the slackness and the sensation of falling. Had the sky been full of trees? It had felt so, howling and creaking and rustling. The sensation of the grass on her back, rushing, a burning on her arms. Had someone been holding her? She thought she remembered choking, her T-shirt constricting around her neck and the stars rushing by. Then there had been silence.

Now this.

What had happened? Someone must have pulled her out of the car. Toby? Then where was he now?

The wind had ceased, and it was now silent out here in the blackness of English countryside. The chill made her shiver and she got to her feet, stumbling as her left ankle gave out beneath her, sending her face down into the dirt again.

Her ankle was sprained or broken, she had no idea which. It was not her only pain. Something had torn in her neck; turning her head caused a sharp stab of pain to shoot down her back. She touched her head and was surprised it didn't hurt.

Lucky Tamar.

She crawled on her hands and knees, trying to get a sense

of where she was. A field? A hill, she decided, as the ground dipped beneath her and she tumbled forward, rolling in sickly agony down several metres of long grass.

She finally found her voice. 'Toby!'

In the distance came a faint answer, and she sighed and crawled her way towards it, testing the ground before her with her hands, not wanting to fall again.

A couple of minutes later, she heard his voice again, this time coming from her left. She sighed, rolled on to her back and shouted his name at the top of her voice. To hell with it, he could come to her. She couldn't go any further.

They kept calling to one another until, finally, Toby saw his wife lying in the grass and came running. He squatted down next to her and she grabbed his arm. She let go of it again due to his screaming.

'Broken,' he explained, out of breath and feeling completely spaced out. Concussion. He knew this from experience, having had his head cracked by a bust of Beethoven some time ago. 'How are you?'

'Ankle,' she said. 'Sprained, I think.'

'Lucky. Both of us. How did you get up—' He suddenly had to turn away and be sick. Definitely concussion, he decided, lying back next to her. They'd move in a minute. They had to, they needed to make sure August was. . .

Toby passed out.

Tamar sat up and tried to wake him up again. She didn't think it was good to let him be unconscious. Or did he need to be? She couldn't remember. She screamed in frustration and somewhere in the darkness, a fox answered.

* * *

When the car finally pulled up outside the safe house – a description it had long since ceased to deserve – Jennings ran to meet it.

'Took your bloody time,' he said to the driver.

'Road was blocked,' the driver explained. 'These two had crashed.' He nodded towards Toby and Tamar on the back seat. 'Said there was some sort of storm?'

His scepticism couldn't have been clearer. From his position a couple of miles up the road he had seen nothing.

'Like Piccadilly Circus out here tonight,' he continued. 'Some bloke went tearing past in a taxi too.'

'Fine time to pick up bloody civilians,' Jennings sighed. 'I'll get an ambulance on the way.'

'We're not bloody civilians,' Tamar told him. 'We are here to help August Shining.'

'Oh,' Jennings sighed. 'I'm afraid it's a little late for that.'

Toby kept slipping in and out of consciousness but he picked up on that.

'August?' he asked, struggling to climb out of the back seat, his balance all over the place.

'Steady,' said Jennings. 'You're in no fit state to—'

'Where's August?' Toby insisted, pushing past him before taking two more steps and stumbling to the ground.

'Christ Almighty,' said Jennings, stooping to pick him up.

'August!' Toby screamed, his voice as delirious as that of a drunk.

April heard him. 'Oh Lord,' she sighed. 'Toby.'

She got up and went to him, waving Jennings back as she took Toby by the shoulders.

'I'm sorry, Toby,' she said. 'August is gone.'

'Gone where?' Toby asked, looking around as if he might see him. 'My head. . .' he moaned, touching it with his good hand.

'He's dead, my love,' she told him, and held him as tightly as she dared as first he stared, shaking his head, then gave in to the tears.

FORTY-FOUR

The last time they had been in the company of Pleasance Bellevue, she had been performing a marriage ceremony. Now it was a funeral.

'We honour the memory of a great man,' she said. 'Someone who worked tirelessly to make this world a better, safer place. His heart was as big as his brain and he leaves behind a memory greater even than both. If the world only knew what a gift he had given it over the years, there wouldn't be a room big enough to fit those wishing to offer goodwill and thanks.' She looked up at the three mourners: Toby, Tamar and April. 'As it is, his work was done in secret. He neither wanted nor needed the acknowledgment of others to endorse what he did. Like all truly great men he gave all and expected nothing. He will be missed.'

She looked to Toby. 'Did you want to say something?'

'No,' he replied and continued to stare at the wooden crate of ashes on the table in front of them. 'What's the point? A few words for the dead? I haven't got any big enough.'

Tamar squeezed his hand.

Pleasance nodded. 'We don't need words to remember him.

Or thank him.' She patted the box. 'And alive or dead, he will always be shining.'

Outside, they filed into the car, April holding the ashes. Toby had wanted to but, with his arm in a sling, he was convinced he would drop them. Besides, he still sometimes found his balance giving out, even now, five days after the accident. The doctor insisted he'd be fine in time.

'Just take it easy for a bit,' he'd advised, popping a piece of nicotine gum into his mouth and grinning with the cheeky pleasure of it all.

Toby had seen no problem with that as a piece of advice. After all, it wasn't as if he had a job to occupy him.

'You can't just quit!' April begged him after they'd returned to the Section 37 office.

'Why not? asked Toby. 'It's only a matter of time before the department's closed anyway. Section 37 *was* August, you know that. They've wanted to close him down for years. Now they can. I'm surprised I haven't had the relocation paperwork through already. It's probably delayed because they can't figure out anywhere pointless enough to dump me.'

He got up from his desk, scattering the papers he'd been shuffling.

'It's all just waiting for the shredder, isn't it?' he said, watching it float to the carpet around him. 'Probably for the best.'

'That's August's life,' April pointed out, not unkindly.

'No it isn't,' he replied. 'It's just paper. August's life bled out of him while I wasn't there to help him.'

'There was nothing you could have done.'

'Of course there was. I should have been there, watching his back. But, as always, it doesn't pay to rely on Toby Greene.'

'Then it doesn't pay to rely on April Shining either,' and this time there was venom in her voice. 'Think how I bloody feel for a minute before you completely sink into self-pity. I wasn't there either and everything that happened when that . . . that *thing*. . .' Her words petered out.

They hadn't talked about the atrocities the higher power had committed while in possession of April's body. None of them quite knew what to say on the subject. They knew it was hardly her fault – and, deep inside, so did she – but it was too big to face for now. It was a conversation that could only burn once ignited.

'Sorry,' Toby said, realising he'd been selfish. 'I just can't be doing with any of it. Not right now. We still don't understand half of what happened. How Tamar and I got out of the car, why Fisher wanted to set August up. . .'

'I think we can guess it wasn't really Fisher,' said April.

'Probably not. But what about Fratfield? What suddenly made him come back here? Was it him that killed August? We know he was there but why?'

'Only one way to find it out,' said Tamar.

Toby nodded. 'And that's my only priority now. Just as it has been for the last few weeks. We need to find Fratfield and get some answers. I only hope I can get it done before every penny of the budget is snatched back.'

As if on cue, the phone rang. Toby stared at it for a moment, knowing it would be a call he didn't want to take. April and Tamar stared at him, neither wanting to do it for him.

He snatched it up.

'Dark Spectre Publishing,' he said.

The two women watched as his face turned even more sour.

'Fine,' he said after a few moments. 'I'll be there.'

He hung up.

'Looks like the axe has finally dropped,' he said. 'Sir Robin. Wants me to meet him at Cornwell's right away.' He shrugged. 'Whatever, the sooner it's started the sooner it's finished. I'll be back in a couple of hours.'

He walked out of the office.

April looked to Tamar who shook her head gently. 'He will get better,' she said.

'Good for him,' April replied. 'I wonder if I will?'

'Thanks for coming, Greene,' said Sir Robin, half rising from his armchair. This was almost a sign of politeness from the indolent bastard but Toby didn't let it dent his hatred for him.

'I didn't imagine I had much choice,' he replied, sitting down in the chair opposite.

A man in evening dress hovered by him.

'Drink?' asked Sir Robin, indicating the well-dressed man. 'Algernon would quite like to know.'

'Algernon can bring me a single malt,' said Toby. 'A really large, really nice one.' He stared at Sir Robin. 'I may as well make one last dent in the budget after all.'

Sir Robin ignored the comment. 'My condolences on the death of August,' he said, with a half-measure of sincerity. 'We were all very shocked to hear.'

'I assume that's why nobody attended the funeral? Hung-over from the party perhaps?'

'Now, Greene, there's no need to be like that. I know I haven't always been the staunchest defender of Section 37 but I still respected Shining's talents. I told Bertie as much when he mentioned his silly investigation.'

'Silly investigation.' The words came out of Toby with difficulty. He was getting angrier by the moment and he needed to try to swallow some of it. For all he may have no future in his current line of work, a prosecution for attacking a peer of the realm would do him no favours, however enjoyable it might feel at the time.

'Very silly,' Sir Robin continued. 'I can only assume work was getting to him. You heard of course? He committed suicide on the same night that Shining was killed.'

'I heard.' Though Toby thought it unlikely it had been a simple case of suicide.

'And then there's poor Clive, of course,' said Sir Robin. 'Shot in the middle of Finsbury Park. We still can't get to the bottom of that. It makes no sense at all. . .'

'If only you had a department that specialised in unusual cases,' Toby replied, taking the Scotch from the silver tray Algernon was poking under his nose.

'Oh, I don't think it's necessarily in your line,' said Sir Robin. 'I dare say there's a rational explanation. We'll dig it out in the end. We usually do.'

'Besides,' said Toby, 'my line is about to draw to a close, isn't it?'

He took a mouthful of the Scotch. Algernon had done well – it was very large and very nice indeed.

'I don't quite follow you.'

'Oh, come on, Sir Robin, let's not beat around the bush.

I'm really not in the mood. When does my new job title get flung at me?'

'Well, as you bring the subject up, obviously we did think this was an ideal time for a restructure.'

'A restructure. That's what we're calling it, is it?'

'A rethink, perhaps. Sounds more cerebral. The PM does like it when things sound cerebral. God knows why, maybe it's brain envy.'

'When?' Toby asked again.

'The paperwork's being dealt with as I speak.'

'Fine, then you can add to it. I resign.'

For the first time in their conversation, Sir Robin actually appeared ruffled. 'Resign? What do you think this is, McDonalds? You can't just resign.'

Toby laughed. 'You know, it's funny. When I was first sent to Section 37, my old section chief suggested I should work there. Maybe it's time I gave in to the inevitable.'

'But if you leave, who the hell am I going to find to run the section?'

Toby stopped smiling. 'What?'

'Section 37. There's no other bugger I can give it to, after all, is there? Nobody would want it.'

Toby stared at him. 'You're not closing it down?'

'Ah . . . I see we've been talking from a position of some confusion. No, I have no intention of closing it down.'

'Why the hell not?'

'You think I should? I must confess I'm surprised to hear you say that.'

'Of course I don't think you should, I just assumed. . .'

'Well, yes, I have been somewhat antagonistic towards it at

times, I admit. I can see why you might think I would take this opportunity to . . . well, yes. But, after the Lufford Hall business, you built quite the following, you know. Mostly thanks to dear old Clive, of course. He was very pleased with you.'

'We did save his life.'

'I'm sure he was grateful, for as long as said life lasted. Oh dear.' Sir Robin made a show of embarrassment. 'How insensitive of me. Anyway, the point is, it has been decided that perhaps your section does serve a valuable purpose within the Intelligence community. In these times of economic awareness and the vital need to ensure that all departments are achieving a solid balance between expenditure and. . .'

'We're cheap.'

'Well, yes.'

'And so we look good on paper.'

'You do.'

Toby laughed and took another mouthful of his drink. 'Unbelievable. Section 37 lives on because at least its books balance.'

'Well, actually you turned a vague profit. Something to do with a novel about lesbian vampires, I believe. Though why people want to read about those, I have no idea. It all sounds terribly oral.'

'Lesbian vampires?' Toby had to think for a moment. 'You're talking about Dark Spectre? But that's just a cover.'

'And people have been judging you by it!' laughed Sir Robin, proud of his little joke. 'One of the titles it published has been optioned by some ghastly American in Los Angeles. No doubt he means to turn it into something starring Joanna Scarlet or whatever she's called. The one with all the lips.'

'You can't just keep us going because we've got a movie deal!'

'Naturally not. We also deeply respect the work you do. Deeply. But it was pointed out in very vociferous tones that it would be counterproductive, what with all the necessary cuts in public spending, to ditch a section that actually brought in money.'

Toby finished his drink and waved at Algernon. 'I'll have another one,' he shouted, causing several members of the club to turn around and stare at him in geriatric disgust. Or perhaps it was wind.

'Steady on,' said Sir Robin. 'Bit early for a party.'

'You can afford it. So you're keeping it on and you want me to run it.'

'Nutshell.'

'I withdraw my resignation.'

'Quite right too. Pleased to hear it. Naturally it comes with a promotion.'

'And increase in salary.'

'You're all about the money, aren't you, Greene? I had no idea you were so venal.'

'I have an expensive honeymoon to pay for.'

'Ah yes, the good lady. We're having her vetted, you know.'

'Good luck with that.'

'I'm sure it'll be fine, they pass anybody these days as long as they don't throw things at royalty. Naturally it would be lovely if we could take this opportunity to, how shall I put it, get things on a more even keel.'

'Meaning what?'

'Well, as you rightly point out, my relationship with Mr Shining — God rest, etcetera, etcetera — was at times somewhat strained. Perhaps, with some young blood in the driving seat, we might welcome in a new era of interdepartmental harmony.'

Algernon appeared with Toby's drink. He hadn't bothered with the tray this time. Toby wondered whether he'd simply tip the bottle in his lap if he shouted a second time.

'You're hoping,' he said, knocking the drink back, 'that I'll be much easier to handle than August was.'

'Well, I wouldn't put it quite so aggressively. But yes.'

'Not much chance of that.'

Toby put the glass down on the table and got up. 'Now, if you'll excuse me, Section 37 has a few loose ends to tie up.'

'Would one of them be Bill Fratfield?' Sir Robin asked as Toby made to leave.

Toby halted and turned to look at him. 'It would.'

'Well now, I heard something quite fascinating concerning our poisonous Mr Fratfield just before I came to meet you.' Sir Robin smiled. Toby thought he looked like a python who had just been offered a wriggling hamster. 'It's quite the most bizarre thing. . .'

Bill Fratfield – though, like any he used, that was not his real name – stood next to the ancient watchtower and gazed across the Spanish cove below. From up here, he looked down on the entire resort. In the distance there was the town, its winding streets leading back from the beach and its cafes. The church steeple jutted up, its ancient bell ready to toll at the slightest provocation. Beyond that, the vineyards and their row after row of stunted vines.

Directly beneath him, the old port, its exclusive, slender beach and the overpriced restaurant that served those who tanned themselves on it. He had eaten a large bowl of mussels there not half an hour ago. That and the copious quantities of bread and wine it had come with being precisely what he had hoped this march up the cliff would work off.

Out to sea he saw a couple of large liners making their way towards the port of Denia, a few miles north. People about their normal business. None of that for him. For now he was having a holiday.

'Señor?' a strained voice shouted. 'Pleases, señor?'

He looked back towards the cliff path to see the young waiter from the restaurant running towards him. He was waving something in his left hand.

'What is it?' Fratfield asked, immediately on edge. He disliked being the focus of anyone's attention. The waiter came up to him, wheezing with breathlessness.

'This is yours, señor,' he said after a moment, proffering the thing he'd been carrying. It was a Manila envelope.

Fratfield tapped the breast of his jacket and found it was empty. That envelope contained his passport – fake naturally, but important while in use – and a rather large quantity of cash. It had been in his jacket throughout lunch. How could he have dropped it and not noticed?

He snatched it from the waiter, still unable to get his head around how he could have misplaced it. Realising from the look on the waiter's face that this abruptness was not quite the reward he had hoped for, he smiled with as much sincerity as he could. 'Sorry, don't mean to be rude. Thanks a lot.' He took a ten-euro note out of his pocket and gave it to the man. That improved the look on his face.

'It is no problem, señor,' the waiter said, heading back down the path. 'The other English gentleman gave it to me. He said you'd be pleased to have it back.'

Fratfield watched him go, a chill feeling of suspicion creeping over him.

English gentleman?

He opened the envelope. His passport was there but no money, just a sheet of note paper wrapped around a folded paper napkin. He opened the note:

Mr Fratfield,

You'll forgive me not coming over and chatting in person, I'm sure. I don't think my company would have helped your digestion.

You'll also forgive me taking your money. After all, it was originally mine. Not that I question the job you did to earn it. You followed my instructions to the letter. Still, I need it more than you, given your current circumstances. I'm afraid I've also refunded the transfer for the balance. In fact, your bank account is now rather empty. Awful of me, I know, but you pick up the odd trick in my line of work. Old line of work, that is. I'm pleased to say I've retired, in no small part thanks to your kind financial contribution.

As it would have been terribly rude of me to leave you with nothing, I do enclose a small gift. Something I believe was once yours that it is my pleasure to return. Its previous owners are better off without it. I did try to give it to you earlier but I'm afraid you're a hard man to pin down.

Yours,

A.S.

'A.S.?' Fratfield muttered, running to the edge of the cliff and looking down at the restaurant below. Standing between the tables looking up at him was a well-dressed man in sunglasses and a panama hat. As Fratfield watched, he raised the hat to him in greeting.

It couldn't be! It was impossible!

Around him, a wind was beginning to build, whipping at the long Spanish grass and whistling through the holes in the ancient brick of the watchtower.

Fratfield searched through the envelope. His passport fell to the ground, landing open. He saw his own photo, and next to it, like a bookmark, a small piece of paper with ancient markings scrawled on it. As the wind caught it, it fluttered into the air, sailing up beyond the edge of the cliff.

No! He couldn't have done!

The wind continued to build, stronger and stronger, until Fratfield was forced to dig his nails into the grass to avoid being pushed along by it.

He looked towards the watchtower as the pale, bloated wind demon appeared, the storm raging from its wide open mouth.

'I cast you!' Fratfield screamed. 'You can't come for me!'

'I am cast,' the wind seemed to say, 'it does not matter by whom. All that matters is promises. We get what is owed to us.'

With one last scream, Fratfield felt his grip give way and found himself sailing backwards, his heels kicking at the grass until they found nothing but fresh air.

Below, the diners looked up in horror as a scream rang out, the dark shape of a man flying through the air before finally, inevitably, hitting the rocks below.

'Madre Mia!' gasped the waiter who had handed Fratfield the envelope. He crossed himself. He turned to the old man who had found it. 'He must not have liked what was in it.'

'Possibly not,' the man admitted, 'but it was all his.'

With that he turned and walked away, his eyes gazing out at the brilliant, shining sea.

ADDITIONAL DOCUMENT: THE SECOND LIFE OF AUGUST SHINING

'I ask you to remember an important thing. Sometimes we do not see what is real. Sometimes, what we think has played out before us is not as we perceive it. Our eyes cheat. Our hearts lie. Sometimes it is necessary to make a little theatre.'

'You said, "Is this now?"' said Shining. 'What did you mean?'

The sudden change of subject seemed to confuse the entity that inhabited Ryska for a moment. She stared at him for a couple of seconds before answering.

'Moving from my plane to yours, it's hard to be precise. Time is not so linear to us. I have found you before but it was never the right time. Sometimes you were younger, sometimes it was too late.'

'Too late? That's reassuring.'

When Ryska didn't reply, Shining paused and turned back. She was looking at him with a quizzical expression that he recognised as a sign that Ryska's consciousness was no longer in residence.

'You again, is it?' he asked.

She nodded. 'Have you thought about what you mean to do?'

'About the rebel?'

She nodded.

He leaned back in the doorway, checking briefly that the others were out of earshot. He could hear them faintly outside, chatting in the porch.

'You're the same as him?' he asked. 'By which I mean you can do everything he can?'

She nodded.

'Then, yes, I know what I mean to do, as much as the idea terrifies me. You said it yourself, I have to give him what he wants.'

'Tell me your plan.'

'Doppelgänger Contract,' he said. 'I need you to go back and make another me.'

Shining watched Toby and Tamar dancing in the courtyard of the Church of the Sacred Mind. Ah . . . weddings, such a shame he didn't get to go to many. Give it five minutes and he'd be on the dance floor himself showing the young idiots what hips were made for.

First, he had to. . .

He stumbled, a wave of dizziness washing over him. Surely he hadn't had that much to drink? He'd been taking it steady, like all of them, but he wasn't a man to hit the bottle too hard. It came again, stronger this time. He sank to his knees and blacked out.

'You all right, August?' asked Pleasance, stepping out of

the kitchen. 'What you doing sitting on the floor? We run out of chairs? I'll fix some more in a minute. I got some pecan and raspberry muffins coming on like hellfire in that oven.'

'More cakes? Dear God, woman, are you trying to kill us?'

'Not with the cakes, it's the punch that'll do that. Come on, I'll pour you another glassful.'

She led him outside.

In Pleasance's office, watching through a crack in the door, August Shining saw himself leave, arm in arm with their host.

He turned back to face the thing wearing Jamie Goss's body.

'How do I know you're telling me the truth?' he said.

Goss shrugged. 'You obviously thought you would,' he said, 'or you wouldn't have sent me back to do this.'

'My head's splitting. Doppelgänger Contract? Aren't you supposed to ask first? Doesn't it have to be some kind of deal?'

'No. The rebel just phrases it that way. It's so he can get something from you that he wants.'

'Whereas this is what I want?'

'Very much so.'

Shining rubbed his aching head. It had explained it to him twice already, he trying to process it as he watched his unconscious body – his unconscious *other* body – sat out in the hallway. He was having a hard time of it.

'So I have to take this extra time to fake my own death. . .'

'You won't be faking. He will die. He has to.'

'But he's me!'

'So are you.'

Shining waved the conversation away with his hands. This

was getting too much for him to cope with. He sat down at Pleasance's desk.

'Let me take some notes, dates, details. . .'

Bill Fratfield had received the email while waiting for his flight out of Mexico. Using the airport's rented computer space, he had logged on to his business email account and there was the message: URGENT: SERVICES REQUIRED.

He'd read the mail. There were no details regarding the kill, just details of where he was to travel to and a number he was to message on arrival. This was normal. Clients didn't like to mention the name of the person they wanted removing until the assassin was hired. In fact, on the rare occasion that a client did mention the name, any professional tended to run a mile – if they'd told you, who else had they told?

Why not? he thought. If he had to run, he might as well earn some money while he was doing it. He sent back a reply and proceeded to book a new flight. He'd let his original tickets stand, and with a bit of luck Toby Greene would end up following him as far as Italy before he realised he was chasing an empty seat.

Shining waved cheerily at the man behind the shop counter and made his way over to the storage lockers.

'Got something nice, have you?' the shop assistant asked.

'Hopefully!' Shining replied, using the open locker door to hide the fact that he was slipping an envelope from out of his jacket. 'Oh,' he said, dropping the envelope in. 'That's annoying. It's empty.' He closed the locker door and pulled out his new phone. 'Better email them and see what's going on.'

'Happens sometimes,' said the shop assistant. 'Probably on its way and they sent you the delivery notification early by mistake.'

'That'll be it for sure,' August agreed, walking out. 'Not to worry. Thank you!'

Heading towards the office, Shining handled the messages from Fratfield. It was all falling into place. With Fratfield hired as the assassin to – how unnerving this thought was – kill his other body, he'd deal with both of their longstanding problems in one fell swoop. Fratfield could handle the higher power and then August would handle Fratfield.

Across the road, August Shining saw himself – his *other* self – step out onto the street. Quickly he darted into the closest shop.

'Hello sir,' said the owner. 'Can I help you at all?'

'Just browsing for now,' he said, immediately turning to stare through the window. On the opposite side of the road, his other self was staring right back at him. He jumped back from the window.

'Browsing for sandwiches?' the owner asked, with no small amount of sarcasm, pointing at the array of fillings stocked before him in the chilled counter.

'Ah, right . . . yes . . . erm, tuna salad please.'

'Certainly, sir.'

While the sandwich was being made, he checked his notes. If he was leaving the office now then they'd be driving him to the safe house. He didn't have time for this, he had to get to his car.

'Sorry,' he said, grabbing the sandwich, 'just remembered a

thing, must run.' He threw a five-pound note towards the owner and peered out of the doorway. Across the road, his other self was looking towards a car that was indicating to pull in.

Shining dashed up the road a short distance and then crossed over, all the time keeping an eye on his other self and the car he was climbing into. He ran around the corner from the office to where his car was parked in a rented garage a few doors down.

He'd given it a couple of runs over the last few days, only too aware of how little he used it. He'd had visions of the damn thing packing up on him when he really needed it. Besides, he'd had time to kill – what an unfortunate phrase that was in the circumstances, he thought. Over the last few weeks he'd been living in the house on Morrison Close, doing his best to run over the plan until he was sure it was as safe as it could be.

The problem was that he had come up with it in a rush, thinking on the hoof and laying down the bare bones of it to the entity that had come back and duplicated him. The second August – him – could hardly communicate with the first, so even though he looked at the arrangements and saw countless ways they could be made safer and better, he couldn't risk altering them. His original self would play his part and that was now fixed. The entity had made it perfectly clear that the risks of altering his timeline at this stage could be catastrophic and, in truth, he hadn't needed to be told. It was vital that he kept out of sight and ensured that everything that had led the other August to that safe house – and the conversation with the entity – remained identical. He would handle Fratfield and ensure that part of it was secure, the rest would just have to play out with no involvement from him.

He got in the car, shoved his sandwich in the bag with the rest of the kit he'd prepared, and drove back to the main road.

He had to annoy a few fellow motorists to begin with, overtaking and cutting between the other cars as he tried to get the car he was tailing in sight. Once he'd spotted it a short way ahead, he settled back and followed, heading out of the city and towards the house where soon he would die.

On the hill above the safe house, Shining brushed the remains of a sandwich from his fingers, raised a pair of night-vision binoculars to his eyes and followed Jennings as he stepped out of the cottage and made his way over to the two other security officers.

Shining had been in position for several hours now, had monitored the movements of the security officers as they took it in turns to make circuits of the building, plodding through their duty in the thorough manner only ex-military could really manage.

You learned a great deal training in the army, but he often thought that one of the most impressive skills you inherited was an ability to do the mundane without going mad with boredom. For himself, as important as his supervision was, he had found himself begging for something to happen within a couple of hours of setting up position. Waiting wouldn't kill him, he knew, but there were times it felt like it would.

He reached for his phone, checking for messages. Nothing. This was no great surprise. Fratfield was waiting on his orders like the good professional he was. Shining wondered when those orders would be given. He trained his glasses on the blank window of the interrogation room, picturing the target beyond the drapes. He wondered when it would be time for August Shining to die.

It would have to be soon. Should he risk it? Was it better to have Fratfield arrive too early or too late?

Too late, probably. Still . . . He glanced at his watch. He'd give it another half an hour and then set the assassin moving.

Convergence.

From his position on the hill, Shining saw it all come together.

He saw the car leave with the security officers inside it, bouncing its way out of the rough driveway, then speeding off along the road, its lights receding.

He saw Fratfield jogging along the road before making his cautious circuit of the house. He received the man's text message and replied accordingly. How strange it was to be sat here, orchestrating events from afar, pulling strings like a puppeteer.

It made him a little bit too much like the enemy for comfort.

Any moment now, he felt sure, August Shining – the other August Shining – would die and then the night's work would be all but over. He checked his weapon. He hated to kill but Fratfield must die. Alive he would always be a threat to Toby and Tamar. Perhaps he should just kill him now? Then kill his other self?

He wasn't sure he was capable of that. Besides, in that split second while he aimed his shot – perhaps more than a split second, he was not the practised killer Fratfield was – might the higher power not see it had been tricked? What might it be capable of then?

Best to stick to the plan, however rough it was. Surely, as long as he was quick, everything would work just fine.

But plans are slippery things and, however much you may think you have anticipated all the possibilities, life invariably surprises you.

The first surprise of the night was the presence of another car on the road. This in itself was not worrying, it was an open road after all and, even at this time of night, traffic was only to be expected. When it pulled into the driveway of the cottage, however, Shining's plans really began to fall apart.

April! What was she doing here?

Everything hinged on the fact that his other self would get everyone else out of the house. No risk of innocent casualties. His possessed body would step out of the front door, Fratfield would take his shot and then August would take out Fratfield . . . but now?

August began to run down the hill. He had to figure out a way of getting his sister out of the house.

The wind began to blow. Harder, then harder still. It robbed him of his balance and he fought to keep his feet as he heard the sound of another car approaching. What was this now? The wind. Fratfield. The curse . . . surely they were out of the country? Toby and Tamar couldn't be here!

He saw the car headlights streaking towards the house, swaying along with the car as it fought to keep to the road. Then he saw it bounce and tip into a roll.

He looked back at the house.

April or Toby and Tamar. That was his choice. Damn him for coming up with such a stupid plan. Damn him for not anticipating better. . .

He ran towards the road.

* * *

Toby pulled himself free of his seatbelt, falling on to the roof of the upturned car. 'Tamar?'

She grunted and he reached for her seatbelt even as the car began to spin again, turning on its roof.

'Oh God,' he moaned. 'Tamar. . .'

The car flipped again and he collided with the dashboard, losing consciousness.

The car nearly hit Shining as he skidded on to the road, the wind forcing him to bend forward, legs wide. Keeping low, the upturned vehicle shielded him from some of it, he could see both passengers were out cold.

Toby was closest, and Shining pulled him out through the shattered window. The car shifted again and he toppled backwards, losing his grip on Toby, who rolled down the incline of the verge, coming to rest at the foot of the hedge.

It was Tamar he needed to get clear, she was the trigger.

He undid her seatbelt and lifted her out, throwing her over his shoulder.

Glancing towards the road, he could see the wind demon, puffing up its cheeks in preparation for another gust. Around it, detritus swirled, a cyclone of dead leaves and small branches.

August had the wind behind him as he ran, moving up the hill away from the road as fast as he could. There would be a point, he knew, where Tamar was far enough away from Fratfield that the curse ceased.

Of course, now it occurred to him that the easiest course of action would have been to kill Fratfield but then he would have been in the position of having to face his duplicate, possessed self. Maybe that would have worked, maybe the whole plan would then have come crashing around him, nobody would ever know. He'd made his decision and now he was sticking with it.

But what if he didn't manage to get back for Fratfield? What if the assassin escaped again?

What would be would be. For now he just had to do his best to ensure Toby and Tamar survived the night.

He stumbled, both he and Tamar falling to the ground. Still too close, he thought, as the wind howled around them. He grabbed her by her T-shirt and began to drag her, his energy fading. If they weren't clear soon, he would never make it. He couldn't keep moving much longer.

He saw the demon at his heels. It had followed him, its pale white face looking quizzically at him as he dragged Tamar a few more feet.

Suddenly, the wind stopped and Shining collapsed, in relief.

'Far enough,' he sighed, lying down on the grass next to the unconscious Tamar.

'Far enough,' the demon agreed.

Shining sat up and looked at it, fighting for breath. 'You can talk?'

'Why shouldn't I?'

'No reason, I suppose. I just looked upon you as a force of nature.'

The demon scratched at the soft skin of its face, its cheeks distended like defaulted balloons. 'A force of nature that can speak.'

'Yes.' He tried to get up. He had to keep moving, had to deal with Fratfield. He sank back down; it was no good, he could barely breathe.

'Why do you want to run?' the demon asked. 'She is safe now.'

'Not while the man who cast you is still alive she's not.'

The demon nodded. 'He is a dark man, I look for a soul inside him but I think he has none. I wish I was not bound to him.'

Shining thought for a moment. 'Can I release you?'

'Only by turning the curse back on the man who cast it. It is possible but not simple.'

Shining nodded. 'You just let me worry about that.'

He left Tamar and worked his way back towards the house. Every part of him ached. He was getting far too old for this sort of exertion. His vision was blurring and there was a pain in his chest as he neared the road. What was wrong with him? He'd never felt so . . . the pain in his chest increased, tightening, crushing. . .

August Shining fell to the ground, barely able to draw breath. A few seconds later he was unconscious.

Light. The sound of birds. Wetness on his face.

He opened his eyes onto a new morning and, just for a moment, he had no idea what had happened. Then he remembered and sat up in panic.

'It's over,' said a voice from next to him. He turned to see an old man stood a few feet away, a gleeful-looking Labrador sitting patiently by his side. 'Your heart broke. I fixed it for you.'

Shining got to his feet. 'But what happened at the house? Did it work? How's April? Is—?'

'The rebel has ceased to be. We owe you thanks. The rest of your people have long gone. They are all alive and well.'

Shining checked his watch. He'd been unconscious for hours.

'My heart broke?'

'I fixed it for you.'

'You said. Thank you.'

'It was a gift.' Then the man's facial expression changed and, in his own voice, he said, 'Hello there, you all right?'

Shining nodded. 'Fine, I think. Overdid it last night.'

'I'll say, falling asleep in the middle of a field at your age. You want to take it easy.' With this advice, he wandered off, his dog trotting on beside him.

Shining got to his feet and walked back to his car.

He felt better than he had for years. So Fratfield had escaped; that was unfortunate but he now had a contingency plan for that. He checked his pocket and found the piece of paper the demon had given him. The ancient symbols on it were quite beyond his understanding but he didn't suppose that mattered. The important thing was that it would work.

He climbed into his car and brought out his phone. He should see how everyone was. They'd be shocked to hear from him, of course, maybe even angry at what he'd put them through. But, once they understood that he couldn't have revealed himself earlier, once they saw what he had done, they would forgive him. For one brief moment, August Shining felt like a man at the top of his game.

Then he checked his emails.

* * *

Across the road from the Church of the Sacred Mind, August Shining watched as the three people who loved him – the three people left alive – climbed into the car and drove away with his ashes.

'You are still hiding?' said a young mother pushing a pram.

'I thought you'd gone. Don't tell me you're going to start making a habit of possessing people now.'

'No. I will leave soon. I just wanted to understand. Why are you still hiding?'

'Because, in the long run, this is better.'

'To have them thinking you're dead?'

'To *be* dead. Just for a moment I thought I was clever, I thought I'd beaten the odds again. I hadn't. Do you know how many people died at the hands of your rebel?'

'Many.'

'Yes,' he nodded, 'many. And all because they knew me. Because they were involved in Section 37, because I made them targets.'

'Is that true?'

'I think so.'

'So you are going to stay dead.'

'I think it's best for all concerned. They'll get over it. Maybe without me they'll all make better, safer decisions with their lives. I'm surrounded by victims. Cassandra, Derek, Alasdair, Jamie, Lucas. . .' He shook his head. 'It's too much. It's all just too much.'

'I understand.'

He looked at the young woman. 'You're not going to tell me I'm wrong, then?'

'What would I know? I am not flesh like you, it all seems chaos to me. Where will you go?'

'I have one more thing to take care of,' he told her, 'then I'll go wherever I want, as long as it's a long way from here.'

Bill Fratfield paid the bill for his lunch and then got up from his table. Time to walk that off, he decided, then I can plan what lazy way I wish to spend my afternoon. Maybe I'll even go for a swim, take a dive from some of the rocks.

'Thanks,' he said, waving vaguely towards the waiter.

He looked out at the sea, glistening in the sunshine.

'Careful!' A young man collided with him, having jumped up from his table.

'Apologies,' the young man said, with a faint German accent. 'I do not look where I go.'

'No problem,' Fratfield replied, still too full of seafood and drink to think too much about it.

Fratfield aimed towards the cliff path as the young German walked over to a different table. He placed the envelope he had just stolen from Fratfield's pocket in front of the man who was sitting there.

'Perfect,' said Shining. 'Many thanks, Gustav. Now watch yourself in future. If I catch you dipping pockets again, you'll have worse to deal with than a little favour.'

Gustav tutted in annoyance and walked off.

Shining opened the envelope, removed the money that was inside and replaced it with his note and the scrap of paper that contained the wind demon's curse.

Job done, he decided, blank slate.

He called over the waiter.

Also by Guy Adams:

The Clown Service

Toby Greene has been reassigned.

The Department: Section 37 Station Office, Wood Green.

The Boss: August Shining, an ex-Cambridge, Cold War-era spy.

The Mission: Charged with protecting Great Britain and its interests from paranormal terrorism.

The Threat: An old enemy has returned, and with him Operation Black Earth, a Soviet plan to create the ultimate insurgents by re-animating the dead.

Also by Guy Adams:

The Rain-Soaked Bride

How do you stop an assassin that can't be killed?

Toby Greene is part of The Clown Service, a mostly forgotten branch of British Intelligence tasked with fighting paranormal threats.

However, the Rain-Soaked Bride is no ordinary assassin. Relentless, inexorable and part of a larger game, merely stopping this impossible killer may not be enough to save the day. . .